Fallen Hopes, Taken Dreams

J. M. Barlog

Library of Congress Cataloging in publication data on file

ISBN : 978-1478353393

To my father and mother

Prologue

December 29, 1890. Dawn crept like a thief in the night over the forty-two teepees pitched along Wounded Knee creek. Painted Ghost Dancer figures adorned the tanned hides. The air was soundless, windless. The temperature clung to zero. Nearby, dozens of restless tethered ponies huddled in an improvised rope corral. A few Sioux women swaddled in blankets hauled water skins from the icy meandering banks. A handful of children dashed about—too young, too innocent to fathom the grave events unfolding in their midst.

At the encampment's core, glowing embers spit skyward from a towering teepee. Crammed inside, a dying Sioux Chief Big Foot addressed callow Lakota warriors. All wore Ghost Dancer spirits painted on their chests. The old chief and his tribe sought no more than to die in peace on the land that had given them life.

"The Ghost Dancers will protect you from bluecoat steel," he delivered in a weak voice laced tightly together with an unyielding conviction.

Ninety-two inspired warriors began a chant to incite courage, bring fire to their bellies. Then, brandishing makeshift weapons, they spilled out in a stream of unshakable determination. But they had not gone far when ...

As the sleepy sun breached the horizon, a massive jagged line of eight hundred mounted silhouettes materialized along a ridge overlooking Wound Knee creek. The sight fired terror into the warriors' souls.

All fell silent. Moments passed. Fear spread.

A tinny warble from an uncertain bugler sent the horse-flesh surging forward.

History failed to record who fired that first terrible shot, but by day's end, more than three hundred of nearly three-hundred-fifty Sioux Indians camped at Wounded Knee creek lay dead or dying. And as cavalry scouts had reported in the days previous, most were women, children and elderly.

This final bloody confrontation ended the Ghost Dancer movement forever, forcing the last renegade Sioux tribe back onto the government reservations. But the spirit of the Ghost Dancer refused to die ....

1

February 27, 1924. A moonless, frigid night. Jimmy spent the waning hours of his nineteenth birthday alone, in a tenuous sleep, curled on a rickety pine bench in the rear of a covered truck. The nasty cold and endless hours of constant jostling drove him to exhaustion. A miasma of noxious engine fumes at his feet wafted up through cracked floor panels.

Brakes screeched. The sudden lurch slammed Jimmy face-first into the bulkhead. His nose cracked against the wood. The jarring movement toppled the bench, casting him into the deadly gases.

Dazed, Jimmy squirmed, desperate to draw his feet beneath him. The vile air invading his lungs burned like hell. Panic flooded his brain, triggering his survival instinct. He clamped his mouth closed, thrashing to rise above the caustic shroud caving in around him. As if the bench itself plotted against him, the leg pinned him to the floor. When his lungs threatened to explode, he gasped. More poisonous air rushed in. He coughed it out.

With his next inhalation, his head spun in wild gyrations. He jerked frantically. But the bench's weight held him hostage. Blackness poured in around him. His oxygen-starved brain began shutting down.

"Celia!" he screamed with a breath he thought to be his last.

Surrendering, Jimmy closed his eyes, wanting to die holding the image of his Celia in his mind. They had taken him from her. Now he would never see her again.

He swallowed blood gushing into his mouth, all the while clenching his teeth against a fire raging through his shoulder into the curve of his neck. He coughed hard to eject the deadly vapors. More rushed in. A single thought consumed his faltering brain: *He must not die*. He must get back to her.

But Death would be cheated this night.

The rear door screeched as it opened, welcoming in a mean winter wind, and with it, fresh breathable air. Jimmy coughed hard to eject the poison from his chest. With a loud sucking sound, he refilled his lungs.

"Move it," the gruff driver snarled, standing in shin-deep snow.

Jimmy squirmed rearward, not in obedience, but rather in frantic search for breathable air. He gulped it in; his sight began to clear. When he reached the opening, the driver snared his straitjacket's collar. Yanking downward, he jerked Jimmy headlong into the icy-crusted surface as if he were nothing more than a sack of soiled laundry.

The driver's callous laugh echoed inside Jimmy's head while shards of jagged ice slashed his cheeks. His coughing turned violent, which triggered his gag reflex, forcing him to purge more than just the remaining fumes from his lungs. Blood splatters tainted the sparkling ice layer.

But he was alive.

"You're home," the driver added with a tongue-in-cheek snicker. He wore a worn leather patch to hide a deformed nose while his left eye drooped as if a claw had permanently disfigured it.

Jimmy gazed up into the perverse pleasure in the driver's inky black eyes. Then a muddy boot slammed his rib cage, urging him to his feet. He struggled to his knees without assistance, leaving behind a crimson crater in the snow. The driver aided him upright by jerking his arm straps until Jimmy thought his arms might pop from their sockets. He silenced an erupting scream. He would never reveal weakness in front of the white man.

Jimmy's head throbbed. His vision collapsed around the edges. An ethereal buzz roared through his brain from the exhaust fumes and the vile drugs they had earlier forced down him.

When he looked up, terror seized his soul. His eyes climbed a two-story brick building with iron grates securing every window. A few windows still glowed with a pale yellow, despite the late hour.

The driver tugged Jimmy up six concrete stairs to enter through the main door, where warm air assaulted them. Jimmy welcomed the heat. He wore only a wool shirt beneath their straitjacket. In the incandescent light, he stared at the paunchy driver, whose unshaven face encircling sparse teeth gave him a wickedly nasty appearance. That smile, and his days-old smell, would sicken even the stoutest stomach.

"You wanna hit me, injun?" the driver said then chuckled. He grabbed Jimmy's straitjacket to throw him into the wall.

Tongue clinched between his teeth, the driver jabbed a buzzer thrice with a grimy fat nub of an index finger, whose tip had been excised at the first joint. While waiting with crumbled BIA papers in hand, his eyes made no attempt to conceal his contempt.

Soft footsteps rose from the interior. Then the wire-reinforced glass window beside the inner door slid open. A woman's appearance momentarily disarmed Jimmy. She wore an unflattering black uniform dress, trimmed with a white apron and white sleeve covers. Her coffee-colored hair she had wrapped in a tight bun neatly on the back of her head. A faint smile crossed thin, almost colorless lips as her deep-ocean blue soulful eyes reached out, attempting in her own way to reassure Jimmy.

"You're rather tardy this evening," she said in an edgy, all-business British voice directed at the driver. She accepted his papers sharply, lobbing back disdain when she noticed Jimmy's blood-smeared face.

"Hey, he fell," the driver offered curtly, avoiding eye contact.

She figured that to be a lie. Her eyes read the papers sufficient enough to ascertain that everything was in proper order, lest she suffer the wrath of her irascible boss.

"Heavy snow coming outta Kansas .... That's why I'm so late ... not that it matters to you."

While they waited, Jimmy took in as much of the woman as he could. She, however, avoided his eye contact. Instinct backed him away when the inner door unlocked. It swung open easily, soundlessly.

Jimmy tried to swallow—found it impossible. The locked door, the grated windows. He knew the kind of place this was. The pungent vile smell of unkempt men assaulted his nose. He knew that odor, that air of sickness and death. Fear propelled him toward the outer door. But before his second footfall, a short, bull-shaped man in dingy white shirt and dungarees snared him at the collar.

Jimmy's upper body turned rock hard in resistance.

Their eyes locked, each sizing the other in that brief second. This one refused to back down, so Jimmy yielded, severing the intimidating link between them.

"Thank you," the woman offered the driver in return, hoping her etiquette might become infectious. She received a grunt for her effort.

"You need to sign ..." the driver pointed out, stabbing the top sheet with his nub to indicate where. "Or I don't collect my bonus."

"I know exactly what I must do," the woman parried back.

She scribbled her signature before returning the top sheet to the driver, who accepted it with a toothless grin. Now he could collect his three dollar government bonus for completing his assignment without incident. His relief swelled. At last he was rid of this nuisance charge.

"We'll have him from here," the man in white said.

Jimmy appraised the short man in that tense second. A stone face. Mean, hard green eyes, riddled with scorn. Smileless. An empty vacant stare designed to unsettle. But Jimmy also detected a trembling hand clamping his collar. A weakness this one failed to realize he was offering up at that moment. His unflinching face, though granite, appeared strictly a façade. Jimmy cataloged his observation.

"Nathan will have him from here," the woman said.

"Gets mean when the drugs wear off," the driver offered. "Tried to kick me in my privates, he did."

"That so? We'll be fine, won't we," Nathan said with a perfunctory smile meant to inform Jimmy intimidation would be fruitless. Nathan's eyes barely glanced into Jimmy's before turning away to shuffle him through the door.

Jimmy offered no resistance, even though at five-foot-eight, he stood half a head taller than this Nathan nudging him along. He could kick this frog of a man then bolt for the door. That desire vanished, however, as quickly as it rose. He could never free himself of the straitjacket. And as such, he would get nowhere without the use of his hands. He trusted his moment would come not now, but at another time.

Once inside the inner door, all friendliness disappeared from Nathan's face. Jimmy seized that moment to appraise the woman more fully. Something about the way she looked at him disarmed him. Did she seek to convey with her eyes that this was not the terrible place he believed it to be?

Then his eyes slid off her to surveil the darkened hall with doors lining both sides. The low light coupled with his muddled vision made it difficult for Jimmy to discern the more subtle details of his new surroundings. He pressed his brain to accumulate information.

"Where do I stick him, nurse Thompson?" Nathan asked.

"In there's fine. I'll advise Dr. Wallace of his arrival." Thompson indicated the room to their left, three doors down from where they had entered.

The sound of Nathan locking that inner door was deafening. Jimmy's heart sank into the darkest pit of his gut. He needed no more to understand where he had been placed. However, at that moment Jimmy had no idea he had been dealt a death sentence. He held no understanding of where he was, nor why he had been placed here. He just knew this place he would come to loathe.

2

"Let me out of here!" Jimmy screamed, kicking and hurling himself into the reinforced oaken door. His effort, however, inflicted such agony that it felt like someone had stabbed his shoulder a hundred times with a gutting knife.

Nathan stared at him through the glass of a small window in the door. His face remained unchanged. He neither smiled nor frowned. He simply stared unflinchingly into Jimmy's brown eyes.

Jimmy spat on the glass. The bloody saliva oozing down kept Nathan from observing him. Nathan's chapped lips never turned up even the slightest.

"I did nothing. Let me out of here," Jimmy pleaded.

Blue eyes appeared. A hint of sadness surfaced that the nurse could never deny. For a moment, Jimmy paused to stare at her, hoping. Then Nathan's unaffected green eyes took her place.

With his back to the window, Jimmy slid from Nathan's sight to stare vacantly at his new world: a twelve-by-twelve room with colorless, peeling plaster walls and nothing more than a slumping bed shackled to rings in the floor beside a rain-stained window with a steel grate over it.

"I did nothing," Jimmy muttered to himself.

At the sound of approaching footsteps, he sought refuge in the room's darkest corner. For a time he rested very still on his haunches. Muted voices crept under the door. Jimmy strained to hear; their words remained indiscernible. When the voices grew louder, Jimmy rose in anticipation. He pressed against the wall to gain the greatest leverage. Then he readied himself by filling his lungs with several deep breaths.

Keys rattled. The lock clanked. The handle turned.

As light from the hall fell into the room, Jimmy launched himself at the silhouette breaching the doorway.

It was that Nathan.

Jimmy slammed into him, driving him against the opposing wall. But without the use of his arms, he could accomplish nothing more damaging, and with a jerk of Jimmy's arm, Nathan deflected him away, regaining control. However, in so doing, Nathan had brought his head too close.

Jimmy lunged, sinking teeth into the base of Nathan's neck. Nathan growled and cracked Jimmy's jaw with a force that sent Jimmy reeling back into the bed in the opposing corner.

Before Jimmy could kick back to his feet for another attack, Nathan strapped his legs to the foot of the bed. Heaving, Jimmy lay as helpless as a calf roped by a seasoned ranch hand.

"Let me out of here," he snarled. He wore Nathan's blood proudly on his teeth.

Nathan finished him off by strapping Jimmy to the bed at the chest. Then he stepped back and crossed his arms, as if his task had been properly accomplished. The unruly frightened calf had been subdued. The moment between them lingered.

"Sonofabitch injun bit me," Nathan said, wiping away blood trickling down his shirt.

"Nothing serious, I'm sure," Dr. Wallace offered. He stood in silhouette in the doorway holding a tray with metal instruments Jimmy had never seen before.

"I've had worse," Nathan replied.

"Let me out of this!" Jimmy insisted.

"It keeps you from harming yourself," Wallace replied in a soothing matter-of-fact tone. He wore glasses that in reflecting the weak light hid his eyes, while his weathered face carried the wrinkled strain lines that came from his years of administering this facility.

"Harming myself?" Jimmy said.

"We're going to help you, Jimmy. Here, you need to drink this."

Nathan tilted a small paper cup to Jimmy's mouth. Jimmy responded by spraying the caustic liquid into Nathan's face. Unfazed, Nathan wiped his eyes with his sleeve and turned to receive another dose. They had been expecting that. The tray held five small cups.

Jimmy averted his face as much as possible against his restraints. Though inconsequential, his defiant act revealed much to Wallace. Despite the restraints, Jimmy still sought any way possible to resist.

"This goes much easier if you cooperate, Jimmy," Dr. Wallace said, pausing to allow his paternal tone to sink in before continuing. *Always respond to outrage with calm.* A simple edict Wallace reminded himself to practice daily. The doctor's voice worked in concert with his eyes to diffuse anger, though Jimmy thus far proved unreceptive.

"You must be thirsty after such a journey," Wallace added.

He handed Nathan another cup, which he pressed again to Jimmy's lips. This time Nathan tilted Jimmy's head slightly to force some liquid down his throat.

Jimmy swallowed against his will, only because Nathan had pitched the medicine to the rear of his throat, limiting its ejection. At the same time, he clamped Jimmy's nose.

"You see, progress already," Wallace commented plainly.

In the faint light, evidence of a smile appeared on the doctor's face. The backlight falling in from the hall made the doctor appear taller, broader than he actually was. Jimmy surmised this Wallace to be no taller than him.

"Why am I here? What are you going to do to me?" Jimmy pressed.

"You'll be fine. I'm Doctor Wallace. I'm going to help you while you're here with us."

"Where is here?"

"The Canton Insane Asylum, Jimmy."

"Why did they bring me here?"

"Because you need help. This is the only place you can get it."

"Help? *This* is the white man's way of helping me?"

Wallace retreated to the door.

"If you wish to help me, unstrap me and release me from this jacket," Jimmy pleaded.

Nathan tried forcing more liquid down Jimmy's throat.

"All in good time," Wallace replied.

Jimmy spat the liquid into Nathan's face. Jimmy knew exactly what they intended to do. A moment later, Nathan turned back to Wallace for direction.

"Leave him for the night. And cut that damn hair," Wallace said as he retreated into hall.

3

Still clamped arm-over-arm in his straitjacket, Jimmy sat in diffused morning sun strapped to a chair positioned near the window while Nathan hacked with dull shears at ruffled shoulder-length hair. Their forced medication anesthetized Jimmy's mind and fogged the periphery of his vision. He could only discern clearly that which appeared directly before his eyes.

Snip.

A clump of hair, black as a moonless midnight, fell through his narrowed field of vision.

Inside Jimmy cringed. A piece of him fell to the floor. A part of who he was had been sheared away by the white man. Others in his tribe—mainly the youth—had begun cutting their hair as a matter of convenience. Jimmy had refrained to honor his father. *New ways must replace the old, he had said to a father's deaf ears.* His father had shaken the words off as if they were infectious. The old man would hear none of the white man's propaganda.

Despite Jimmy's goodwill gesture, their relationship still deteriorated—the logical outcome when young men challenged the ways of the old. The past year had been a tense one. Centuries-old traditions fell to the rise of modern, white man's ways. Unsheared hair had always separated them from the white man. Jimmy feared he might surrender part of his culture if he parted with his. Now *they* had decided that for him.

Nathan paused. For a moment, Jimmy thought the orderly had at last finished. Then a scissor point pricked his Adam's apple. Only the faintest sensation of pain wormed through their medication. But Nathan plied his intent indelibly into Jimmy's brain.

"Any savage shit, you never live to walk out of here," Nathan whispered with a diabolic glint. He said no more, allowing silence and time for the words to penetrate Jimmy's thick Indian skull.

Snip. Snip. The shears resumed.

Jimmy flushed Nathan's words from his mind while blood trickled down his neck. He knew for now he must temper his anger; he must learn everything possible about this place and these people. He must prepare for when his time came. And his time would come; he knew it.

"There, now ya look human," Nathan added to punctuate this disgrace.

Jimmy hung his head. He now understood why so many tribal elders grew angry when the young cut their hair. It changed them from who they were, into what the white man wanted them to be.

At last Jimmy's straitjacket came off. For the first time in two weeks, he would feed himself and be able to sleep with his arms outstretched. He flexed his aching limbs. But there came a price for this modicum of freedom: he must take his medications as directed by either Nathan or nurse Thompson without retort.

Wallace accompanied Jimmy from his room into the hall. Jimmy's world again changed, expanding. Would it be for the better or for the worse?

"Day room privileges run from nine in the morning 'til nine in the evening. *And they are privileges*, subject to revocation if you fail to comply with any of our rules. We offer activities of therapeutic value to keep you busy while you're here," Wallace said plainly. He never once looked at Jimmy as they approached the door at the end of the hall.

Jimmy listened, all the while reconnoitering his surroundings. To his left, the door he had entered this place through stood ten strides down in the direction opposite the day room, which Jimmy surmised to be the windowed door ahead. He saw men milling about through the glass. An orderly worked a mop with his head down at the far end of the hall, while nurse Thompson busied herself at a desk situated just outside the day-room door. Another orderly crossed the day-room-door window. Nathan was nowhere in sight.

Despite the persistent application of their mind-numbing drugs, Jimmy pressed his brain to focus on what became most important to him: A way out of this place.

"The slightest infraction gets you locked down in your room. Do you understand, Jimmy?" Wallace asked, stopping him before reaching the day-room door.

Their eyes met.

Wallace's thin frame and meek appearance behind his glasses made him seem less intimidating now than upon Jimmy's arrival. The doctor made no gesture for the door handle until he received Jimmy's response, as if without it, Jimmy would be barred from entering some secret exalted place.

"I understand," Jimmy replied.

Only then did Wallace unlock the door. Apprehension crawled up Jimmy's spine. He had no idea what to expect. He swallowed hard. Would he be accepted? Would he be challenged? He felt his pulse rise while the back of this throat went bone dry.

They entered the asylum day room cluttered with Indians of varying ages, all belonging to many different tribes. Some were tall, some small; many were fat from lack of physical activity, with a few as gaunt as broomsticks. Some found solace slumped into chairs alone in the corners, working hard to avoid eye contact with either Jimmy or Dr. Wallace.

Others spoke amongst themselves, gazing briefly Jimmy's way while he stood there at a loss for what they expected of him.

He turned to find Wallace had backed out of the room to speak to Thompson at the desk. Every face he peered at was Indian. The only white people were the nurse, doctor and orderlies. Despite a room crowded with his own brethren, he felt utterly alone.

Immediately Jimmy picked out the three orderlies scattered about the room like guards. They also wore the white shirts with denim pants, while asylum patients wore faded blue shirts with pocketless denim pants that looked as if they had been the discards of the asylum employees. While their shirts wore no markings, their odd color would easily distinguish a wandering Indian amongst the locals as an errant asylum patient. Jimmy realized he must steal an orderly's shirt in order to be less conspicuous among the locals.

A loud '*whooping*' across the room snared Jimmy. He wandered toward the sound coming from an Indian who looked his age; one of a dozen that Jimmy surmised must also be in their twenties. Many others were older, with subdued faces Jimmy concluded had come from the same medication they administered to him. None were younger.

The 'whooping' one stared vacantly out a window while incessantly pounding its sill with a left arm in a grimy plaster cast.

Jimmy elected to maintain a safe distance from this one, at least for the present.

"Feelin' at home now, boy?" Nathan jabbed from behind Jimmy. "Let's find you a place to stand."

Jimmy turned only to be shoved toward the wall away from the door. He knew better than to resist, though part of him wanted to crack Nathan's jaw. *Patience.*

Jimmy retreated even further from the flow when a withered, gray-haired Indian with a sullen drooping face rolled by in a wheelchair that squeaked with each revolution of its large wheels. Had Jimmy not yielded, the old man would have rolled over his feet without regard. Jimmy's glare went unnoticed by the departing old man.

Then Jimmy spied something that captured his interest. A hulking, massive Indian, towering a full head taller than he, began easing his way toward the very same window that the smaller Indian now stood at pounding the sill. As the hulk closed in, the other Indian pounded harder and faster, as if sounding alarm. Yet no one in the room, other than Jimmy, took notice.

Jimmy scanned the orderlies, including Nathan. They were all busy with something, unaware of the obvious unfolding confrontation. The hulking Indian's eyes grew wide with perverse anticipation. A smile glimpsed his face. Even with his smile, his eyes intimidated. There remained three other vacant windows on either side of the occupied one, yet the hulk honed in on that particular window.

Jimmy made no move toward the window, but rather weighed his options. His brain urged him to turn away—this was none of his concern. His conscience bid him to do something.

With eyes full of attitude, the massive Indian marched up to the window, where he proceeded to cast the smaller Indian aside with a shove powerful enough to topple the smaller from his feet.

Despite being out-bulked, the smaller Indian refused to be intimidated. He plowed his way back before the window, where he resumed his pounding. The hulk thrust back with an explosive grunt. The smaller jammed his way back in between the hulk and the glass until his cheek became pressed firmly against the glass.

The hulk's gnarled fingers, most likely the result of fractures gone unset, curled into a knotty fist.

Whack!

The smaller Indian took the hulk's punch without raising a hand in defense. With blood gushing from both nostrils, he forced his body back in front of that window. He absolutely refused to yield that precious square of real estate that looked out onto a world denied him. Not a single orderly showed the slightest interest in the conflict escalating at the window.

When the hulk drew his fist back for another shot, Jimmy, heart thumping, wedged between the two. With a sure hand, he slashed the hulk's punch downward, deflecting the blow, and causing the lumbering girth to trip over Jimmy's outstretched foot and tumble to the floor like a grand old tree coming down.

The smaller Indian merely stared at Jimmy over bloody fingers clutching his battered nose.

When the hulk straightened up, with silent, dark eyes full of fire, and ready to attack Jimmy, Nathan intervened, jamming himself between the two Indians. The hulk, despite his size over Nathan, immediately backed down.

"Harold, I'll lock you down," Nathan cautioned like a vicious dog poised to bite. He stood undaunted despite their formidable disparity in mass.

For a long moment, Harold met Nathan's unyielding eyes.

"We gonna have a go?" Nathan pressed in an almost taunting way.

Two other orderlies rallied behind him.

Harold knew better.

Jimmy suddenly felt himself being measured. He came about. Wallace stared at him through the glass—not at Harold nor at Nathan—but at him. The doctor's face lacked expression, forcing Jimmy to ponder how the doctor had interpreted his actions. Or perhaps Wallace chose to merely observe without passing judgment? Jimmy could only wonder if he had passed, or failed, his first test in this place.

Jimmy offered no expression of victory, but rather straight-faced, he turned back to the window where the smaller Indian now stared out while thumping his sill.

"Thanks. Don't mention it," Jimmy muttered with a sarcasm lost on this one. Perhaps he did not speak the white man's tongue?

The Indian refused even to look at him. Instead, he wandered away without comment, which confused Jimmy even more. After spilling blood to hold his precious ground, he now abandoned it rather than engage Jimmy in innocent conversation.

"Nice talking to you, too," Jimmy added, perplexed.

He was indeed, it would seem, the only sane one locked in this place.

He drifted from the window to settle in a position beside an Indian near his age staring intensely at the wall. Jimmy promptly decided it best to avoid conversation altogether, rather he should wait and see how things developed.

Out of boredom, Jimmy took to scrutinizing the orderlies. He made a point of glancing at the nurses station opposite the window. The doctor routinely glanced up from his work to observe the room. Jimmy knew Wallace meant to keep an eye on him.

Before he realized it, an hour had passed without his position changing. Was he so quickly becoming like those around him? Could he actually be one of them? He noted that so far he had seen a single nurse and a handful of orderlies in this place. Of the orderlies he observed, Nathan seemed the most attentive to the patients, but in a manner more like a guard than someone concerned with these men's well being.

"When do we eat?" Jimmy queried the man beside him, who maintained his stare at the wall. Receiving no answer, Jimmy concluded this one might simply be deaf.

An orderly passed. Jimmy repeated his question to him. Again no response. Jimmy shifted positions, which allowed him to monitor the man that had taken the punch, who while attempting to be stealthy, kept checking the clock situated over the day-room door. As if timing some strategic advance, he eased his way toward Jimmy, who for a second, thought he might be coming over to thank him after all.

Instead, the Indian rubbernecked the room to assure himself no one might be watching. When he came within three paces of Jimmy, and Jimmy thought this one would actually speak, he altered his course to plant himself before the day-room door, staring into the corridor. Such an odd behavior, Jimmy thought initially.

Jimmy concluded everyone here was indeed crazy. Despite an overwhelming urge to wander over to the Indian to see exactly what had garnered his attention, Jimmy decided against it for fear it might spark a confrontation. One confrontation in this place was more than Jimmy wanted to deal with in a day.

After but a few minutes at the window, the man drifted away, wandering opposite Jimmy's direction, avoiding eye contact. Jimmy obliged by turning away.

5

Dinner time. A famished Jimmy sat at one of a dozen long tables in a noisy, drafty, poorly lit mess hall with the other patients, consuming tepid stewed vegetables flavored with a few scraps of gristly venison. Orderlies sat sprinkled amongst the patients, spoon-feeding some their dinner while it mostly drooled down their chins.

Jimmy captured the last of his carrots with his spoon—the only eating utensil allowed—while studying those around him. Some seemed completely helpless, others bordered on self-sufficient, while others appeared animated, perhaps even normal. Disgust crept onto Jimmy's face. Why had they placed him here amongst such disordered people?

Yet his eyes always gravitated back to the one whose nose had swollen and turned the color of a plum. This one's eyes never strayed from his food, and while he shoveled carrots in with his left hand, his right tapped the table to the point of irritation. Despite that, he seemed to transmit some strange connection that Jimmy could hardly avoid. Although never having exchanged a single word, Jimmy sensed a growing bond between them. It had to have been the way this one earlier had kept a furtive eye on Jimmy's movements in the day room. Each time Jimmy tried to confront his stare, this one quickly averted his eyes.

Despite overcooking and underseasoning the dinner, Jimmy emptied his bowl, relishing the last bite of the stale wheat bread. He realized he had eaten little in the previous five days, during which time he had retched up anything he did ingest while acclimating to their vile medications.

Jimmy rose with his tray to leave.

"Where you think you're going, Jimmy? Sit down. We tell you when to get up," Nathan delivered as an order.

He seemed in a sour mood for having to shovel food into an old man's mouth with little compassion. That which failed to go in, dribbled down to stain the old man's shirt. Clearly, Nathan found no inner reward in this particular duty.

Then it became clear why Jimmy had to remain seated.

Medication time again. The nurse entered with her tray of small paper cups. One by one, Indians rose from their tables, returned their trays to a long clearing shelf at the side of the mess hall entrance, after which they accepted the cup Thompson carefully selected for each of them.

Jimmy accepted his, hesitating as he brought it to his lips. He had endured about as much retching as his stomach could handle. He despised having to drink their vile liquids. But his pause brought Nathan's stern glare, which rekindled Wallace's heavy-handed words inside his brain. So Jimmy knocked back the cup the way he knocked back whiskey, hoping to force the liquid down without having to taste it. Despite his attempt, the vile medicine caught in his throat, triggering his gag reflex. He swallowed in spite of its vile acidic taste, crumpled the little cup into a tight wad, which he returned dutifully to the nurse's tray.

Did he, for just that moment, detect a glimmer of empathy in the nurse's eyes? Maybe he saw nothing more than her perverted white pride convincing herself she was helping the poor Indians. Anger and hate rose into Jimmy's throat. He swallowed hard to get it back down.

As Jimmy turned to leave, he caught a glimpse of the bruised-nose one. When Nathan placed the cup in this one's steady hand, he shifted it to his trembling hand. Nathan returned it, but this one insisted he take it in his other. Nathan finally abandoned his insistence. The Indian tried to take his medication, but the shaking caused most to dribble down his chin.

"We're low on his. You think I need to prepare another?" Thompson asked quietly.

"Nah, Charley's a good guy. He doesn't cause trouble," Nathan replied, dismissing Charley's action.

Anyway, Nathan was occupied administering medication to the old man he had just fed. Their exchange proved just as disastrous. The old man leaned his head forward after receiving the medication, causing most to mingle with the food scraps on his shirt.

"Charley," Jimmy whispered.

The sound of his name brought a sideways glance from Charley, who was using his spoon handle to scratch beneath his cast.

Jimmy thought he detected a glint of a smile beneath the bruising. Years would pass before Jimmy realized it, but he had just received his first lesson for surviving in this place.

Exiting the mess hall, Charley climbed the stairs and ambled back to the day room. Jimmy followed ... but not too closely.

Sharply at nine on the clock, orderlies herded the patients from the day room to the latrine then back to their rooms, where one-by-one, they locked them in for the night. Jimmy remained just inside his door after it closed. The clank of the lock settling into place stabbed into his soul. Darkness caved in around him as if it were burying him in the earth.

Jimmy remained at the door for a long moment, still unable to comprehend what had happened to his life. After awhile, he shifted to the window where he gazed absently at a gibbous moon crawling into a night sky crowded with stars. A giant oak two hundred paces from the building formed a cascading silver-tipped silhouette against the night.

6

The following day Jimmy wandered the day room alone in a crowd of people. Harold caught his attention across the room. Try as Harold might to look inconspicuous, he again flowed toward the window where Charley stood staring out while pounding the sill. As Harold neared, Charley pounded faster. When Harold came within a dozen steps of the window, Charley *whooped* like a frightened crane.

Jimmy strolled toward the window, not too fast, but neither too slow. He timed his arrival at the window to be precisely one step before Harold's.

When Harold realized Jimmy's intent, he abruptly altered course, shoved Jimmy on his way past, then continued across the room to stand at the window on the opposite wall of the day room.

Jimmy relished his small victory in this place.

"It's the only way," Charley said, responding to Jimmy's presence beside him at the window without looking at him. Jimmy could see Charley making eye contact with Jimmy's reflection in the glass rather than look at him directly.

"I thought you didn't talk, Charley," Jimmy replied, surprised at first that Charley spoke without prodding.

Charley snapped his head around with the viciousness of a rabid dog.

"I am Mana! Charley only to them," Mana growled with genuine anger stoking the fire in his eyes.

"I am Tesqua. Jimmy Sparrow Hawk to them. I am Apache."

"No one here cares what your name means."

Mana returned to staring out the window.

"How'd you break your arm?" Tesqua asked innocently.

For a long moment Mana stared at his grimy cast, pressing his brain for an answer to the question.

"I don't know," he replied.

Mana peered into Tesqua's eyes. Tesqua detected a deep despair he had never witnessed before. It was as if he were delving into the soul of a man whose spirit had been taken from him. A man with nothing to live for. He had never gazed into the eyes of a man with no soul before. It terrified him.

"How could you not know?"

"Know what?"

The innocent question triggered something troubling in Mana's memory. Tesqua could discern that much.

"How you broke your arm."

Mana stared out the window.

Could he be speaking the truth? Could he really not know how his arm came to be broken in this place?

"What's Harold's problem?" Tesqua queried when the eerie silence lingered between them.

"Evey. And his name is Grano."

"Evey? You always talk in riddles?"

Mana stared blankly at him for a long second, then he started to wander away. Tesqua's next words, however, stopped him in his tracks.

"What's the only way?"

Mana just stared back at him.

"The only way? What's the only way?" Tesqua reiterated, his voice releasing an edge of irritation.

"The only way you'll ever leave this place."

Mana indicated with his eyes out the window.

Diggers. Tesqua turned to black dirt arcing out a hole as two men hollowed out a grave fifty yards north of the building near a giant oak. Tesqua's heart froze. Breathing became difficult. Bile backed up into this throat. He tried to swallow but couldn't. He spun about, taking in the entire room in a glance. The orderlies distributed themselves throughout. No one, it seemed, monitored the door. Tesqua shifted away from looking out the window to provide a watchful eye on the door.

He waited. Small beads of sweat accumulated on his furrowed brow.

A few inches at a time, Tesqua eased over to stand near the day-room door. No one seemed to notice his subtly changing position in the room. In fact, no one noticed much of anything that went on in the day room. A crude plan came together while he waited for opportunity to present itself. Tesqua would be ready.

While offering the appearance of daydreaming, Tesqua patiently waited, listening. First came footsteps. Tesqua's heartbeat lurched. He held his position steady. A moment later came the sound of the lock turning in the door. Opportunity had just arrived! He had to hold himself back. It took an eternity for the lock to release before the day-room door opened.

An orderly entered, oblivious to Tesqua hovering less than two feet away. Tesqua slid his foot over just enough to contact the door as it swung closed. The pressure he exerted kept the door from closing completely, thereby preventing the door catch from engaging. In a glance it appeared the door had closed, but Tesqua's foot held it just enough that he could open it with a little effort.

He scanned the breadth of the room. His breathing became louder. He could hear frantic thumping inside his head. No eyes were observing him; no one paid him any attention. His heart hammered inside his chest. He had to act on instinct; now was not a time to debate. It might be his only moment.

Maybe ... maybe he should wait. Indecision stomped all over his mind. Fear choked his breathing. Fear cripples, he scolded himself. He must block it from his head. His mouth turned to cotton. His palms sweated as he waited for a better moment. What if no better moment came? He made fists trying to dry his hands. He knew he must grab the handle tightly. If he slipped, his chance would be gone. He filled his lungs, scanned one more time.

He grabbed the handle, pulled the door open enough to slip into the hall.

He was in motion. No stopping now. Freedom dangled just beyond his reach through that reception-room door. He glanced right to the nurses' station desk. He was alone. The door leading out of the asylum—his door to freedom—waited twenty strides on the right. He raced to the reception-room door, focusing only on how to crash it.

His heart pounded out of control. Thoughts of his Celia flooded his brain at that moment. She would be waiting for him. He would fall into her loving arms.

Tesqua reached the door. But at that same moment, Nathan emerged from the staircase thirty paces to his left. Time sped up. Damnit!

Tesqua yanked the door. *Locked.* He rammed it twice.

"Hey!" Nathan yelled, bolting toward him. "I need help!" he screamed even before he approached Tesqua.

Tesqua spun. There had to be something he could do.

Out the corner of his vision, Tesqua spied the day-room door opening—two more orderlies spilled into the hall. He had only seconds left.

Nathan closed in.

Tesqua rabbit-punched him squarely on the jaw, dropping him in his tracks. Time stopped. Tesqua wheeled. He went for the linen cart across the hall. Raising it chest-high, he rammed it at the glass window, missing it squarely, but clipping it near the edge. The wire-embedded pane held. Jagged cracks radiated from the impact point to the corners, but the glass remained in its frame. Tesqua swung the cart at the onrushing orderlies. He missed one, caught the other in the thigh. However, his action slowed neither.

Tesqua flailed his arms with all his might. But his efforts proved futile. In another moment, Nathan had regained his footing and Tesqua went down, wrestled onto his stomach by the threesome. A knee slammed into his spine. He felt all the air being crushed from his lungs. For a moment, Tesqua fought only to inhale. He had only seconds before he passed out.

The orderlies worked Tesqua's arms to his back to lash them with leather straps they unfurled from their pockets. Tesqua's first ill-conceived test of his captors and their prison had failed—miserably. But he would continue to test them until he uncovered their weakness and his way to freedom.

7

With closed eyes, Tesqua brushed his fingers lightly along Celia's warm sinewy flesh, gently coming around to cup her small breast. Her chocolate-brown nipple tightened under his touch.

Celia wanted to sleep, her night had been difficult, but at this moment she wanted Tesqua more. Her body tingled. The delicate hairs on her arms rose in response to the gentle kiss Tesqua bestowed at the base of her neck, all the while his hand journeyed slowly over the contour of her pear-shaped six-months-pregnant belly.

She opened, welcoming his playful petting that teased her until she thought she could stand it no more. They kissed, both breathing urgently. Despite the fact that sunrise remained an hour away, Tesqua was fully aroused and awake. Celia knew well what stole her man regularly from his sleep.

The two had married contrary to her mother's concern that Tesqua seemed too wild to make a fit husband. She believed Tesqua undeserving of such a wonderful young woman. Celia, his junior by two years, believed in her heart Tesqua was the only man who could give her a life of simple happiness, a kind of happiness that one could never purchase with the white man's money. Contrary to most of the other women her age in their tribe, she sought no more than the tradition of her people. Nurture the land, and the land would in turn nurture them. Love could take care of the rest.

"Careful," she whispered when Tesqua expressed his yearning to mount her. She responded in kind to his foreplay, using her hand to heighten his excitement; she wanted him as badly as he wanted her at that moment. But her mother's stern warning rang insistent inside her head. Keep him at bay during the last months of carrying their baby. Much too dangerous to allow a man to have his way, her mother had cautioned with a look that left no room for loose interpretations. Would he be able to withstand the many weeks remaining until giving birth? Would she?

She hated to, but she pulled away from him, removing his access to her.

Tesqua understood. He loved her too much to ever allow anything to steal away their moments of bliss. He gently kissed her cheek, then her lips, electing instead to wrap his arms over hers and hold her close. She always felt safe in his arms. Yet neither had the slightest inkling they would not be sharing their bed when the next sunset faded into night.

Celia had always been the rock in their relationship. If anyone could rein Tesqua in, Celia would, his mother had shared with her on the eve of her wedding. And for the first nine months of their marriage, she had been able to tame him. At least so she thought.

"You don't want to harm our son," she whispered, offering encouragement for his discipline.

"You're sure it's a son?"

Celia turned over, pressed her nakedness against him, which brought him pleasure.

"Of course. In my vision, a bear comes out of the river. My mother said the bear means our first-born will be a son. You will have a warrior to follow in your footsteps."

Her smile magic, Tesqua could see the excitement of motherhood taking over her face even in the faint predawn light.

"We are no longer warriors. Our lives are not our fathers."

Tesqua could only offer a lover's indulgent smile. He had long ago abandoned the foolishness of Apache visions. *They were the old ways.* Ways that forced them to live on government reservations. Not the ways he would instill in his family. They must embrace the new world, a world the white man thrust upon them. Refuse to accept that world—spend your life in misery, he had argued to his father. For many days after those words, his father refused to even speak to him. As a result, there grew a distance between them when they spoke.

"What?" Celia pressed in response to his smile.

"Nothing."

Suddenly Tesqua sprang awake, angered it was all a dream. His bed and his pregnant wife were a thousand miles away. They had locked him in their asylum, so far from her that she would never be able to see him at a time she most needed his comfort.

"Celia!" he screamed at the empty room. He yearned to stroke her softness and feel her warmth against him. At this moment, he felt utterly alone, defeated; and his jaw hurt like hell. Nathan had whacked him good while he had him on the floor. He remembered that much.

Celia would be crying for him. He would miss that moment when his son entered their world. His first-born's initial view of life would be experienced without his father. Would they have a son as Celia believed? He could only hope. He realized, as he lay in his bed staring at barren crumbling walls, that he knew nothing more than they had imprisoned him with no means of freeing himself. What if no one had informed Celia as to what had happened to him? She might think he abandoned her, ran away when she most needed her husband.

Damn them!

The lock clanked.

Tesqua pulled his muscles to sit up in his bed. Wrist straps held his arms against the mattress, with the lashings secured to the floor rings.

Once the afterimages of his Celia faded, reality pressed against his brain. He was hungry, thirsty and the pressure in his bladder shot jabbing pains into his lower spine. It seemed in a fleeting moment, his life had become so wretched. Everything, even the simplest necessity, became a luxury he had to beg for from the white man.

Nathan strolled in, a broad grin illuminating his face. He approached the bed, stopping safely out of spitting range.

"I sense you and I will never become friends, Jimmy," he said, jingling his keys to taunt Tesqua.

"You going to unstrap me?"

"I don't know. You learn anything from yesterday?"

"I learned all of you have imprisoned me against my will."

"When will you realize we're here to help you," Nathan said, mimicking Wallace's words in a way that singed Tesqua's nerves.

Nathan's smug tone triggered an acidic eruption in Tesqua's gut. The orderly wanted Tesqua to understand who held the real power over him in this place.

"I need to relieve myself."

"You should have thought about that before you cracked my jaw. Oh, the sniveling fool you rammed with the cart quit an hour after your outburst. Took twenty stitches in his leg." Nathan moved in a little closer. "You've made my job harder now. So excuse me if I don't care about your problem."

Nathan chuckled as he strolled out, savoring each step. The jingling keys only further tormented Tesqua.

"Let me out of here!" Tesqua screamed. He stopped when Thompson peered in as she passed. Her eyes held his, but she made no move to enter to aid him in any way. Tesqua needed water, but he never believed anyone would provide it. He lasted little more than an hour more before he peed in his bed. He imagined he would be sleeping in it before anyone would do anything about it.

8

Tesqua's punishment consisted of two days strapped to his bed plus five more days confined to his room. Wallace informed Tesqua he was being lenient for Tesqua's first offense, holding to his staunch belief that people, if given sufficient time, will acquiesce to anything ... even an insane asylum. Could Tesqua, however, prove the exception?

After serving his days, Tesqua rejoined the day-room population to find Mana circling from window to window, this time pounding his thigh.

"Get a-way from me," he barked at no one. Not a soul dared venture within ten feet of him while he paced. But his snarling outbursts, nonetheless, agitated the meeker patients, inducing them to huddle on the opposite side of the room. Some cowered, others faced the wall, believing that if they just avoided looking at Mana, they would remain safe from him.

Tesqua found amusement watching a half dozen patients clinging together like frightened rabbits and flowing en masse from one side of the room to the other to avoid the ranting Mana.

"You're still alive," Mana said evenly without looking up. The man acted crazy one second, perfectly sane the next.

Tesqua snared his arm.

"I'm not like you. I'm not like any of you," Tesqua scowled, "I will not die here!"

"Figured they were digging for you."

Mana motioned diggers at the giant oak.

"How long have you been here?" Tesqua asked.

Mana slapped the wall as if in pain.

"Too long."

"I won't be here that long."

"That's what I said," Mana replied, for the first time looking at Tesqua.

His eyes slid off Tesqua to Nathan, who strolled about, heading toward them. Mana abandoned the window, putting distance between himself and the orderly. After a moment, Tesqua followed.

On their journey across the room to avoid the orderly, they passed Ko-nay-ha, a fifty-year-old Kiowa in a chair positioned against the wall, clear of the flow of those patients now shuffling back across the room to avoid Mana. Ko-nay-ha sat hollow-eyed and unsmiling.

"This one here hasn't spoken a word in four years. His eyes never blink. I think his brain got switched off, like the way the lights go out here at night," Mana commented.

Tesqua's mind reeled. He thought not about the Kiowa occupying a chair, but rather the fact that Mana had been imprisoned at least four years already. Tesqua's son might be growing up without his father. Celia must hate him. By now, she must believe he had deserted her. He held no doubts that their Indian agent would withhold Tesqua's whereabouts from his family. Most likely, no one back on the reservation would know what happened. Tesqua realized he had grossly underestimated the power the white man held over him. He had failed to heed his father's words. He wished for a moment that he could go back to correct his err. He knew how foolish it was to wish … for anything.

Mana glanced at the clock. As if late, he hurried to the day-room-door window. Less than a minute later, he left the door to return to his window. Those few moments, however, had dramatically altered Mana's face. He remained smileless, but his eyes seemed more content than they had been when Tesqua first entered the day room. Something had drawn Mana's spirit up from the dark depths that this place sucked everyone down into.

For hours, Tesqua did nothing but stare. A few played checkers at the table, others occupied chairs scattered about the room, gazing blankly into space. Still others found places at the windows from which to observe, and possibly dream about, the outside world; their view of that world spoiled by an iron grating that forced them to take in everything through a mosaic of checkerboard squares.

The old Indian wore a scowl as he rolled his chair along, oblivious to those around him. He rammed a few unabashedly during his travels from one side of the room to the other, grumbling at them when he did. His actions seemed almost intentional. Maybe he hoped to spark cross words between them, ignite a flame of life back into them. He never once uttered a word of apology for his rude collisions.

As Tesqua roamed, he made it a point to avoid the wheel-chair-bound old man. For a brief time he amused himself by moving directly opposite wherever the old man rolled. The very action brought a faint glimmer of a smile to Tesqua's face—it brought a sneer from the old man when he, at last, figured out exactly what Tesqua kept doing.

Tiring of the pointless game, Tesqua lingered near the corner closest to the window overlooking the nurses' station. Thompson worked diligently at her desk, looking up regularly to check on her patients. When her eyes met Tesqua's, she quickly returned to her work. Tesqua's brief contact, however, had affected her. He could see she became self-conscious of herself knowing he was observing her. She withdrew a strand of hair that floated into her face and checked the collar of her uniform dress.

At that same moment, Tesqua realized he had not seen Dr. Wallace observing him since the first day the doctor had escorted him into the day room. In fact, only when the doctor sought to administer some new medication to Tesqua did they encounter each other. Only orderlies tended the patients in the day room, and only the nurse administered the routine medications, though the orderlies served as her enforcers, ensuring each patient swallowed what she gave them.

Tesqua started across the room for the fifth time that day when a booming thunderclap rattled the windows with the voracity of an exploding bomb. The violent percussion triggered a fellow Indian's excruciating scream.

"Get down!" he cried out incessantly, his hands clutching his ears as he flattened himself to the floor. When Tesqua erred by passing within arm's reach, the man snared Tesqua's leg to pull him down alongside him.

"They'll see you. Get down 'fore you get your head blowed off," he warned in a quivering voice.

No one in the room other than Tesqua paid this one any attention. Tesqua yanked at his trapped leg until he at last freed it. He wasted no time getting as far away from the man as possible. The terrified Indian slithered snake-like to the corner, where he curled into a fetal ball while pressing his hands tightly over his closed eyes.

Tesqua had heard the stories, but now he had actually witnessed what the white man termed shell shock. He never could understand why any Indian would volunteer to fight in a white man's war. Hadn't their people fought the white man enough to know better than to get involved in their internal squabbling? And risk their lives for what?

A few Indian agents had tried recruiting for the war, with a handful of men Tesqua knew falling for their foolish talk. Indians weren't United States citizens, yet they urged them to take up arms, put on a uniform and travel far away to fight for the same people that had ravaged the Indian nations over the last hundred years. They now must learn to live with the white man; they didn't need to die for them.

What would be the result of their patriotism to a nation that despised them? A war medal? More likely, death, maiming or landing in an insane asylum with shell shock. Tesqua had listened to the graphic stories from a few of his own tribe who suffered as a result of fighting in the white man's wars. The tales usually came out over a jug or two of bootleg whiskey. He wondered for a moment if the old Indian in the wheelchair had received his injury fighting in some distant land.

Tesqua harbored no sympathy for those fools, only sadness that they were again taken in by the white man's empty promises. Their courage earned them nothing. They returned from the war to squalid reservations suffering from hunger and neglect; they received apathy or disdain from every white man whose path they crossed.

Just thinking about such maltreatment churned disgust in Tesqua's stomach. His face contorted with an angry grimace, which Mana mimicked from across the room. Then incorrectly concluding that Tesqua had meant his expression of disgust for him, Mana turned his back on him.

Tesqua's anger bubbled at a low boil. His eyes darted about the room, taking in everything in a split second. The orderlies were scattered about. No eyes watched him. Nathan was nowhere about. Maybe he had left his job for the day? The nurse busied herself at the desk. After a few moments, she walked away. But Tesqua remembered the vicious repercussions of his last failed attempt. His courage evaporated. He scolded himself for his weakness, but he realized he must stop acting on impulse. He must scrutinize his surroundings for answers as to when and how to escape this place. Only through observation coupled with flawless planning might he succeed.

9

Darkness came ... along with loneliness, anger and the dreaded night screams. They had been locked in their rooms for less than an hour when shadows created by movement in the hall snared Tesqua's attention. He slipped from his bed, eased to the door to gaze out the small window. In the corridor, Wallace pushed a bed along, using Nathan to guide it from the front.

Mana was strapped to the bed.

As they rolled past Tesqua's room, his eyes met Mana's. Mana never resisted the four broad leather straps holding him fast. Yet, Mana's wide eyes revealed unmistakable terror. His face overwhelmed Tesqua, who pressed his cheek against the door so he could see them for the longest possible time. Swallowing became difficult. He had never witnessed such fear in a man's eyes before. It was the fear of death that he saw. After they disappeared, Tesqua remained, staring at nothing.

Some time later, Tesqua had no way of knowing just how long, the hall lights dimmed, sizzled, then came back to full brightness. Down the hall, someone shrieked.

"Shut up and go to sleep, you monkeys," Nathan called from the nurses' station.

Tesqua shifted, catching only a glimpse of Nathan's feet hanging off the desk's corner.

****

Morning arrived. An exhausted Nathan trudged his way out when Thompson arrived for her day shift at the same moment Tesqua strode down the hall toward the day room. He listened clandestinely while Nathan briefed Thompson on the night's activities. Every little scrap of information could prove important to him. He never knew what tidbit might become crucial to his plan.

"I'm not working another double shift," Nathan moaned, louder than he should. "When the hell is he going to hire ..."

Tesqua continued into the day room. Double shifts meant overwork, which led to exhaustion, which led to carelessness. He moved to the table, watching two men play checkers for many minutes before realizing Mana was absent from the room this day.

After Nathan had finished speaking with Thompson, he entered the day room.

Tesqua approached him.

"Where's Charley?"

"Don't ever come up and talk to me," Nathan spat.

"I wish to talk to him."

"Yeah, well, we all wish something, don't we? I wish to go home and sleep, but I can't. Now get away from me."

Tesqua abandoned Nathan, seeking a place to isolate himself in the crowded room. He counted fifty-six Indians scattered in various locations throughout the space as if tossed in willy-nilly. He thought there were more Indians now than when he arrived five months ago.

"I'm Apache," Tesqua blurted as the old man rolled past.

The old Indian continued without acknowledging Tesqua's words. The elder also pressed his chin to his chest to avoid Tesqua's eyes.

Tesqua glanced up to the clock over the day-room door. Realizing it was the time Mana regularly stood at the day-room-door window, Tesqua shifted to the glass.

He stared at nothing for the first few moments. Then it happened. A string of Indian women crossed the corridor in the wing opposite theirs. *There were women here!* Tesqua's heart leapt at the thought of being able to speak to an Indian woman, any Indian woman, again. A few appeared even close to his age.

He left the day-room-door window to rap on the glass at the nurses' station.

Thompson stopped her work at the desk, slid the glass open.

"Why are we kept separated from the women?" Tesqua asked.

"Do you want to sit?"

"I don't want to sit. Why are men and women kept apart?"

Tesqua's rising voice brought Nathan to the window.

"We got a problem?" Nathan's cold stare penetrated Tesqua's eyes.

Tesqua said nothing. Instead, he moved from the window back across the day room. He wanted as much distance as possible between himself and the orderly. He learned it was wise to avoid Nathan at any cost when his mood turned cross. Having to work double shifts meant Nathan would be cross until they hired a new orderly.

For the first time since his arrival, Tesqua's face actually broke a slight smile at the thought of mingling with women. He missed being with Celia so much. The worst time was when evening came. Back at home as the sun set and Tesqua returned from the fields, they would sit together across from a blazing fire. Celia loved to talk, but she also loved to just sit in silence with him. Their last few weeks together had been spent talking about the baby, seemed it was always about the baby, and what he would look like. She said a dozen times that their son would be as handsome and as strong as his father. Tesqua chose not to disagree with her.

"Sioux," the old Indian said.

Tesqua spun about. The old man in the wheelchair stared up at him with a sort of admiration in his eyes.

"What?"

"I am Paraquo."

"Paraquo," Tesqua repeated, surprised the old man had chosen this particular moment to speak to him. Paraquo leaned forward in his wheelchair, motioning Tesqua closer.

"The white man fears me," Paraquo confided, his dark eyes darting side to side, making certain no orderly might overhear.

For a moment, the gravity of Paraquo's actions convinced Tesqua he might become privy to some grand Indian secret. A revelation meant to change Tesqua's life forever.

"Why should the white man fear you?" Tesqua asked, returning the same conspiratorial tone.

Paraquo unfurled a calloused fist to reveal a palm-sized leather medicine pouch secured with a frayed black shoelace. The old Indian then tucked the pouch beneath his belt, finishing with a crooked withered finger to his wilted lips.

"I am a powerful shaman," he whispered.

"If you're so powerful, free us from this white man's hell-hole," Tesqua whispered back.

Neither spoke. Paraquo's lips drew tight across his jowly face. His eyes froze. Then he released a grunt and rolled away toward the window looking out upon the giant oak. In Mana's absence, that prime piece of real estate was temporarily up for grabs. Or was it temporary? Were there diggers out there right now preparing Mana's grave? Seemed only the old man was interested in it. Even Grano displayed no interest in standing before it without Mana in the room.

Tesqua sought solitude in another corner.

Two hours later, the day room came alive as patients jammed their way in to crowd the day-room-door window. The main hall became the arena for all the patients' interest.

10

Outside the locked day-room door, Grano stood with restraint straps dangling from his wrists while Nathan struggled to force him back to his room. What had began as a minor scuffle in the latrine escalated into a confrontation in the hall when Nathan mistakenly thought he had secured Grano in restraints before single-handedly transferring him back to his room.

Grano, however, had decided once in the hall that he no longer wished to cooperate. Nathan's long work hours with no increased pay had made him irascible. He exhibited zero sense of humor anyway, and the additional stress made him more difficult than usual. Most patients, despite being crazy, had enough sense to avoid the unpredictable orderly. But not Grano.

Nurse Thompson tried her best to assist, but she knew better than to approach Harold when he fell into one of his anti-social moods. Besides, she could have little impact opposing one of Harold's size. Strangely enough, though, she harbored no fear of him. For all his outbursts of anger, he never once directed violence toward her. Nathan, however, was a different matter. The orderly derived his pleasure not from intimidating the weak, but rather antagonizing the strong. Nathan thrived on terrorizing the likes of Grano despite their formidable disparity in size. It appeared now he had pushed the giant Indian just once too often.

"You want me to summon Wallace?" Thompson asked while the reception room buzzer rang insistently.

"I'm okay," Nathan muffled from the headlock Harold held him in. "Everything's under control."

Thompson skirted the struggling pair to reach the reception room door. She threw it open.

"Your bloody finger stuck on my buzzer? We're in a bit of a ..."

"You're expecting me," a tall, broad-shouldered chestnut-haired man with a thick goatee on a cherub face said, displaying a youthful innocent smile. He offered his hand, though Thompson had no time for it. In that moment, she measured this one to easily match Harold's size.

"The new orderly! Come along then. You're needed inside straight away," Thompson replied, ushering him through the door without delay then locking it.

No sooner had they entered the main hall when Nathan came sliding by on his arse. Grano, standing akimbo fifteen feet away, grinned like a man who had just vanquished his opponent in one of the local wrestling competitions.

"I'm warning you, Harold, we're no longer friends," Nathan said.

Grano said nothing, only indicated with his eyes that he would repel anything Nathan might throw at him. However, Grano's expression turned grim when the newcomer passed his coat over to Thompson. The giant Indian took pause to assess this new threat, but only for a moment. Raising his brows,

Grano spit into his palms and rubbed them together vigorously, ready for both Nathan and this new challenger.

Nathan picked himself up, glanced over at the man beside Thompson, then started toward Grano again.

"Too much sugar," Nathan said, also spitting into his hands in preparation for his next assault.

"You go right. I go left. Meet in the middle of his back," the newcomer offered with a cocky smile that disarmed Grano for the moment.

"Go," Nathan commanded. Having someone equal in size to Grano beside him inspired Nathan. A premature victory smile even broke across his lips.

And they were off. The newcomer circled one way, Nathan the other. Grano instinctively backed up a few steps to brace for their onslaught. He extended his massive hands to arm's length in anticipation of their surge.

Wild cheering erupted behind the day-room door.

Nathan attacked first. The newcomer lunged from the opposing side. Grano swung his mighty arm, flinging the newcomer into the wall while Nathan jumped unsuccessfully for a headlock. Grano only laughed as he pulled Nathan around by his belt to plop him at the Indian's size fourteen scuffed up shoes.

The newcomer launched himself off the wall in a dive for Grano's left arm. He successfully latched onto it then worked it quickly to the center of Grano's back.

"Don't you medicate these patients?" the newcomer asked.

When Nathan returned to his feet, Grano locked his head under his armpit.

"This is medicated!" Nathan muffled as he slid his head out the rear. Snaring the dangling wrist strap with a wild swipe of his left hand, he brought Grano's right arm to the furrow of the huge Indian's back. In a clever finishing move, Nathan swung Grano in a circle, propelling him against his will toward an open door.

But Grano, for the moment defeated, refused to surrender. He threw his massive girth sideways, knocking the newcomer into Thompson, which toppled them one atop the other on the floor. Their compromising position brought a new chorus of cheers from everyone crowding the day-room windows.

As much as Grano admired his little offensive maneuver, it was nonetheless flawed. His momentum carried him into the patient room, where, before he could regain a charging stance, Nathan slammed the door and snapped the lock into place.

"Let me out of here," Grano growled.

"Later, after the sugar wears off," Nathan said, hands on hips as if *he* warranted the credit for subduing their unruly giant of a patient.

On the floor, Thompson lay nose-to-nose with the newcomer in a position that held everyone's attention.

"Dr. Barry, you're early," Wallace said, approaching them from the staircase.

Dr. Barry hastily pulled himself up, after which he aided Thompson back to her feet. He liked the feel of her soft hand in his. It was so delicate. She also exuded the most pleasing fragrance that lingered in Dr. Barry's mind.

"Doctor? Sorry. Thought you were ..." Thompson offered profusely in apology.

Barry, however, never heard a word she said. His gaze remained fixed on her shimmering blue eyes. Her smile immediately captivated him. Despite the altercation, he knew he was going to like being here.

"Thought we were getting a new orderly?" Thompson added, hoping to soften her error. She straightened her uniform with one hand while hastily adjusting crumbled hair with the other, hoping her true intent went unnoticed by the new doctor.

"Sorry about my neglect. The new orderly had a last minute change of heart. He won't be starting after all," Wallace offered.

"Great," Nathan muttered.

Dr. Barry straightened his clothes, smoothed his hair with one hand while offering his other to Thompson. He actually just wanted to touch her again.

"Very pleased to meet you, nurse?"

"Thompson."

The nurse made no move to shake his hand.

"I'm sure we'll be working closely. I mean not that close, of course."

"Of course."

While Grano pounded the door, Wallace led Dr. Barry up the staircase to their offices on the second floor.

Life returned to normal in the asylum—yet it had also inexorably changed.

11

Once ensconced in Wallace's office, Dr. Barry settled into the chair across from the doctor, dabbing the small cut he suffered to the corner of his lip. The bleeding had all but stopped.

"We currently house ninety-six patients."

"All Indian?"

"Full-blooded right down to the half-bloods. Only Indian insane asylum in the country. Congress wants them segregated. They're more challenging."

"I do enjoy a challenge."

"Then you've chosen the right place. But I must apologize, Dr. Barry, it's most uncustomary for new staff to draw blood on their first day. As you can see, we do have a few problems that we deal with regularly."

"I must say, I wasn't expecting quite the exhilarating welcome."

"I'm glad to have the help, though. I'm the only attending, and I'm currently engaged in finding another orderly to replace the two that recently left. It's quite the challenge to find people willing to be around them on a daily basis. Most wish these people didn't exist. But let me be frank with you for a moment, because I am curious about one thing."

"Why here?" Barry offered with his boyish smile. He had expected the question. At times, even he asked himself the same thing.

"Exactly. You're Ivy League. We're hardly cream of the crop. Seems at the very least, there would be greater rewards at St. Elizabeth's, or any other large institution, for that matter."

"Like you said, doctor, it's all about the challenge. So, when can I begin working with patients?"

"Have you familiarized yourself with the findings from the congressional study of incidents of mental illness among half breeds?"

"Not yet."

"Then I recommend you start there. The report poses many interesting postulates. We're certainly finding extreme cases among our population. It presents a number of irrefutable arguments. I feel it substantiates their claim for a genetic predisposition toward mental illness in half-breeds. If only the government had taken that notion seriously twenty years ago, our jobs today might be so much easier."

"I wasn't aware any serious study had been conducted in that area. I'm not sure I would have subscribed to such a notion even if I had known."

With his brow furled, Wallace dismissed Dr. Barry's statement as naive. He will have a much different attitude, given a few months in this environment.

"Take some time to settle in. Observe our patients awhile to get comfortable with their cases. When you're ready, we'll discuss each of the patients as we make rounds, during which you can select your case load. But it's advisable you take your time studying the patients here before jumping in. They're considerably more complex than others you might have been accustomed to treating. The half-breeds are especially prone to fits of uncontrollable rage. I've had them under study for quite some time now."

"I'll follow your lead, doctor. I do look forward to working here. I've received many excellent comments about your work from the Bureau people in Washington."

"Ah, yes, our BIA bureaucrats. I'm not sure they can even understand what it is we contend with here. I've been pleading with the commissioner for years to allocate more funds to help us improve our facilities. We're habitually underfunded, understaffed, and for the most part, neglected. But that's the bureaucracy. For now, doctor, just take some time to form your own judgments. I do look forward to our working together."

Barry's face turned puzzled as he rose to leave.

"Were you..." he asked, indicating a cavalry hat with officer insignia on Wallace's side bureau beside a sepia faded photograph of a cavalry officer on his mount.

"My father."

12

Barry spent his first two months in Canton observing asylum patients. He meticulously captured every detail of everything he saw, heard and felt. He had always been a copious note-taker. He never trusted anything to memory. He learned as a young graduate to assume he would forget the important details. It bothered him greatly to come into a facility with such otherwise poor record keeping. Patient records were the single most important tool in performing his job. He ventured that so much had been lost due to negligence, that it would make his job here difficult—if not insurmountable—in the short term. It appeared as if Wallace had documented almost nothing of his interactions with patients. Nor were adequate medical records maintained to provide the illness and mortality statistics the government bureaucrats regularly required. Barry attributed the poor habits to the understaffing the asylum faced, which, of course, stemmed from the limited funding the Bureau of Indian Affairs allotted to maintain such a facility. Hence, the problem was not one with the asylum, but rather in Washington, or so Barry thought.

New requests for admittance arrived weekly, but with every bed occupied, Wallace became forced to turn away most who sought their medical expertise. That struck Dr. Barry personally at first, feeling they were part of the problem rather than the solution. However, he came to realize after rummaging through file cabinets, that not a single patient had been released from this asylum in the past six years. The only way beds opened up in Canton were through patient deaths. And Barry was having difficulty ascertaining exactly how many patients that had been. To add insult to injury, of those records he successfully uncovered, the majority had been simply marked 'DECEASED' then filed away with no medical data to identify cause of death or even a signed death certificate.

Slowly Barry began to grasp the multiplicity of challenges here. More than he even imagined when he first accepted the assignment. But he resolved to find in each day an opportunity to improve not only this facility, but also the quality of life for each of the patients he attended.

****

Tesqua entered the day room to a dismal gray day beyond their windows. The slate sky threatened rain. A unseasonal chill seeped in through the window frames, infecting the room.

Mana, as always, stood at the window staring out at hundreds of small brown birds flocking to the safety of the giant oak. How many patients before him had stood there staring at that magnificent tree? How many would come after he was gone? Grano had long abandoned his campaign of bullying Mana, so for weeks the day room lacked any spirit. Few spoke to each other. Some played checkers, though too many times games ignited arguments, which deteriorated into shoving matches that eventually brought the orderlies. On a few occasions blood flowed, but it was never Tesqua's or Mana's. They had learned to avoid the petty fighting that the others engaged in.

Nathan went about tending patients while Tesqua made a game out of avoiding Nathan when he could. To keep his mind sharp, he memorized Nathan's routine, then found pleasure in successfully predicting Nathan's moves, which also allowed him to avoid coming within close proximity of the compassionless worker. Tesqua saw his actions similar to a human checkers game between him and the orderly. Except the orderly was unaware that he was even playing.

Tesqua casually shifted across the room when Nathan finished rolling Paraquo over to a corner. He now stood beside Sequall, a recent admission who refused to utter a word while exhibiting multiple signs of paranoia, though Tesqua could care little for what seemed to be ailing this one.

Sequall occupied his days shifting from foot to foot, like he had to pee, all while standing before two chairs. He carefully spaced the chairs two feet apart, checking them habitually to reaffirm they maintained their exact spacing. When he paused before one, Tesqua sat in the other.

Sequall screamed!

Tesqua jumped up. The last thing he wished was a confrontation with this crazy one, or worse, to bring Nathan over. But as soon as Tesqua abandoned the chair, Sequall's screaming ceased. He returned to bouncing between the chairs as if nothing had occurred. So Tesqua decided to sit in the other chair, which brought more screaming. When Tesqua left that chair, Sequall stopped. Tesqua found humor in switching the Indian's screaming on and off like a faucet. Finally, Tesqua gave up, migrating over to Mana at the window.

"Our fathers are why we suffer. They were spineless men who surrendered to the white man," Tesqua moaned while gazing out at the giant oak that had stood for likely a hundred years. It would grow a hundred more, unless the white man destroyed it, like he had decimated so much of their land.

"My father never surrendered," Mana replied.

"Nor will I. Nothing they can do will make me ashamed of who I am. They will never break my spirit. I'm getting out of here," Tesqua announced.

"Not very wise," Mana commented. After a silent moment, he indicated the leaves, all shades of crimson and yellow, fluttering from the giant oak. Overhead, a flock of Canadian geese flapped by in their v-formation.

Tesqua sought an explanation with his look.

Mana, in his own way was toying with him, savoring the moment.

"This isn't like your New Mexico. South Dakota winters are brutal. You'll have nothing when you leave here."

Mana paused, allowing Tesqua time to contemplate his words.

"Do you know what happens to those who fail?" Mana queried with a raised brow.

"The Apache knows no word for failure."

Mana offered his empty smile then drifted way, leaving Tesqua to ruminate over what he had told him. Tesqua knew he must head due south once free of this place. The sooner he traveled beyond the snow's reach the better. He just couldn't know how far south he must journey before escaping winter's paralyzing grip.

After a few minutes he drifted back to Mana, who now stood before a window facing west.

"Why are you here? Despite all you do, you don't seem crazy like those others," Tesqua asked.

"Inebriation psychosis, manic depressive, suicidal tendencies. For starters."

"Oh."

The moment lingered between them. Tesqua searched for something to say, came up empty. Mana turned away from the window, located Nathan in the room. Mana had more to say, but he knew better than to speak where Nathan might overhear.

"I was seventeen. I got drunk and ended up in jail. The next thing I knew they stuck me here."

"They can't lock you away for being drunk."

"Oh! I should go then."

"Sorry, stupid thing to say."

"They do whatever they want to us. Like you said, we pay the price for our fathers' surrender."

Mana started to walk away. Tesqua snared his arm.

"I will find a way out," Tesqua said.

"You want out? Convince them you're crazy. Then they cannot steal your soul."

"You mean like him over there?" Tesqua indicated Sequall still bouncing from foot to foot before the two chairs.

"No. He really is crazy. You need only convince them."

Mana crossed the room. Tesqua lingered, allowing Mana to get halfway across, then he started after him. Mana stopped at the window facing south, staring at the road leading up to the asylum. Their prison sat in the midst of sun-drenched open fields. In all directions on the compass, not a single other building could be seen.

"But if they believe you're crazy, they're never going to let you out," Tesqua said.

"Does the Apache have a word for wishful fool?" Mana said, pausing.

Tesqua understood his meaning.

"We're Wallace's rats to treat as he pleases," Mana replied.

"I'm no wishful fool," Tesqua shot back.

"You really think they stuck me here because I got drunk?"

Tiring of yet another pointless conversation that would never lead to substance, Mana drifted away to return to his window facing the giant oak. Tesqua abandoned any further attempts to gain answers.

13

Darkness surrounded him. Layers of clouds hid the moon. Tesqua left his bed the moment the lock clanked. Another dreadful night. So many had passed he had given up counting. The wretched night screams began. He crept to the door to carefully inspect the point where the bolt penetrated the doorjamb. Very gently he rocked the handle, hoping that unlike so many times in the past, this time he would uncover something that might somehow help him. The door remained securely latched, refusing to offer up any clue as to how it might be breached.

Giving up, he shifted to the window. With no moonlight to aid him, Tesqua inspected every crack in the window's frame. Six bolts anchored a rusted steel grate over the glass to the building's brickwork. But one bolt, Tesqua uncovered, had rusted so badly that half its diameter had eroded away. Maybe if the rust penetrated the core, he might successfully snap off the bolt head to release the anchor.

But sizing the grating in his head, he realized it would take at least two free corners before he could slide through to freedom. There appeared no simpler means of disengaging the grating to allow his escape out the window.

Like he had attempted so many times before, he tried the window only to find it held fast. But this time, he felt a nail head securing the window to the frame. He rubbed a finger along the window's opposite side to locate another nail head. Two nails bonded the window shut. To get the window open, he must carve the nails from the wood. Intending to do just that, he scraped at the wood surrounding the head repeatedly with his fingernails. After an hour, he had made a slight groove in the wood. But his fingers bled from his effort, which in the end proved insufficient to work the nail head out. It was, however, just enough to realize that if he could gain some type of makeshift tool to gouge deeper, he might some day pry the nails up.

He realized as he stared into the night, dreaming about the only thing that mattered to him now, that his entire escape plan would have to play out in the course of a single night. He must pry the nails out, open the window, then snap the grate off its rusted anchors to be able to jump to his freedom. Anything less would alert them to his intent. Then they would respond with more nails and new bolts to secure the grate.

No, he must be patient; he must wait for the moment when he could break out cleanly without them being able to intervene and foil him.

The hours of darkness would allow him to travel far from this place undetected. With the first dawn of his freedom he would be many miles from here.

Frustrated, an angry Tesqua finally gave up for the night. He leaned his head against the rain-stained glass.

"Celia," he whispered into the darkness, hoping somehow one of his ancestral spirits might snatch up his voice to deliver it to his wife. She would hear him calling her name and know that wherever he was, he still loved her and he had not abandoned her.

Overcome with longing, he returned to his bed, where he curled tightly beneath his blanket to stop his shivering. The frigid night air crept over him. Patient rooms went unheated on all but the coldest nights of winter. Each patient received a single blanket to warm themselves regardless of temperature. In time Tesqua fell asleep.

"It is my voice. Our heritage," Celia's words rang inside his head while he slumbered.

"That is your mother talking now," Tesqua spat back. "My children will be born in a house."

"Like the white man? That is not who we are," she argued. Their exchange had made Celia so angry that night.

"Those were the ways of our fathers. Our sons will know a better life," he retorted, fueling her anger further.

"Or daughters. How long will you run away from who you are?"

"Listen to me. It's the only way we can survive. The only way our children can thrive. We no longer have a life as Apaches."

"They will never make me ashamed of who I am. I will never become one of them," she replied.

Tesqua grabbed her arms.

"I *am* a proud Apache. I will teach my children to be proud Apaches. But we *must* adapt."

Celia turned away, breaking their contact.

"Stubborn woman," Tesqua said between clinched teeth.

Tesqua awoke to passion's fire raging in his loins. His dream left him yearning for Celia more than ever.

14

"Tell me about your people," Barry said after a long silence.

Tesqua sat across from him in a room with no windows, no pictures, no distractions. In all his time at the asylum, Barry became the first to ever attempt to really talk to him.

"Why? You don't care," Tesqua responded drily.

"It may help me understand you better."

"And then?"

"Tesqua. That's your Apache name, isn't it? I heard them call you that in the day room. Would you prefer I call you that also?"

"I would prefer it if I were home with my people."

"I'm working to make that happen."

"Work harder! I've been in this place a year, and no one will even explain to me why they put me here."

"According to Dr. Wallace's notes, you've made progress. I hope together we can continue that."

"Progress? The only progress I've made here is I'm now a year older."

Barry scribbled on a pad in such a way that it prevented Tesqua from seeing what he wrote. Of course, Tesqua couldn't read anyway, so his actions were meaningless. Beside him on the desk sat a folder with more papers in it. Tesqua surmised that folder held the answers he sought. But even Barry would be reluctant to help him, despite his words.

Silence ensued. Tesqua crossed his arms, refusing to speak any further. Barry said nothing until their time ended.

15

Many weeks later, Tesqua sat at the table in the day room playing checkers with Paraquo. The old Indian seemed unable to grasp the idea of how to play such a simple game. Yet he enjoyed moving the pieces, while under the impression he was winning regardless of the outcome on the board.

Mana stood in his position at the window facing the giant oak, whooping on occasion and slapping the wall. His actions had become so ingrained in the daily routine of the asylum that few paid attention, including the doctors. Since their last talk, Dr. Barry had spent little time in the day room or with Tesqua. Maybe he concluded Tesqua no longer deserved his time, that his skills would be better applied to patients who needed help.

Tiring of the checker game with Paraquo, Tesqua wandered over to the window where Mana stood. The giant oak, alive with brilliant green hues, turned Tesqua's mind to thoughts of home. His son or daughter would be approaching their first birthday. He would not be there to celebrate with them.

"If you're not crazy, and I'm not saying I believe you, why continue the act? Wallace certainly doesn't care," Tesqua queried.

"Trust."

"I do."

"So do they … when they think you're crazy."

Mana noticed the clock, which sent him to the day-room-door window. Tesqua lagged a step behind.

"And?"

"Trust leads to complacency."

The women crossed the corridor. Tesqua watched Mana's expression change when one in particular passed.

"She is why you do this, isn't she?"

"Evey," Mana said. His voice revealed his feelings for the first time when he spoke her name. He said her name the same way Tesqua spoke Celia's name, though Tesqua had never uttered his wife's name aloud amongst anyone there.

"Evey!" Tesqua chimed. It all became clear now.

"The smallest. Evey-sha-nay-a Moon Dancer. My Evey."

"She's very beautiful." Tesqua concluded, even though he had caught only a glimpse of her in passing. When she gazed directly at Mana, her face brightened into a smile for that brief moment the two held eye contact.

Tesqua's words seized Mana.

"She will be my wife … someday. We were together here before he separated us. I ache when I see the sadness in her eyes."

"Complacency leads to escape!" Tesqua said in excitement. He had unraveled Mana's latest riddle. He spun about in panic, realizing the orderlies could have overheard his words.

"Not if you don't learn to keep your mouth shut," Mana scolded, all the while rubbernecking himself to determine if an orderly had heard.

"We're supposed to be crazy, and crazy people don't try to escape," Mana added.

He withdrew from the day-room door to return to his place at the window facing the giant oak. He would have to wait for tomorrow to see his Evey again.

Tesqua wandered over to him after becoming bored with standing at the day-room-door window and taking in nothing of interest.

"So, you stole Evey from Grano. That's why he beats you."

Tesqua savored the rush of pride in making the connection between the love triangle of this place without having it spelled out to him.

Mana just shook his head.

"No. She despises him. He's why we're kept apart. I caught him touching the women. When I stopped him, he broke my nose."

"What's Evey's story? Why she here?"

"Stabbed her teacher with scissors," Mana said, then he wandered away again, no longer wishing to talk to Tesqua.

"Any you want to marry her?"

Tesqua came around. He was talking to himself.

After roaming the room aimlessly, Tesqua returned to the window facing the giant oak, where he began clandestinely scrutinizing the steel grating. He studied each of the grating's attaching points to the window frame. The bolt in the lower right corner looked as if it, too, had rusted through. It would let loose with one determined shove. *Every detail could be impor-tant*, Tesqua reminded himself. Surely none of the staff gave any consideration to the building's integrity, at least not until someone broke out. Then it would be too late. Tesqua would be free and far away.

Before Tesqua's hopes could rise, he spotted three nail heads on each side securing the window to the frame. There would be no way he could easily raise the window to get at the grating. But there might be a way to ...

"All the windows are barred," Mana said, coming up beside him.

"Every one?"

"Except those in the basement."

Tesqua smiled.

"But you would be wise to hide your ..."

Before Mana could finish, Tesqua attacked, nailing him in the jaw with a fierce right hook delivered more forcefully than he intended.

Nathan swarmed in to lock Tesqua's arms behind his back and throw him into the wall. Mana, face bleeding, stared in shock as Nathan dragged Tesqua away.

"You ever say that again I'll ... let me go!" Tesqua screamed while Nathan dragged him from the day room.

16

The following morning, despite being famished, Mana lingered in his room after Nathan unlocked his door. He felt empty inside, as if he had lost his only friend, and as such, dreaded facing another day in the day room.

For a long moment Mana stared at the hall. Then he forced himself out of his room. He knew if he lingered too long, Nathan would return and lock the door forcing him to remain in his room until lunch.

He passed Tesqua's room. Tesqua's door had been thrown open wide to place Tesqua on display. Tesqua sat immobile in a restraint chair with all the trappings of a medieval torture device. A broad leather strap secured Tesqua's head to a wooden back. The same kind of straps secured his limbs. A tightly constricted chest strap forced Tesqua to breathe in short gasps.

Mana stared for a moment, feeling no gratification at Tesqua's brutal punishment for his actions. He knew he should for what Tesqua had done to him, but he felt only pity for his comrade. For whatever reason they locked him in this place, it would be a long time before Tesqua might ever feel free again. That was if any of them might ever be free again.

As Mana moved on to the day room, Thompson slipped into Tesqua's room. With fumbling fingers, she quickly released his chest strap. Tesqua inhaled deeply, relishing the sensation of normal breathing. His night had been tense and arduous.

"Just avoid Nathan. You'll be fine if you ..." Thompson whispered.

"Nurse, there a problem?"

Wallace filled the doorway, his expressionless face hard as stone.

Thompson spun about to Wallace's narrowed brown eyes.

"No, sir. Just making sure he can breathe."

"He still alive?"

"Yes, sir."

"Then he can breathe."

"Very good, sir."

Thompson glanced back at Tesqua with eyes meant to convey what her silenced voice could not. He uncovered pain in those watery eyes. Something he had failed to recognize before. She really was not one of them. She might be one he could trust.

While Tesqua looked on immobile, Wallace snared Thompson's arm as soon as she entered the hall, stopping her in her tracks. She looked him dead in the eyes ... then looked away—his stare being fierce and penetrating.

"We must instill a sense of control in these patients."

"He was breathing with difficulty," she offered in her own defense.

"You can't help these people. Just tend them. Never countermand my orders again. Understand, nurse?"

Thompson started for the nurses' station, expecting Wallace to release her. But he didn't.

"Yes, doctor."

The words proved terribly difficult for her to eject.

Only then did Wallace release her arm so she might leave.

At the periphery of her vision as she returned to her desk, she caught Nathan with the linen cart hovering near the reception door, taking in their exchange. His smug smile caused her stomach to convulse. Wallace had demeaned her, lowered her to the level of an orderly the way he condescended to her. Inside she fumed. Nonetheless, she held her tongue behind a stoic face. Having this job was more important than venting her anger. Anger that had been slowly, constantly expanding inside her since the day she started work at the asylum.

She returned to the nurses' station desk to find Mana collecting up the wire wastebasket to empty it. He routinely volunteered to perform menial chores around the asylum. It made him feel important amongst the others. He took his duties seriously despite the ridicule he endured from those around him. Even Nathan badgered him for his efforts.

Thompson focused her attention on a patient chart on the desk. The last thing she wanted was for anyone to see the humiliation on her face. She had long ago learned not to shed a tear in these situations. And she had endured easily a hundred of these humiliations in her tenure here.

"Excuse me, ma'am," Jake said, standing on the other side of the desk like a lost puppy but with innocent green eyes. He stood taller than her by a few inches, mainly because he wore a mop head of unruly strawberry-colored hair. His broomstick arms had matching red splotches where he had been scratching, but his youthful cherub smile disarmed everyone immediately.

"I'm sorry, Jake, is it? I got so wrapped up I nearly forgot about you."

"That's quite all right, ma'am," Jake said, smiling.

Thompson waved for Nathan to set aside his current chore to join her at the nurses' station.

"Nathan, Jake here is your new assistant. How about you two start by fetching up the kitchen supplies. Jake, Nathan's in charge of all the orderlies. He'll teach you everything you need to know around here."

Straight-faced, Nathan led Jake past Tesqua's room just as Dr. Barry entered.

17

Entering Tesqua's room, Dr. Barry proceeded directly to the window, staring at the long grass swaying with a lofty breeze. He intentionally positioned himself beyond Tesqua's line of sight.

"I thought we were making progress. Why did you attack Charley?" he said finally, still staring out.

"Mana! His name is Mana. Why are men and women separated?" Tesqua replied.

Tesqua's question raised an eyebrow, brought Barry from the window to face him. It seemed an odd response for one in the excruciating confines of the restraint chair.

Barry had to fight down the urge to release the straps so Tesqua could breathe easier. But he knew Wallace's policy regarding punishment and decided now was not the time for a confrontation. The very thought of patient restraint in such a manner convulsed Barry's stomach. Canton had to be the last facility with such a terrible device still in existence. At least in Barry's mind. He despised the method, and though the chair had disappeared from other institutions around the country, Wallace, for whatever reason, still felt it appropriate to bridle patients as punishment for outbursts of temper.

Barry set his sights on someday allowing his patients to smash the device to bits with a hammer. He imagined the chair might still find use in remote areas of Europe, but certainly the day had come in the United States when such barbaric measures had outlived their purpose. There was no evil dark enough to ever warrant such torture. And this method clearly bordered on torture, not a civilized treatment for mental illness.

Any confrontation with Wallace would only serve to disrupt Barry's nascent treatment programs for his patients. He'd sooner take a stick in the eye over a fight with Wallace. But Tesqua *had* attacked Mana without provocation, according to Nathan's report, and until they could discern exactly the root of Tesqua's violent outbursts, they had little hope of helping him.

"Answer my question, I answer yours," Barry risked. He had no idea where this might go, but decided to allow Tesqua to lead in hopes of gaining some new insight into the complexities of his mind.

"His name is Mana, not Charley."

"Fair enough. Why did you attack Mana in the day room?"

"Answer my question. I answer yours."

"Fine. But perhaps you should let us determine what's best for you."

"Taking away our freedom, that's best for us? Then you strip away our dignity as men."

Barry raised a bushy eyebrow again. Tesqua had offered up something of himself, but as yet, Barry failed to understand where he meant this exchange to go.

"It's more complex than that. Our highest priority is the welfare of every one of our patients."

"We're no different than you. You think we don't desire the company of women? I see the way you look at Thompson."

Tesqua's revealing statement drew the doctor further in. A tinge of embarrassment surfaced on Barry's face. He failed to realize until that moment that his interest had become visible. Certainly, he detected in Thompson's eyes an equal interest in him, but their overt actions had somehow become detectable to others. Barry now wondered if Wallace had noticed the signals he unconsciously sent the nurse.

"Well?" Tesqua injected to break the silence.

Barry appraised Tesqua's words for a lingering moment while they stared at each other.

"Past problems force us to be more cautious."

"We are not animals that you house in separate cages," Tesqua spat.

The words bit into Barry. How might he expect these men to respond to his efforts when they believed they were being treated no better than animals? Tesqua viewed this place not as a safe haven but rather a prison. Caged animals exhibit aggressive behavior. How much control could they hope to exert over these patients before they feel as if they were stripped of all dignity?

"We're bartering!" Barry chimed, suddenly realizing that Tesqua hoped to manipulate him into giving him what he wanted.

"Okay. Suppose I did allow the women to visit. What do I get in return for my gesture of goodwill?"

"What do you wish?"

"I wish for you to control your anger. I wish for you to come to me when anger threatens to control you. Together we can get to the cause of your emotional distress."

"Perhaps in doing this, you provide me reason to stay my anger," Tesqua offered.

"Fair enough. I shall see what I can do. Now my turn. Why did you attack Charley, Mana?"

"I'm sick of his petty whining."

"So, how can I trust that you'll control your anger?"

"I've answered your question. We are done."

Tesqua turned his eyes away slightly. Barry came to understand that as Tesqua's sign their conversation had ended. There would be no further exchange.

Barry departed, feeling as if he had, for the first time, found a way into Tesqua's mind. But he still had a formidable hurdle to climb to keep his word.

18

Nathan led the way into the basement dry goods room. He switched on the dim bulb dangling overhead to shed meager light on a ten-by-twenty space of shelves loaded with various sacks of dry goods scattered throughout. They stored everything six inches off the floor, since the asylum basement suffered flooding during heavy spring rains and rats during the harsh winters.

Once Nathan closed the door, they slapped each other five.

"Told you all you needed were the right answers to their questions and you'd be in," he said.

"Thanks, man. I really needs the job. And I can learn real fast, as long as I don't have to remember too much all at once."

"Don't worry about that. Follow my lead, you'll do just fine. Shitty work, I know, but fantastic fringe benefits."

Nathan slid onto a table in the corner. He offered Jake a smoke, lit his, then Jake's. Jake followed suit, though he thought he should get busy doing what the nurse had asked him to do. So a moment later he slid back off the table.

"Relax, Jake. Cool your heels a while," Nathan said in response to Jake pulling an eighty-pound sack of potatoes off a shelf. His skinny arms quaked from the weight.

"Lesson one: Be too efficient, they just find more crappy work for you."

Jake immediately slid the sack back and rejoined Nathan on the table.

"Two things you must remember. One, they watch you like a hawk the first two months. Be careful of Wallace. Don't screw up. Do everything I told you. *Everything*. Once you get your keys, they leave you alone. Second, and most important, everything we say and do is kept on the down-low. Never say nothing about anything. Got it?"

Jake nodded and jumped from the table, quick to press out a half-smoked cigarette under his heel. He was anxious to show he had a proper work ethic.

"Do I gets more money after I's trained?"

"Shitty pay, I know. But I got that covered. We steal the stuff these crazies get from their families, blankets and stuff, and I got a guy we sell 'em to in Sioux Falls. But I get half of everything you get for the first six months like we agreed, right?"

"Sure. I said I would."

"Don't worry, you're going to love it here."

Nathan pressed out his cigarette then grabbed a sack of beans. Jake found Nathan's impish smile reassuring.

19

The Monday started out as it had done a thousand times before. However, on this day, Mana stood around in the day room on the side opposite of Tesqua. He refused to look over at him when he entered, and though he tried to conceal it, Mana monitored Tesqua's every move.

After two hours Nathan left the day room, leaving Jake with one other orderly to tend patients. The near constant drafts seeping in through the loose window frames kept the room cold, so a few patients slung blankets over their shoulders. They now sat in their own space, curled up in their wraps, staring at nothing.

Tesqua waited until Mana turned his back toward him. Then he eased a few steps in Mana's direction. Mana came about. Tesqua froze, looking anywhere but in Mana's direction, forcing his smile to remain beneath the surface. He hoped his eyes concealed his intent.

Mana turned around again. Tesqua moved again, stopping when Mana came back around. Tesqua's movement this time had been noticed. Mana turned. Tesqua moved. This time Mana moved away, stopping at the next window over.

Tesqua inched closer. Mana wandered away, electing to stray across the room.

Tesqua remained at the window watching Jake. Then moments later, he wandered in Mana's direction. Mana moved faster this time, crossing in a wide arc to avoid Tesqua. When Tesqua altered his direction, Mana scurried to evade him.

"Stop, will you?" Tesqua scowled in a harsh whisper.

Jake ceased his activity at the table, but he offered no more than a casual glance in their direction.

Tesqua, now desperate, cornered Mana at the window, where he refused him an escape. Mana retreated until the glass facing the giant oak stopped him.

"Why did you attack me?"

"I had to," Tesqua replied.

"You had to? Little voices inside your head told you to?"

"Just listen for a moment. I didn't want to jeopardize the trust you've built for yourself. Nathan was coming up behind you while we were talking. I needed to convince him we weren't plotting against them."

"Sure."

"Besides, you said to convince them I'm crazy."

"Not by beating me. I'm the only one who can help you."

Mana's words struck a dissonant chord in Tesqua's mind.

"What makes you think I need your help?"

"Isn't it obvious?"

Tesqua stared out the window at a truck climbing a shallow rise a distance away. Its dust trail hung endlessly in the air.

"That road to the north, where does it lead?" Tesqua asked.

"Sioux Falls. A day's journey from here."

"There will be train tracks there," Tesqua muttered. He realized the quickest and easiest way to get south is to climb aboard a slow moving train.

"So?"

"They can take me south."

As Tesqua stared at the rolling dust cloud, his mind drifted back to a ten-year-old Tesqua with long braided hair, brimming with the exuberance of a hopeful warrior. He dashed full pelt after a wild turkey in a craggy field. When the bird zigged, young Tesqua zigged, when the bird zagged, young Tesqua zagged in relentless pursuit. Out of breath with his lungs ready to explode, young Tesqua dove for the bird, snagging its neck. The fowl, in its final effort to escape, squirt excrement into Tesqua's face. But a determined young Tesqua refused to release the creature. He tucked the huge bird under his arm while he worked his way back to his feet. Then he vaulted his catch high in the air to cheers from his father and his uncles.

"Less if I run," Tesqua said after the long pause. The ten-year-old heaving warrior in the glass disappeared.

"Then find a way to avoid their medications. It is how they control us," Mana replied with a skeptical edge to his voice.

Mana drifted away when Nathan, upon entering the day room, took particular notice of them talking at the window. Tesqua smiled, watching the truck until it disappeared over the distant rise.

20

Using a fulgent moon as his calendar, Tesqua marked the passage of another month with a scratch on his wall. In days, it would be two years since he had last seen his family. Celia would have given up on him by now. His son would be playing with other children without ever having experienced the joy of being with his father. The child would not even know what his father looks like. Tesqua's mother would blame him for all this. She blamed him for everything that went wrong in his life. Try as he might to please her, she always found fault in everything he attempted. She expected him to fail at his marriage, and through no fault of his own, she turned out to be right.

Darkness caved in around him as he lay amid an unearthly silence. No night creature sounds permeated the brick and glass of their prison. No crickets, nor owls, nor coyotes. They had taken from him all the natural sounds of how his life was meant to be, of the harmony he once knew within his world.

With the morning's light, Tesqua joined Mana in the hall. They ate breakfast together in the mess hall in abject silence.

Afterward, they proceeded to the day room without having spoken more than five words to each other. Every patient executed the exact same motions every day, as if all their spirits had been stripped away in the asylum.

After hours of boredom, Tesqua attempted to cajole Mana into a game of checkers, but Mana hated playing what he termed 'the white man's games of chance.' Tesqua never could convince him checkers was anything but a game of chance, like the card games they played on the reservation.

Before his marriage, Tesqua spent most of his free time drinking, gambling and talking with friends about what their futures might be. A future dictated more by what they were rather than what they could become. He gambled less frequently after marrying Celia, but still had been known to lose everything in a reckless night of cards and alcohol, never mind being in the midst of prohibition with poverty on the reservation rampant.

Mana snapped at Tesqua when he asked a question, another meaningless exchange that consumed part of every day they spent there. So Tesqua left Mana in a corner to wander over to the window at the nurses' station.

Something was happening out there.

Thompson offered a rare smile to Tesqua when she looked up to see him standing there. Over time, he came to cherish such fleeting moments in this place. Her smile could be so intoxicating. He wondered what it would be like holding a woman again. But those very thoughts also brought sadness. They brought Celia to the forefront of his mind. She was always quick to smile. She loved to laugh. She also required many doses of affection. Tesqua now wished he had given her so much more than he had. He never kissed her enough, and there were times when she reminded him of that. He never could understand what she expected of him as her husband. He believed his hard work and fidelity were most important, but over time, he learned that for some reason—unknown to him—they were insufficient. She needed so much more, and now he wished he had taken the time to give her what she truly desired.

Outside the day room, Barry approached Thompson at the desk. They spoke briefly turning their backs toward Tesqua to prevent him from deciphering their conversation by reading their lips. Not that he could know what they were saying anyway. Nor at that moment did he care. Then Barry left.

Tesqua wandered over to Paraquo, offering to walk him around the room. But Paraquo refused, instead wheeling his chair to place his back to Tesqua. It seemed everyone in the room who wasn't crazy had suddenly found a reason to shun him.

The day-room door unlocked, though no one inside noticed, including Tesqua. It became over time one of those actions so routine that it failed to register in anyone's mind anymore. Mana stared out his window at the giant oak, his right hand incessantly pounding the sill. He didn't turn around to notice twelve Indian women enter the day room. All wore wrap-around dresses in the same blue cloth as the shirts the men wore.

Entering last, Evey paused just inside, panning the room. Her soft fawn-brown eyes exuded a seductive innocence when they caught Tesqua's. They found gentleness there. A slight smile broke on her face, a smile so sweet it nearly stopped Tesqua's heart. But then she continued until she saw Mana.

Mana caught her reflection in the glass first. His face alighted, something Tesqua had never witnessed since arriving at this place. Mana came about to Evey, standing less than a dozen paces from him. He had long ago given up on the dream of holding her in his arms again. Her simple smile brought goose flesh to his skinny arms. They came together, brushed hands briefly, much to Nathan's dismay, who stood just inside the door. The orderly leaned against the wall with crossed arms under a disapproving scowl. Dr. Barry stood beside him with arms likewise but brimming with his smile. It was as if a brilliant light had awakened them. The men began to stir, gravitating to the women.

Evey's insides still fluttered whenever they touched. She had missed him so and could hardly believe they were again together in this place. A wish she had held so dear for so many years had just come true. She wanted to kiss him, to wrap her arms around him and feel his warmth against her. But she dared not.

Mana and Evey's contact, though momentary, was unbelievable beyond words. Her soft warm skin touching his hand took him away from the dread of this place, if only for that second. It had been so long since they were even able to be this close to each other, let alone touch.

"Evey," Mana said. So many words raced inside his head that he had difficulty assembling what to say next. She stood before him. His urge to kiss her raged irresistible, but Mana knew that act might cause them to yank the women out as quickly as they had entered. Yet he would find a way to kiss her; he could see in her eyes that she wanted it also.

"How did you arrange this?" she asked. Her smile melted Mana's heart.

They roamed together to find a corner away from the others. In this place, one square foot of personal space became precious, especially when it could be shared with someone special. Their intimacy proved short-lived, however, when Tesqua wandered over.

"You going to introduce me?" he said, smiling as big with his eyes as with his lips. Evey's soft eyes had a way of crawling under a man's skin. Tesqua had to cross his arms to refrain from touching her, which he knew would alienate his friend. At all costs he must respect what was Mana's—even in this place.

Yet there was no mistaking the mutual interest between the two. Tesqua stood taller and stouter than Mana, like a man who worked hard in his life. His callused hands confirmed that. And he exuded confidence in his smile. Tesqua easily attracted women. Mana seemed the more fragile and timid of the two, one who made a good friend, not such an exciting lover.

"No," Mana said flatly. He moved with Evey to sit at the table with the other women.

Lizzie, a fiercely talkative Seminole with a cheeky face over a slender frame in her early thirties, sat beside Ko-nay-ha, talking about anything that came to mind. Just having someone different to talk with exhilarated her. The other women in the institution shunned her, finding her most annoying. Their visitation had breathed new life into Lizzie. Ko-nay-ha, however, sat at the table staring straight ahead as if he had turned to stone, ignoring every word she spoke. Regardless, Lizzie put her own positive spin on it. He would never interrupt her, and he, of all the patients, would never attempt to silence her.

"I don't trust him," Mana whispered to Evey at the table when he glanced back at the corner to Tesqua feeling alone.

From opposite sides of the room, Barry and Tesqua exchanged a clandestine smile. None of the patients now chatting amongst themselves would ever realize Tesqua had engineered this. He had done it for his only friend. Dr. Barry would garner all the credit. For the first time since Tesqua's arrival, the day room filled with vibrant chatter. *Everyone* seemed so alive now. Tesqua was witnessing a different Mana at the table. He still pounded the surface with his right hand in his usual nervous manner, but his face had been transformed. Tesqua realized he gained a glimpse of the man who existed before they locked him away in this place—the real person they had tried to take from him. Tesqua had manipulated circumstance to bring that person back to the surface.

Watching Evey made Tesqua's heart pain for his Celia. Someday he would get free of this place to return to her. That hope kept him going with each sunrise.

Then something snared Tesqua's attention. While Evey and Mana chatted innocently at the table, Evey casually positioned her thumb between her middle fingers. She held it until Mana nodded slightly, then she extended two fingers while curling the shorter two under into her palm. Mana nodded once again, so she shifted them again. While they talked, they were exchanging information using a code only they could understand. Tesqua studied the hand gestures, hoping to decipher bits of what they were really communicating to each other.

Moments later Mana scanned the room for the orderlies. Then his left hand began similar gyrations. They had developed their own hand language that kept the orderlies unaware of their true exchange. Tesqua pressed his brain to remember the signals he saw in the hopes he could convince Mana to reveal their substance.

The women's visit lasted precisely two hours. A short period after being separated for years, but long enough for Mana to feel alive once again. Nathan seemed particularly anxious for it to end, expecting problems at any second. At its conclusion, the orderlies promptly rounded the women up to escort them back through the locked double doors that separated the men's wing from the women's wing.

What Nathan had secretly hoped for never materialized, which meant another visit would be forthcoming, unless the orderly could find some way to sabotage Barry's latest patient program. And Nathan figured sooner or later one of them would slip. They were Indians, savages at their core. Before long, they would ruin the privilege for themselves. At least, that was the belief Nathan held.

Tesqua detected sighs of relief from not only the orderlies but also Dr. Barry when the visit went off without so much as one cross word. Grano had been the one to watch. But he sat quietly in a corner, feasting on the females with only his eyes. Maybe even he realized the benefits of their new doctor. Tesqua hoped that, for Mana's sake, this would not be an isolated event.

Alone once more, Mana returned to stare out his window. Tesqua gave him a few moments to relive the experience in his head before drifting over to him, staring off in another direction.

"So, she had a lot to say," Tesqua commented.

Mana offered no response.

"I watched your hands. What do the gestures mean?"

Mana turned to him.

"Perhaps you're not as crazy as I thought," Mana said then wandered away.

21

Friday morning came with heavy rain. It poured so hard at times that it dampened everyone's spirit. Nurse Thompson busied herself preparing the daily medications at the desk when Jake strolled up coincident with Mana passing on his way to the day room.

"Miss Thompson, Dr. Wallace said I see you about getting my keys," Jake said.

Mana swung his arm, toppling the papers Thompson used to record her patient doses. His nudge turned out to be just enough to scatter them about the floor.

"Stupid, stupid, stupid," Mana muttered, slapping his head hard as punishment for his mistake.

Nathan, working nearby, scurried up with his tongue locked in his cheek.

"Mana, what did you do?" Thompson asked in her diminutive non-threatening tone.

"You stupid idiot injun. What's the matter with you," Nathan scowled.

Mana cowered, falling to his knees while shielding his head as if anticipating Nathan's beating.

Nathan, however, caught himself. He returned his balled hands to his sides, despite an undeniable glare in his eyes. Thompson suspected—no she knew—that had she not been right there at the moment, Nathan would have struck Mana for such a minor mistake. In her absence Nathan probably used any incident as justification to inflict pain on these people. She could only wonder how often Nathan beat the patients when she was off site. Certainly Wallace cared little to prevent the orderlies from taking out their frustrations on the patients.

"It's okay, Mana. Collect them up and return them to the desk. Nathan, you've got rooms need tending."

Nathan tightened his lips. He returned to his linen cart parked outside a nearby patient room. He despised dealing with the nurses; he especially disliked Thompson with her condescending British demeanor, as if she thought herself superior to him. Her every utterance had a way of grating upon his nerves.

"Yes, ma'am," he mumbled beneath his breath as he rolled the cart away.

Nathan's rise to supervisor of the orderlies came by default. It turned out he was the only orderly willing to endure such a difficult job with such low pay for so long. But he still ranked beneath the nurses on the asylum hierarchy. He knew he could never advance higher than his present position, but he accepted that his eighth-grade education had gotten him this far, and aside from the patients' aggression, the position rarely challenged his capability. What other job could he get away with smacking the crap out of Indians? But he had also developed his own way of getting the most out of his position.

At the desk, Mana stacked a few papers, meticulously arranging them before collecting up the next few.

"Jake, yes, your keys. Right. Just a bit."

Thompson fumbled about, retrieving a single key from her desk drawer, which she used to unlock a cabinet on the wall behind the desk. When she opened the cabinet door, Mana stole a glimpse of what hung inside.

Keys.

His heart raced. He averted his eyes quickly, focusing them instead on arranging the papers on the floor before picking them up. His mind swirled. He could hardly believe what his eyes had just witnessed. The implications came too fast for Mana to process.

Thompson glanced over at him before removing a set of keys kept on a hook inside the cabinet.

Mana, however, cataloged the fact that another set of keys remained, hanging from another hook in that cabinet. *Keys led to freedom.* Mana could hear his heart thumping in his chest.

Thompson locked the cabinet then returned her key to the wide desk drawer. During the entire exchange, Mana collected up spilled papers to return them in a nice neat stack on the corner of the desk.

"These never leave your person, understand?" Thompson instructed as she handed the ring with three keys to Jake, who clutched them tightly, for he knew what they meant to him. His probation finally over, he gained new freedom in the asylum. He became a trusted one, which meant a lot to Jake. No one had ever trusted him before. Not even his mother. For the first time in his young life—being only twenty-four—he had accomplished something. To the other orderlies they were just keys, but to Jake they were his shining badge of accomplishment.

Thompson glanced to Mana again, making certain collecting up the disheveled papers occupied him. She lowered her voice as she placed her back toward him.

"There are three masters. Brass is the exterior. Silver patient rooms. The small one's for the basement rooms, except the drug room. Only I and the doctors carry that key."

"Yes, ma'am," Jake replied, attentive to every word she spoke.

"Lose your keys, come to me or the doctors immediately. Got it?"

"Yes, ma'am, absolutely."

"Very good then. Dash upstairs to give the two rooms at the north end of the hall a good going over."

Jake clipped the keys to his belt, the exact same way Nathan carried his. He smiled at the sound they made as he strolled away. Nathan had told him life would greatly improve around the asylum once he got his keys. Jake could hardly wait.

Mana remained on his knees, collating the last of the fallen papers into a stack before returning them to the desk exactly where they sat before his mishap. He avoided looking over at the cabinet or meeting Thompson's eyes as she stood over him. With the last papers upon the desk, Mana returned to the day room. He hid his beaming smile from Thompson. How he would use his newly gleaned information, he had yet to determine. He just knew what he had learned would be important to his future.

22

Maggie, the women's wing night nurse worked at the station desk beneath the glow of a small incandescent desk lamp. The light shed warmth upon her cold hands from the unseasonably cool air. She stopped writing when the light flickered, went dim for a few seconds and then came back to its usual intensity. Over time everyone had become desensitized to the building's shoddy electricity.

Rough calloused hands sprang up from behind her. They clamped her neck then playfully squeezed.

"Let me out of here," Nathan screeched in a strident voice meant to mimic a patient.

Maggie screamed—she nearly jumped out of her seat.

"Jesus, you scared the heck out of me. I never heard you coming," she said, slapping him harder than just a playful smack on his shoulder.

"Ouch."

"You deserve it!" she scolded.

Nathan eased a hand toward her breast, but she intercepted it in time to deflect it to her arm. He bent down to kiss her neck, but she resisted his advances by scrunching her shoulders, which forced his face away.

"What are you doing here, anyway?" she asked sharply, growing annoyed with his unwanted and uninvited advances.

"Thompson sent me over. Take dinner. I'll watch the monkeys."

"It's that late already? Don't need to tell me twice. I'm starving," she said, wasting no time collecting up her purse and heading out the double doors.

Nathan smiled, settled into the chair and threw his feet up to rest on the desk's corner while he scanned the paperwork neatly arranged on the surface. That lasted only a moment, though. Once Maggie's footsteps evaporated, he erupted from the chair to proceed to the first room on the right just inside the wing. He rapped the door lightly.

An ashen Jake slipped out.

"Okay. Last room on the right. Be quick. I'm covering your back. Name's Kit."

"Y-y-you're sure about this? I mean this can't be ..."

"Told you, shitty pay but great fringe benefits. Besides, I checked her file. In for nymphomania. You're doing her a favor, man. Now move it."

Jake swallowed hard. Refusing meant he might be ridiculed. He had to decide in that second to trust Nathan, though he wasn't completely comfortable with this whole plan. After a moment's thought, Jake hurried away to disappear into the last room on the right.

Nathan remained near the double doors, which allowed him to observe anyone approaching the wing. As he watched, the overhead lights dimmed, then buzzed, before returning to their full brightness.

Muffled screams arose from the room Jake had entered. Nathan trusted Jake knew how to handle himself on his own. As dumb as he was, Jake had to know how to do it.

Minutes passed. Nathan paced. Sweat beads dotted his brow despite cold air wafting through the drafty hall. Jake had been in there longer than Nathan expected. He had built in a safety margin using the fact that most duty nurses routinely stretched a thirty-minute dinner to forty-five, since no one monitored their time, least of all Nathan.

But if Jake didn't get it done, he might …

Finally, Jake exited the room, fumbling to button his trousers with one hand, hastily stuffing his shirt back into his pants with the other.

"Do you understand what 'be quick' means? Don't play with 'em, man. Just get it in, get it off and get it out," Nathan scowled.

"Sorry, man. She was …"

"Get outta here. You were in the basement the entire time. Don't forget."

Jake exited through the double doors.

"Thanks, man," Jake said back through the glass.

"Go, will ya!"

Nathan's face beamed an insidious smile while he returned to the nurses' station desk. *Do a favor, get a favor.* That's how it worked. Now Jake owed him. Debt is a good thing. Nathan savored in his mind his next chance to collect from Jake.

23

A frigid Sunday morning broke in the middle of a mean January. Overnight snow hid the barren plains surrounding the asylum, dappling the charcoal branches of the leafless giant oak.

Nathan waited just inside the reception room with coat buttoned snugly. Thompson busied herself at the nurses' station, while patients filed into the day room as they did every other day.

But this day Thompson kept an unusual eye on the fidgeting Nathan. After a few moments, Dr. Wallace descended the stairs with suitcase in one hand, black worn satchel in the other.

Dr. Barry, who accompanied him, held the reception-room door while Wallace transferred his suitcase to Nathan, who then exited.

"Be back in five days. I'm staying a extra day after the conference to visit friends I haven't seen in many years," Wallace said.

"Very good, doctor. I'm sure Little Rock's warmer than here. Enjoy your time away from the asylum," Barry said. Then he continued about his business.

Minutes later, Thompson watched out the reception-door window as the truck came about and steamed off down the rutted, snowy road.

Wallace was gone.

The moment the truck accelerated away from the asylum, the halls came alive with a bevy of activity. Thompson herded the men into the day room. Afterward, she unlocked the double doors separating the wings to allow the women to join the men.

Minutes later, patients crowded the day room, all looking to one another for some indication as to what was about to happen. Some wore faces of doom, the least little change in activity sent them into a panic; others seemed excited at the possibilities of experiencing something new.

After a few more minutes of confused patients milling about, Barry entered, wheeling in a cart heaped with cans of paint and painting supplies, which he parked in the room's center. One by one, he transferred the paint cans to the table, where he opened them. The patients pressed in like curious children.

"All right everyone, something profoundly different today," Barry started. He detected something he had not witnessed since arriving at this place more than nineteen months earlier. He saw curiosity—that first spark of enthusiasm spring to their eyes. They were actually watching him full of anticipation.

"I want each of you to use these paints to express yourself in the day room," Barry said.

Most exchanged confused looks, wondering what had befallen the doctor. They had never participated in any activities. The orderlies, including Jake, merely leaned against the wall near the door shaking their heads.

"What do you mean?" Tesqua asked, already a flame of suspicion in his mind that spread into his voice.

"Exactly what I said. Use these brushes to paint wherever and whatever you feel. The only thing I ask is that you find your own place so as not to intrude on another patient."

No one, it seemed, wished to be first. Could they not comprehend Barry's instructions? Or had they become so numb from being in this place that they could no longer muster desire to participate?

Barry took up a brush and held it out to Tesqua. He refused it. Evey nudged Mana.

Mana stepped up first. He sized up a narrow-tipped paint brush as if he knew exactly what to do with it. But he instead handed it to Evey, who looked at it as if it were some foreign gadget. Then he took one for himself, followed by two small buckets of paint. As they moved away from the group, Evey glanced back. The urge to see what Tesqua intended to do overwhelmed her. Her interested glance, however, did not escape Mana's notice.

Another stepped forward to take up a brush with a can of paint. But after dipping the brush into the syrupy liquid, he began absently painting himself.

"I actually meant the walls," Barry said, stopping the Indian before he could take a second stroke aimed at the doctor.

It only took one to start the others. Within minutes, five more stepped forward selecting brushes. Before long, everyone had taken to painting an area on a wall. Everyone except Tesqua. He chose to be the last one to take a brush; he did it begrudgingly, selecting a location away from as many of the others as possible.

He grumbled to himself during the long minutes he spent idle, trying to decide exactly what he would place on his wall. Then after noticing the shapes of other patients' attempts, he knew exactly what he would create. If only he had any talent for this. He doubted anyone would ever be able to guess his design when finished.

By afternoon, the day room had been transformed into a different place. Drab lifeless walls came alive with all the hues of the world beyond this place. A rich palette of color and texture adorned every wall. Patients moved about freely, appraising, even chatting as they worked. No one, except Barry, took notice of Nathan's entry into the room when he returned from Sioux Falls. He stood frozen a few steps inside.

"Listen, friend, Wallace isn't going to like this. We don't allow this kind of activity," Nathan commented dryly to Barry.

Those words were the boldest Nathan had ever said to the doctor in his short tenure at the asylum. It even surprised Nathan the way he doled out the expression. They certainly delivered a message devoid of respect for the doctor.

The remark brought nothing more than a raised eyebrow from Barry.

"Dr. Barry, orderly," Barry started, using his finger to illustrate his point. "That means *I* say what we're going to do; and *you* carry out my orders, friend."

Nathan shrugged off the comment with a smirk. He shoved his hands into his pockets and exited the day room. On his departure, Thompson walked over to Barry standing at the table refilling the small paint buckets.

"The mate's right, you know. This really is radical. Even for you. There'll be the devil to pay when Wallace gets his gaze on this."

"One thing I learned dealing with bureaucracy. It's far easier to beg forgiveness than gain permission. Besides, we've got five days before Wallace returns. I'll deal with him then."

"All right, doctor. I think."

Thompson strolled away. Her own enthusiasm for Barry's little experiment had taken her away from her daily routine, which she knew if she did not return to promptly, her duties would go undone. The last thing she wanted was an excuse for Dr. Wallace to take out his anger on her when he returned to see just what Dr. Barry had done. She planned to make certain she was not the first person to cross Wallace's path after he saw the change in the day room.

"It beats ink blots. Trust me," Barry added unconvincingly.

"Not me that needs convincing."

"I've purchased two buckets of whitewash, just in case," Barry mumbled to himself as he took in the orderlies' faces watching from the periphery. By their cold expressions, they obviously shared Nathan's belief.

"Great job, everyone. Don't be timid with your brushes."

When Barry drifted across toward Mana and Evey, and while his back faced Tesqua, Tesqua set his brush into his bucket and moved quickly for the unlocked day room door. On Thompson's departure moments earlier, she had failed to lock it. Tesqua, upon realizing her err, seized opportunity.

Tesqua entered the hall to find Thompson absent from her desk. He moved quickly down the hall without looking back. An orderly descending the staircase opened his mouth to speak, but Tesqua answered him before he could pose his question.

"Latrine," Tesqua said, motioning.

That satisfied the orderly, who continued toward the day room.

Barry had created so much stir with his 'new' day room activity that no one paid attention to anything. Seizing the moment, Tesqua entered the latrine, where he paused for only a moment, then exited to launch himself down the staircase to the basement, barely hitting any stairs with his feet. Wallace never allowed patients unaccompanied in the basement. Only when working with an orderly would they see the lower level, which of course, meant some crappy task needed doing.

This became Tesqua's first venture into the unknown depths, since he refused to assist anyone in this place, and most orderlies would have nothing to do with him for fear that anything they did would turn into confrontation. His heart raced faster than his feet.

Reaching the basement main corridor Tesqua moved methodically from door to door. At each one, he yanked the handle—all locked—then he tried to jar the latch by slamming the knob with his hands. All the while he kept an eye on the staircase.

They were all so damn secure. If only he could get into one of the rooms. Mana had said the basement windows were unbarred, so he could easily slip out one if he could get through one of the doors.

At the last locked door, Tesqua battered his full weight into the wood. Crushing his shoulder in the attempt, the oaken door held fast. His muscles felt like a fire had ignited within them. He rammed it again. Again he bounced off without inflicting the slightest damage. Tears welled in his eyes from the excruciating pain. His excitement deflated. His heart sank into the pit of his stomach. He needed something more to get through the doors down there. As far as he could discern, this might be the best chance he had for ever escaping this place, if he could somehow get to those unbarred windows.

Shuffling sounds from above seized him. How long had he been gone? It seemed like a few minutes—maybe it was too long. Were they coming down to look for him? Had they noticed his absence and taken to scouring the building at this moment? Sweat beaded his forehead; his shoulder ached. His breathing came in shallow gasps. He could feel his heart hammering in his chest. He had to find a way out.

Moments became critical. Panic set in. He squashed it. So far, his absence may have gone unnoticed. There would be another time. For now, he must give up. He spent a few seconds convincing himself otherwise, but the fact remained, he couldn't get through any basement doors to reach freedom through an unbarred window.

24

Tesqua slipped back up the stairs unnoticed in time to fall in behind Mana and Evey entering the mess hall. A smile slipped out. He had successfully ventured off and returned undetected. He would find another opportunity, another time. He would escape from this place. He would see Celia and his child again.

Tesqua sat beside Mana, who sat beside Evey. He stared at his dinner of mashed squash and pinto beans. Both Mana and Evey ate their dinner with paint-splattered hands, which forced Tesqua to check his hands. They were untainted, a sign he had failed to take into account. Would Barry notice this?

Rubbing his shoulder brought Mana's acknowledging smile. Try as he might, Tesqua could not massage away the excruciating pain from his basement excursion.

"The doors were all locked, weren't they?" Mana commented as he separated the squash from the beans, never making eye contact with Tesqua.

"What?"

"Doors ... they were all locked."

"Yes."

"Even though the windows have no bars, you can't gain access to them, can you? Did you think *I* wouldn't notice your absence?"

"Thanks. You could have told me that before I broke my shoulder."

"You needed to learn for yourself. As I did years ago. We would need three men larger than Grano to break through one of the doors. The commotion that would cause would bring the orderlies down upon us before we could get out the window."

Tesqua grunted an acknowledgment. He stared at his spoon for a long moment. Turning it over in his hand, he suddenly realized a new use for this utensil. After scanning the room, he leaned forward to slip the spoon inside his sock.

"Keys," Mana said.

"What?"

"They are the secret to our escape."

"Maybe," Tesqua said, paying little attention to Mana.

"Are you ready now?"

"Ready for what?" Tesqua replied, raising a skeptical eyebrow.

"If you must ask, then you are not," Mana added.

He rose to leave. Evey rose beside him, though she had barely eaten her dinner.

Tesqua remained after the two departed, staring at his food for a long time without touching it. He took pleasure in feeling the spoon tucked in his shoe. Maybe there was another way ...

Tesqua was the last to return to the day room to continue where he had left off. A renewed spirit swept over him. Now he wanted to complete what he had started earlier. He realized that in so doing, he would leave his mark on this place. Long after he was gone, they would know he had been here by his drawing on the wall, just as his ancestors had done with their glyptography on the rock formations in the desert. He would leave behind something that would uniquely represent him. Something others like him could see and understand why he had made it. Something whose meaning the white men would never be able to understand.

"I like it, everybody. I see you in your work," Barry chimed, standing proudly in the center of the day room. He circled to take in the breadth of the artwork now adorning the walls.

There were reasonable facsimiles of buffaloes, wolves, bears, along with eagles, teepees and human-like figures of varying sizes. Many were discernible, some so abstract only their creator could provide the answer as to what they were meant to represent.

Mana's very complex collection of symbols showed some true artistic ability, along with creative depth. Barry tried to find meaning in Mana's work but resigned himself to waiting for Mana to offer some explanation before drawing conclusions of his own.

"You have a wonderful talent for expression," Barry offered as encouragement for Mana. "Are you trying to tell us something with the children you've painted, Evey?"

Evey smiled, looking over to Mana. He was so hard at work he never noticed her interest. She had hated her attempt when she first stepped back to survey it. However, now that Barry had identified what she had actually tried to create, she found great pride in her accomplishment. She had sketched the children who would become part of her life. She decided it best not to reveal to anyone the man beside her in the drawing. That must be her secret. Looking at what she had designed in paint gave her renewed hope that someday she would leave this terrible place. She would fulfill the dreams she experienced now only in the peaceful silence of her sleep.

"Tesqua, yours fascinates me."

Tesqua stared blankly at his painting, which seemed more a blob of red bordering black that only loosely resembled human form. He knew the nature of the spirit he had fashioned on the wall, but assumed no one else would understand. *Especially Barry.* It had to be that Barry's lavish, albeit insincere praise sought to induce some kind of reaction from the patients. After all, what possibly could he know about Tesqua's culture, or any of the others here for that matter?

Barry continued talking—Tesqua ignored every word. In his mind, he held Celia in his arms after each had surrendered their virginity to the other. He was sixteen and it was the first time in his life Tesqua ever felt this way. He knew in that moment that their lives would become one. He would do whatever was necessary to bring her happiness.

"You are my warrior," Celia whispered, molding into his arms.

"We are not warriors anymore. They took that from us long ago along with everything else," he heard himself say.

"They can never take away what's painted in our hearts," she had whispered back.

"It's an Apache spirit warrior in war paint," Mana said sharply, with disdain.

The words yanked Tesqua back to this dreadful place against his will.

"I suspected something like that from the bow," Barry replied.

"Is that really what that's supposed to be?" Mana asked, chuckling.

"Keep laughing," Tesqua shot back, clearly indicating a deeper meaning to the figure on the wall, a symbol meant to convey hatred, violence and war.

Mana's face went slack.

Tesqua laughed.

Despite the drawing, Barry seemed pleased with Tesqua's effort. Perhaps the doctor misunderstood the message behind the paint? Did he not realize it was meant to strike fear into the enemies of the Apache?

"You're such a fool, Mana," Tesqua snapped just before stomping away.

"Will we be able to continue this?" Mana asked of Barry.

"I can only hope," Barry replied, his words laced thinly with faith, which failed to inspire Mana, who suddenly lost interest in continuing on.

"Hey!" Mana yelled, dashing back to his work.

While Mana was standing with Barry before Tesqua's painting, Paraquo had rolled himself to Mana's work. Snatching up Mana's brush, he smeared paint over Mana's figure on the wall.

"Stop!" Mana yelled, dashing back in time to grab hold of the brush. He spun the old man hard to roll him out of arm's reach of his wall.

"What are you doing, crazy old man?"

"Why did you make that? You are too young to know," Paraquo scolded, indicating the figure that stood almost as large as life.

"Make what?"

"The Ghost Dancer. How could you know?"

"My father. He spoke of them many times. He once drew one for me from memory."

Paraquo grabbed Mana's arm so tightly that it inflicted pain.

"They were evil. They brought death. You'll bring evil upon this place."

"They were not evil. My father was proud to be a Ghost Dancer. How do you know of them, stupid old man?"

"I also was one."

Their eyes held in a locked stare.

Mana's face dropped. His heart sank.

Paraquo rolled away before Mana could apologize.

Mana returned to his wall to repair the damage Paraquo had inflicted while Barry retreated to the day-room door to stand beside Thompson, who wore a rare, sweet smile upon her face. She became so much more fascinating when she smiled. Yet Barry dared not tell her so for fear she might feel slighted by his remark. Thompson displayed a most unpleasant knack for always spinning positive statements into negatives. To her, his comment would be interpreted as he meant she was boring when she wasn't smiling.

"You sparked life into them. Haven't seen this much enthusiasm in the eight years I've been here," Thompson said as Paraquo rolled by.

"Unfortunately, I doubt I'll be able to capitalize on this experiment," Barry responded.

"Don't remind me," Thompson said.

A few minutes later Nathan led the orderlies in to herd the patients from the day room for the night. Barry remained long after the last patient had departed. Only pallid artificial light now illuminated the various drawings on the walls. They had transformed their lifeless day room into part of their world. He stood proud of what they, as patients, had accomplished. They eradicated the sterile prosaic environment they had known for so long with one day's effort. In doing so, this room became theirs, a part of their culture. In reality, it became a place that could only feel vaguely like home. But the walls were still an improvement over what they had been at eight o'clock that morning.

Thompson also returned for one more look.

"I don't care what Wallace says or does. This was good for them," she offered.

"I hope so. It offers at least some insight into who they feel they are. Tesqua's deeply rooted anger. Evey's despair. I'm not sure yet how to interpret Mana's. But it has a very special meaning to him by the way he protected it. I suspect it links back to his father."

Barry's eyes said he wished to say more. Yet during the uncertain pause that ensued, he surrendered the moment between them.

Thompson started for the door.

"Will that be all for now, doctor?" she asked, her eyes practically begging him for more.

"Perhaps, Adele, you'll give me the pleasure of your company over dinner?"

With another of her rare sweet smiles, Thompson accepted without hesitation. She had been secretly hoping for this moment since the day Barry arrived at the asylum. She had forgone male companionship for too many years. The yearning inside her, like a candle's wick sputtering in a puddle of wax, had all but gone out.

"I'd love to, Dr. Barry," she replied with her softest voice.

25

In the glow of moonlight filtering through a thin stream of clouds, Mana removed a loose floorboard in his room to slip a paintbrush along with a small paint can into his secret hiding place. He smiled when he thought about how easy it had been to smuggle them out of the day room. The articles joined a collection of other bits and pieces. Mana laughed as he replaced the board, then he slid back under his blanket.

In the next room over, Tesqua stood at the window using the same moonlight to illuminate the nail heads securing the frame. With his absconded spoon, he scrapped at the wood, creating an indentation he hoped in time would become deep enough to allow him to remove the nails that would free his window. He still needed a way of removing the grating covering the glass, but it this terrible place, Tesqua had developed the patience and persistence to eliminate his barriers one at a time.

WIth each measured stroke, he thought of his Celia and what she would look like at their reunion. He would return to her. She would know then that he had never abandoned her. They would have many more children together. Their life would go back to the way it was supposed to be. Those were the thoughts that drove him. After many hours of effort, exhaustion moved him from the window back to his slumping bed. Sleep overtook him at will and brought Celia's smiling face into his mind.

26

Exactly on schedule, Wallace returned five days later. Nathan wasted no time informing him of what had occurred during his absence.

With a day room full of sunlight, Wallace entered, stared at the walls with Nathan at his side then closed the day-room door. A second later, it locked. For a change, Nathan had not exaggerated.

Three hours later, in a special basement room that stored the array of drugs available to the doctors for treating patients, Wallace sat on a high stool over a table with pestle and mortar, preparing small envelopes with the appropriate dosages for the patients.

This was a place of solace and meditation for the doctor. Alone, he could contemplate without distraction or interruption. Only Wallace, Barry and Thompson had access to the room, with Wallace requiring them to lock themselves in whenever they entered. He insisted they make certain there could be no unauthorized access to this place. Wallace also required periodic inventories to account for every drug they purchased, except for the alcohol, which the government allowed despite prohibition, since studies had deemed alcohol as useful in treating certain maladies. Most of the time Wallace maintained the alcohol inventory in his office, where it served to medicate him from his own malady of failing to live up to his expectations for his career.

While Wallace ground one of his concoctions, Barry unlocked the door and threw it open, slamming it against the wall, which jarred Wallace at the table.

The doctor, however, maintained his usual unaffected professional demeanor and kept working with his back to Barry, which forced Barry to be the first to speak.

"There is no reason to lock out the day room and confine the patients to their rooms," Barry blurted.

Wallace remained head down while he ground a powder mixture with his pestle. But anger slowly crept into his eyes.

"All patients remain confined until the day room is restored to its proper appearance."

"Don't do this. For the first time since my arrival, I see hope in their eyes. Taking away what we've accomplished is ludicrous."

Wallace spun about. Face to face, both wore anger across their brows. Wallace's eyes narrowed, transforming him into an icy, inhuman visage.

"Ludicrous? You want ludicrous. Allowing them to revert to their savage roots, that's ludicrous! The last thing we need here is a bunch of wild Indians."

"But they're showing us who they are. It's their culture. We shouldn't be trying to erase that."

"That's exactly what we're attempting to do. They must conform to our society."

"They should be allowed to hold on to who they are."

"Are you aware one of the drawings up there is a Ghost Dancer?"

"So?"

"Do you realize how long it's taken me to get them to adjust to our ways? They now trust us to medicate them over the foolish ritual chants of some tribal shaman. I saw nothing but remnants of their wild, savage existence in that room."

"These people are not savages. You came here to help them," Barry persisted. "I came here to help them."

"Are you done?"

The veins on Barry's forehead pulsed. His face turned ruddy while his breathing surged to keep up with his pounding heart. He was far from being done. But something inside his head was cautioning him to remain on his side of that professional line that separated the two men.

Wallace, however, remained calm, ruminating for a moment before continuing.

"You forget I'm in charge. I'll not allow those disgraces to remain. The day room remains locked. The patients remain confined to their rooms until *you* correct the damage you've done to my treatment programs. End of discussion."

Barry stormed out of the drug room.

Wallace calmly returned to his task at hand.

27

Demoralized patients stared at whitewashed walls. A few played checkers. The day room had returned to the spiritless milieu that had prevailed since its inception twenty years ago. It was as if Wallace could destroy their spirits with a simple edict.

Barry could only observe through the nurses-station window as all his work disappeared. The glimmer of hope he had nurtured for those five days had evaporated. Even Thompson seemed adversely moved by the decision. She barely spoke to him. The stalemate between the two doctors forced Barry to repaint the entire day room himself, since the patients were confined, and of course, no orderly dared volunteer to assist him. Clearly, Barry stood alone in his conviction. Aside from the nurses, Barry felt friendless in his job.

Inside the day room, passing Tesqua, Mana signaled with a slight head nod. Tesqua believed their clandestine signaling unnecessary in this place, but Mana seemed to derive pleasure from it, so Tesqua humored him.

As they passed the table, Lizzie, as always, chatted away to Ko-nay-ha.

"A year ago, I worked the laundry with a woman who thought she had a fox trapped inside her head. I told her, no way she had a fox inside her head. It was a raccoon."

Lizzie could adroitly transition from topic to topic without the slightest pause to breathe. Tesqua knew he could never live with a woman so inconsiderate of a man. He was glad his Celia indulged him during his quiet times. She was always considerate of his feelings; she rarely spoke the way this one spoke to a man. Even though Ko-nay-ha couldn't hear her anyway. He simply stared straight ahead, oblivious to Lizzie's cackling.

"What's the matter, my friend? You seem more crazy than usual," Tesqua said to Mana. He thought he had made a joke, but Mana failed to see humor in it.

"Barry and Thompson."

"So?"

"They've been together."

"Oh."

"They have each other while Evey and I are kept apart. We're as much one as any two people are. It isn't right."

"Since when does right have anything to do with anything around this place?"

Mana grunted. Anger bled from his eyes.

"So, your latest dribble is you think those two are lovers?"

"Watch, he'll touch her."

As they watched Barry and Thompson working together at the nurses station, Barry eased closer to her. Then, while jointly looking over a chart, and when the moment seemed right, Barry set his hand on her forearm.

"See."

"You two really serious?" Tesqua asked.

"As much as possible in this place."

"Don't you think you should know why she stabbed her teacher before you marry her?"

Mana walked away. Tesqua followed a few seconds later, settling beside him in the opposite corner of the room.

"Well?"

"He was raping her. She was thirteen."

Mana stormed off, began circling the day room. With each pass, he stared at *them* outside the day room. After his third pass, he rammed into Paraquo, who had strayed into his path.

"Move away from me!" Mana stammered. His right hand curled into a fist.

Paraquo grunted, wheeling his chair to further impede Mana.

"Move, stupid old man, or I'll yank you from that chair and stomp your face," Mana shouted.

"You think you can?" Paraquo offered, bringing his fists up to protect himself.

Mana grabbed them.

Tesqua grabbed Mana's hands and pulled them off the old man. He then spun Paraquo away from Mana to the window facing the giant oak.

"I don't need your help against this little fawn," Paraquo ridiculed.

Mana lunged for him, but Tesqua successfully pulled him away before Jake could come between them.

"No problem here," Tesqua offered to Jake with hands up in surrender.

He nudged Mana away until he had put at least a dozen paces between the two. Mana, it seemed, would need some time to work through his latest anger. And he was trapped in a place where he had nothing but time. Tesqua managed to calm Mana during their remaining time in the day room.

After being confined for the night, Tesqua stood just inside his door listening to Mana pacing in the room beside him. He stared out as Nathan approached his door, slipping to the side when Nathan glanced in. Once Nathan moved on, Tesqua returned to the window. If he leaned just right, he could see Nathan throw his feet up on the desk when he leaned back in the chair. The lights dimmed once again. A moment later, they came back full bright.

At last Mana had become silent in his room. So Tesqua retired to his bed. This night brought no night screams. In the eerie still enveloping him, Tesqua realized he indeed needed Mana's help. His chances of success alone were slim at best. But with Mana's help, they could devise a way out.

Tesqua closed his eyes. He visualized himself running free through the open fields with the wind against his face. Mana ran beside him. But where were they running? Tesqua tried to focus. He needed to know exactly where they would go once they escaped. That detail became critical to maintaining their freedom for longer than just a scant few hours.

His thoughts turned to a more pressing problem. *Was Mana actually losing his mind in this place?* Would he become crazy like so many others here? Tesqua realized he must find some way to preserve Mana's sanity and thereby improve his chances for gaining their freedom. Escaping the asylum, for the moment, became secondary to his more immediate need. He had to find a way to help Mana; at least enough so Mana could in turn aid him.

28

Five days passed. It took that long for Tesqua to devise a workable idea to help his friend. Dr. Barry, on the other hand, was quite pleased when Tesqua came to his office of his own volition, rather than being forced to attend their sessions, as he had to be so many times in the past. However, within the first five minutes of their time together, Barry realized Tesqua had come with his own agenda for offering cooperation.

Twenty minutes into their session, an exasperated Barry pushed his chair back, watching Tesqua pace. The doctor was witnessing a different Tesqua than the one who had been in his office a hundred times before.

Tesqua, for some reason, had decided to reveal yet another side of himself.

"What harm does it do?" Tesqua insisted with passion-laced words.

It became obvious to Barry that Tesqua refused to accept his response to his request graciously. Barry's eyes probed for hidden meaning.

"I'm not sure it can do any harm. But that doesn't mean we should do it."

"Does your law forbid it?"

"That has nothing to do with it."

"Then do it."

"At times I wonder, Tesqua, who's manipulating who?"

"You do this thing, I make no trouble."

Barry leaned forward in his chair. That was the first time since he began treating Tesqua that Tesqua had ever volunteered such words to him. For a brief moment, Barry felt like he had made a breakthrough.

"But ..." Barry started.

Tesqua had nothing more to say. Having said what he came to say, he saw no further need to converse with the doctor. He left.

"Okay, we're done here," Barry muttered to the empty office.

Barry closed his file, weighing the pros and cons of what Tesqua had requested. Then he turned to how he might actually accomplish it. The idea wasn't so crazy. He could find a way to make it work despite the many obstacles. No doubt, what Tesqua offered could do immense good for the people involved. But with the doctor's tenuous relationship with Dr. Wallace, Barry knew he would never gain the doctor's approval. This wouldn't be the first time Barry had acted so rash on his own without a superior's approval. It would certainly not be his last.

The idea was bold; his plan must be equally bold to carry it out. Besides, he felt like he owed Wallace something in retaliation for the day room debacle. Now he just needed to find a way to pull it off without Wallace catching on. The very thought excited him. He smiled broadly but hid the smile when Wallace strolled by. Their eyes met. Just the cold way Wallace stared

convinced Barry he must find a way to do this thing and prevent Wallace from ever finding out.

Barry leaned back in his chair, steepled his fingers before
his face and began the first stages of planning his little cabal
against his boss. A smile crossed his lips at the thought of what
he might be able to do. Tesqua would have no idea of the fire
he had ignited in the doctor with his request.

The doctor sprang up out of his chair to begin his work.
Today was going to be an excellent day in the asylum.

29

The entire staff of twelve crammed shoulder-to-shoulder into Wallace's office with the door closed. The oppressive summer heat caused the room to take on pressure cooker qualities. Wallace liked to employ this tactic when serious problems distracted him from his other duties. He sat back in his chair while his eyes grazed from face to face, grabbing eye contact for a few seconds with each of his employees. He dissected each for signs of guilt. Those who too quickly averted their eyes became suspects. During the entire time his jaw remained locked tight; his lips drew a thin line across his face. This latest disturbing problem was the last thing he wanted to have to deal with here.

Thompson had never seen Wallace in such an angry fervor in all her time there. Having learned from previous experience, she held his eyes with hers. Wallace habitually turned mean upon those from whom he detected weakness. She held her ground.

After a few strained seconds, his eyes moved on. She had uncovered Wallace's intimidation techniques early, along with a profile of the employees he targeted for his psychological abuse.

"Someone's going to explain how this happened before we leave this room," he snapped. Wallace symbolically checked his gold-plated timepiece set on his desk before him.

The funereal silence held the room. Not a single head turned to look at another. Every orderly, every nurse, stared straight ahead. Barry stood clearly in a position of exemption behind and to Wallace's side.

"Don't look at me. I was in the men's wing," Thompson offered at last when Wallace settled his chilling stare back on her. *The guilty one always talks first*, Wallace thought to himself. He sought to intimidate her; she knew that much for certain, yet she would have none of it. She would *never* allow herself to make such a serious breach of security in the facility.

During that tense moment, Nathan must have thought himself safe, for he stole a sidelong glance at Jake, who stared unblinking, blank-faced straight ahead, avoiding eye contact with Wallace, Barry or Nathan. So many things churned helter-skelter in Nathan's mind at that moment that sorting them out to arrive at the truth seemed impossible.

Wallace detected Nathan's sudden interest in the new orderly. Was Nathan trying to send a signal to the doctor to indicate who he thought the guilty party to be? As a result, the doctor leveled his stare upon Jake. The new guy might be the one to attack. He should fold easy ... if he's guilty. In this game of intimidation who would falter first? Rarely did Wallace. He who finds swallowing difficult, like Jake did right now, should advance to the top of the list.

Jake averted his eyes, casting them downward immediately. This being Jake's first intimidation, maybe he was just nervous. His hands sweated so profusely they slipped off the seat, which he had clutched to keep his tension from buoying to the surface.

"I check the doors every shift, exactly like I been instructed by Nathan," Jake offered in a voice with hollowed out confidence. He still refused eye contact with Wallace. Instead, his eyes bounced nervously between the two doctors. Maybe he secretly hoped Dr. Barry would come to his aid. But Barry wisely remained silent.

Wallace surmised he had just narrowed down his suspect list to one.

"I'd be a laughing stock if this gets out," Wallace said, then he paused to scan the eyes of every employee. His intimidation had snagged him a suspect—but no confession. He would let them stew a while longer.

"We're finished here for now," Wallace said while lowering his eyes to paperwork on his desk, his subtle way of dismissing them.

Everyone jostled to file out quickly. Jake maneuvered his way out so as not to be the last to exit, fearing Wallace might snag the last man out for further interrogation. Only Barry remained.

"I'll see what I can turn up. I can make a few phone calls if you like," Barry offered.

"Unnecessary. I've a friend at the Canton police. No paperwork for now. No one outside these walls need know about this until we know more."

Barry nodded concurrence, leaving Dr. Wallace to ruminate over their latest problem.

****

Hours later as the late afternoon sun blared in, Jake stowed the mop bucket in the latrine closet. So entangled in his thoughts was he, that he never sensed Nathan standing silently behind him. Nathan rammed Jake into the storage room then pinned him against the wall with a forearm to the throat. The bucket clanked against the cast iron sink, creating a horrible racket. However, Nathan cared little about the commotion they stirred.

"What did you do?" Nathan growled with a fierce anger in his eyes. He bared his teeth the way a vicious dog transmits a warning to beware.

"Nothin'. Swear," Jake pleaded, presenting his sternest face against his supervisor.

At that moment, Jake's insides were coming apart at the seams. On the outside, he must have convinced Nathan, because the head orderly slowly released his clamp. Jake's hands shook so visibly he just knew Nathan would refuse to accept his words. The blood that had flooded his face as a result of his constricted throat slowly receded.

"Fucking Barry's gonna be sticking his nose up our asses now," Nathan barked into Jake's face.

Jake dared not move, dared not even swallow. Nathan's face hovered inches from his; those dark eyes kept drilling deeper into his for an answer.

"Keep your mouth shut," Nathan spat.

The moment lingered far longer than Jake could handle.

Then Nathan released his hold. He eased back. A tense pause ensued, during which Jake believed Nathan would slug him anyway. Instead, Nathan just turned about, leaving a disheveled, shaken Jake against the wall, taking in his first breath since Nathan took hold of him.

Jake felt a sudden need to retch. He spun, leaning over the sink to heave up his lunch.

30

At nine o'clock patients trudged from the day room to their rooms. The temperature hovered near eighty, the humidity ninety percent. The oppressive heat had zapped all the spirit from the patients. There would be no air movement to cool them since all windows were nailed shut. With sweat rolling down their faces all throughout the day, the patients could only stare out as the orderlies milled about outside, smoking in the shade the building afforded them. A southerly breeze brought them at least some small measure of relief.

No one called out; no one created the least disturbance this night. The orderlies locked everyone down without a single cross word.

Barry and Thompson exchanged a tentative look while they busied themselves at the desk outside the darkened day room. Wallace's footsteps rose in the still. He descended the stairs with satchel in one hand while dabbing the sweat from his neck with his other.

Jake strolled down the hall with hands stuffed in his pockets after locking in the last patient.

"Good night," Wallace said, his voice drained of energy. "Please have the drug order ..." he continued.

"On your desk first thing in the morning, sir," Thompson finished the sentence for him in her usual cheerful voice.

Despite having days that were just as long and probably more arduous than Wallace's, she always saw fit to keep her spirits up with a pleasant voice. She believed it vital to consistently project a positive face toward patients and staff. Often times she wondered if Wallace's demeaning attitude contributed to the anger and depression infecting all who lived and worked here.

"Very good then," Wallace said.

He made his way out the reception room door while Barry and Thompson looked on. They waited, avoiding eye contact, until they heard the lock slide into place.

Both took deep breathes. They looked at each other the moment Wallace exited the building. Thompson's eyes cast uncertainty; Barry's eyes sought to reassure her.

"You're bloody certain about this?" she whispered.

"Yes, I am. What about them?" Barry replied, indicating Nathan as he exited a patient room, while Jake straightened day-room chairs.

"Trust me," she said.

"Nathan, you and Jake need to clean the dry goods room. Wallace said he saw cockroaches the size of his shoe."

She followed up her order by handing Nathan a clipboard stuffed with papers.

"Also, do an inventory. Make sure you count everything twice. *No mistakes this time*. We'll send an order to Canton on Friday."

That solved that little problem, Thompson thought, listening to grumbling as Nathan and Jake slogged away, making it evident that they had hoped to sit around rather than take on more asylum tasks.

"How long?" Barry queried.

"The way Nathan works, least an hour. You're sure this is right?"

Barry paused before answering. He had never been one to allow authority to stifle his judgment. If something felt right, he went for it, then he endured whatever consequences might follow in its aftermath.

"Not really sure, actually. Just know we might be able to help two people. Besides, South Dakota doesn't recognize it. Only we'll know. After extensive conversations with them both, I'm confident this is what they want."

"We're going to be in so much trouble if this goes wrong on us," Thompson said just before heading off one way while Barry headed another. Both were certain they were doing the right thing, yet they were equally uncertain they could actually pull it off without Wallace getting wind of it. Thompson's own strategy, however, was to let Barry take all the heat if his little plan soured.

****

Nathan lounged on a long side table in the dry goods room with his feet dangling. A cigarette drooped from his lips while Jake jabbed the broom at the scurrying cockroaches he flushed out from beneath the shelves. Wallace hadn't exaggerated when he claimed the cockroaches had been the size of his shoe. Neither Jake nor Nathan ever guessed that Wallace would care about the room or its squatters.

Jake stopped mid-swat.

"I needs your help," he said in a weak, guilt-laden voice that cracked as it trailed off. His eyes searched Nathan's.

"Right. They're just cockroaches. Get those over there."

But Jake remained frozen in place. Rather the only movement came from his hands wrenching the broom handle.

Nathan realized something was seriously wrong.

"I fucked up, man. You knows Kit, when she disappeared?"

Nathan flew off the table as if he had been launched. He grabbed Jake at the throat and flung him into the shelves, where he slapped his face repeatedly.

"I knew it!" Nathan scowled.

The broom toppled from Jake's hands when he tried to bring up balled fists to protect himself.

"I fucked up. I weren't thinking. I got carried away with her," Jake cried, trying to fend off Nathan's hard slaps now battering his face.

"What did you do to her? She dead?" Nathan yelled.

He continued slapping, even though Jake's hands now protected his cheeks.

After a few more whacks Nathan stopped, but he kept Jake pinned against the shelves with a knee to his groin. Blood trickled from Jake's nostrils. Tears rimmed Jake's eyes. His right cheek bloomed crimson from the beating.

"No. No. She's not dead. She's tied up in my room at the boarding house. I was gonna brings her back, I swear I was. But I fell asleep. I knew I was gonna get caught if I tried sneakin' her in. I didn't think, man."

"You *fucking* cockroach!"

Nathan shoved Jake to get him away from him. He snatched up the broom ready to whack Jake across the head with it. Instead, he knocked the broom into the overhead light, causing it to swing in a wide arc.

31

Tesqua stood hand-in-hand with Celia, bathed in vibrant springtime sunshine in the midst of a grassy green meadow nestled in a valley on the south end of their reservation. In her native dress and crown of delicate white flowers, Celia had never looked more beautiful than at that moment. She also never seemed happier. Their combined families, wearing traditional Apache dress, encircled them.

With misty eyes, Celia accepted the cup Tesqua offered; she handed him her bread. While she drank, Tesqua took a small bite of her offering.

"From this day forward, you two shall live as one. Your life shall be his life. His life shall be your life," Paraquo said.

The words snatched Tesqua away from his daydream of his wedding day with Celia. Reality rushed back in, pulling him back to the present. But the afterimage of her smile stuck inside his mind. He felt a lump rise up in his throat. Goose flesh rose on his arms. Then anger replaced them.

"That it?" Barry whispered. He shifted nervously beside Tesqua. The two stood behind the couple facing Paraquo. Thompson flanked Tesqua's other side.

"What?" Tesqua asked. He sighed inwardly. Celia was gone.

Barry's words kept Tesqua from returning to his daydream, forcing him to abandon the image of his lovely wife.

Paraquo began his chant, his voice growing more forceful with each measure.

"Must he do that?" Barry pressed.

"It's a blessing. He prays for sons," Tesqua said.

Barry turned to check the day-room door. So far, they were safe.

"Must he do it so loud? But that's it, right?"

Panic spread through Barry's insides with each passing moment. The entire ceremony was supposed to last under ten minutes. Tesqua had promised. Well, twenty minutes later, Paraquo still droned on in his native tongue. Both Barry and Thompson hoped it might end quickly. They were running out of time. They had been lucky; Nathan lived up to his reputation for dawdling when he should be working. The two orderlies probably feared being assigned more work once they finished the dry goods room.

"Dai k'ehgo lil noijoo li dahaazhi," Tesqua said.

"What does that mean?" Barry asked.

He realized this had been the first time he had heard Tesqua speak in his native tongue. Wallace forbade using any language other than English in the asylum. He feared the Indians would conspire against them if they were allowed to communicate without his staff being able to understand them. Wallace's severe punishments in the past had all but squashed any native words.

"May you continue to love each other forever. My father wished that ..." Tesqua stopped himself. The pain in his heart stole away any further words, leaving an awkward silence between them. Tesqua knew he was expected to speak to break the silence.

"That's it. Will they be allowed to join as husband and wife?" he forced out.

Barry didn't immediately respond.

Mana kissed Evey once more, lifted her into his arms, where he carried her from the day room with Tesqua pushing Paraquo. Barry led the way while Thompson extinguished the day-room lights, exiting last. They had one more task to pull off before calling their little secret a complete success.

****

Nathan paced the dry goods room with the fury of a caged animal. He had a new cockroach to deal with. Jake remained against the shelves, terrified that if he moved a muscle, it would bring another onslaught from Nathan.

"She's been gone two weeks," Nathan grumbled, his eyes on this scuffed-up shoes, certain that if he even looked at Jake now, he would beat him until his brains dribbled out his ears.

Nathan had worked hard in the past two years positioning himself to exploit this shitty stink-hole job. Now a stupid ass-hole like Jake could fuck him out of everything he deserved. He wasn't going let that happen. He wouldn't, not without at least trying to find a way out of this mess.

"What they gonna do to me?" Jake ventured, hoping Nathan had cooled off enough to allow them to talk without erupting into another beating.

"It's kidnapping and rape, you dumbass."

"Fuck, Nathan, help me get out of this. I don't know what to do."

Nathan lit another cigarette while he paced. Jake could see Nathan's temper receding beneath the surface. Nathan took to thinking more, swinging less. That was a good sign. Though his jaw remained clinched, Nathan no longer balled his fists instinctively with each step.

"She's all tied up. I feed her and stuff when I get home at night."

"Go home. Suffocate her with a pillow in her sleep."

Jake's eyes widened.

"Then how do I gets her body out of my room? She'd be real heavy after she's dead. Can you help me?"

"Are you fuckin' nuts? I'd be an accomplice. You tryin' to get me thrown in prison, too? You have to kill her. You have to get rid of her body yourself."

"Shits. Oh, fuck. No. She's crazy. You said it yourself. No one's gonna believe a fuckin' crazy injun bitch."

Nathan stopped his pacing just long enough to slap Jake hard across the face. Jake refused to defend himself. After all, he deserved it for what he had done. After kidnapping her, he had been raping her three times each of the nights he had her.

"Then go to prison, you stupid backwoods fuck."

"How do I gets the body out without someone's seeing me? If I go dragging a big thing like that ..."

"Right, right, right. Dumb shitass. Okay. Don't kill her in your room. Sneak her out at night after everyone's asleep. Tell her you're bringing her back here. No. No. Better yet, tell her you're taking her back to her family. That's it. Instead, drive her into the woods where you'll shoot her. Yeah, yeah, that's it. Somebody else finds the body. You're off the hook. They'll all think she wandered off and a hunter shot her by mistake. Hey, they may never even find the body."

Nathan liked his current solution. He liked it so much he offered Jake a cigarette.

"I can't shoot her," Jake said, with the welcome cigarette trembling between his lips.

Nathan ripped the smoke out.

"Fine. Go to prison."

"I means I don't got a gun," Jake pressed.

Nathan returned the cigarette to Jake's mouth. Then he resumed his pacing for a few seconds. He had to think of every-thing for this bonehead shit brain. Nathan knew if Jake remained in his sight two seconds longer, he'd put him in a hos-pital. Instead, he opened the door and flung Jake into the hall.

"I'll figure it out. Just get the hell out of my sight so I can think," Nathan growled.

Jake wandered the basement hall cursing himself. He paused for a long time at the staircase, unsure of whether to go up or return to the dry goods room. He prayed Nathan would find a way to get him out of his mess. Sooner rather than later, this whole situation would blow up in his face, and he'd find himself someplace a hundred times worse than where he worked. And at times, he thought of this place as nothing more than a prison for Indians.

Jake reached the top of the stairs with head hung and hands balled in his pockets. His ruffled shirt still out of his pants, he looked up to Barry pacing outside Mana's room.

Barry stopped mid-stride. Surprise took over his face.

"Finished already?" Barry asked, trying to tamp nervous-ness out of his voice.

A red-faced Thompson intervened.

"Jake, I need a favor. Check to make sure the lard blocks were placed in the kitchen for the morning?"

Jake, already burdened, failed to comprehend the situation's significance. He nodded absently and trudged off, keeping his hands tucked away to hide their trembling.

Relief washed over Barry's face when Jake disappeared.

Finally, Mana's door opened to a smiling Evey. She revealed such happiness in her eyes that Barry knew in that moment that he had done the right thing.

"Thank you, Dr. Barry," she said in her timid voice, barely audible above the thumping of Barry's pounding heart. At last, it was over. They had pulled it off. Now Barry could smile.

"We should hurry," he said.

They had pulled it off without a hitch.

Almost.

Neither Barry, Thompson nor Evey noticed Nathan watching from the staircase. He had witnessed Evey's departure from Mana's room.

A smile of vicious intent consumed Nathan's face. Perhaps things were not as foul as he had thought just five minutes earlier. A little leverage against the good doctor could be made to go a long way.

32

Days passed with no one suspecting that the relationship between Mana and Evey had changed dramatically after that night in the day room. But Barry and Thompson knew. Tesqua knew. And Paraquo knew. And life went on in the asylum as it did before. Each time Tesqua watched Mana and Evey exchange a brief contact, he missed his Celia all the more. Would she wait for him? Would he ever even see her again? How would she feel when they were at last together after his long absence? What must his son think of him as a father? The little one had to feel abandoned without ever understanding why his father had left. What would Celia tell the little one?

In the mess hall during dinner, Mana pounded the table as he always did while talking to Evey. They seemed to have so much to say to each other. Mana's eyes always brightened when Evey entered the day room. Conversely, he became visibly depressed when the orderlies herded them away. Mana had learned after his years there to savor every opportunity that presented itself.

Tesqua had yet to comprehend that lesson.

As she spoke, Evey risked covering Mana's pounding hand with hers, squeezing it gently. His hand stopped. He smiled at her.

Lizzie sat across from them, Ko-nay-ha seated beside her, staring straight ahead. She had learned the best way to guarantee visitation was by volunteering to feed him, a chore no orderly relished. Besides, she rather enjoyed the task despite his apparent lack of enthusiasm in what she had to say. She just pretended that Ko-nay-ha so enjoyed her voice that he dared not interrupt her.

She would place a small spoonful of food at his lips, and he would actually draw the food back to swallow it. He never chewed, never looked at the offering nor indicated that he saw anyone around them.

"I should braid my hair. What do you think? They overcooked the meat again. I hate the way they cook. I should work in the kitchen. I could teach them how to prepare meat. It looks like snow. I think we'll see an early winter. Where I'm from ..." Lizzie droned.

"Stop talking!" Ko-nay-ha blurted out with such force that it brought the entire mess hall to silence. Every pair of eyes went to the old Indian, who had not spoken, had not blinked, had not lifted a hand in his own behalf for as long as anyone could remember. After speaking his peace, he returned to his catatonic state.

"You could've at least told me what you think of my hair," Lizzie moaned, then continued feeding him.

33

Wallace leaned over his desk with Tesqua across from him. A brilliant afternoon sun shone in through the windows, hitting Tesqua's face. Yet Tesqua refused to squint despite the discomfort it caused. He thought doing so might give Wallace an advantage over him. Tesqua kept his arms wrapped tight across his chest.

"Your anger keeps you here," Wallace said plainly.

"You are my anger. Dr. Barry says I've made progress."

"I do not concur."

"Allow me to go back to my wife and child. They need me."

"It is their welfare that concerns us most. Your anger makes you a danger to your family."

Wallace exuded great pleasure in telling Tesqua that. He spoke as if he wanted to stab Tesqua with every word he delivered. He could see despair looming in Tesqua's eyes—it appeared to Tesqua that Wallace enjoyed placing It there.

"How many times must I plead for my life before you doctors?"

"Doctors? Only I have the power to release you."

"And you're never going to do that, are you?"

"I cannot, in good conscience, consider your release at this time."

The indifference in Wallace's icy, inhuman tone tore into Tesqua's soul. His heart was breaking. His vision of his Celia that he held so dear was slipping away.

"You have no conscience. And I have no more time."

Defeated yet again in his plea for freedom to return home, Tesqua left the doctor's office. He hated everyone and everything in this terrible place. Despite all his efforts, they repeatedly denied his request to be set free.

****

Outside the asylum, parked near the front stairs, Jake sat behind the wheel of the truck with the engine idling roughly. Nathan leaned in through the passenger side window with a smug smile across his face. His eyes, however, delivered a more serious intent.

"Under the driver's seat," Nathan said. Those eyes indicated exactly where he meant.

Jake leaned forward, groping blindly with his right hand.

"Not now, you dumb dirt clod. I'll tell Wallace you're taking the truck to Canton for service."

"I gotta do it in broad daytime?"

"Shut up. We tell him they had to keep the truck overnight. Once it's dark, take the squaw bitch into the woods and handle it. Bring the truck back in the morning."

"I don't knows."

"Look, I've done this before."

"You killed somebody?" Jake eeked out.

"No, you dumbass. I had to leave the truck overnight. Wallace won't suspect a thing."

Nathan backed away.

Relief flooded Jake's face. He eased the clutch out with a trembling foot to slowly pull away while Nathan stood there watching.

Another problem solved, Nathan thought as he bounded up the stairs two-at-a-time to return to the asylum. Now his life could go back to normal. Albeit, Nathan's version of normal.

That evening after Nathan locked the patients in their rooms for the night, he returned to the nurses' station and kicked his feet up onto the desk. He lit matches as a way to fight the boredom. A smile crossed his face when he thought about what Jake would be doing at that moment. A little creative thinking and bang! situation under control. He wanted everything back to the way it should be. After all, he had plans for himself. He needed the cloud of Kit's absence lifted. He was proud of himself for coming up with a way to take care of a difficult problem.

While he stared at a match just moments from scorching his fingers, the lights dimmed, emitting a buzz that lasted more than a moment. It distracted him just long enough for the flame to sear his fingers.

Nathan, the habitual slow learner that he was, renewed striking matches within a few minutes just to study the fire. Only this time he made certain to extinguish them before his flesh felt the first warmth of an encroaching flame. Boring of that, he leaned back to nod off. An hour later, the sound of footsteps snapped him awake.

He leaned out from the chair as Wallace emerged from the staircase with satchel in hand.

"Night, doctor," he said then paused for effect. "Oh, Jake had to leave the truck overnight for service."

"That's fine. Thank you, Nathan," Wallace replied, exiting through the reception-room door.

"Yes, sir," Nathan replied, more for himself. He leaned back, intertwined his fingers together at the back of his head with a broad smile lighting his face. Fantasies crept into his brain about what awaited him in the coming months.

34

With the morning, patients exited rooms, heading for another meaningless day in the day room. Thompson worked with her head down at her desk when Barry approached her. She immediately stopped working.

"What's going on?" Thompson asked.

"I don't know. What do you mean?" Barry replied.

"Wallace is in his office with the door closed. When I knocked, he scowled through the door, admonishing me for intruding then telling me to come back later."

"Beats me. No one tells me anything around here," Barry said, then left to check on a patient.

In his office, an incredulous Wallace stared across at Jake, who kept nervously working his knuckles with a pale, stricken face. Jake looked like a man about to face the gallows.

"Your actions are unconscionable," Wallace spat. His face never changed from the stone-hard visage he wore.

"I weren't thinkin', sir."

"Weren't thinking? Weren't thinking! Do you have any idea the position you've placed me in?"

Jake opened his mouth to answer.

Wallace held up his hand. He didn't want an answer. Nothing Jake could say could alter what Wallace was thinking at that moment.

"Who else knows?"

"Just Nathan."

"And?"

"I swears."

Wallace paused to think. There had to be a way out of this that would allow him to save face. Their little situation with the missing female patient had gone from bad to terrible in what seemed a blink of an eye. Now he wished she had just remained missing. Ignorance meant innocence. Now that all changed.

"I'll find a way to fix this," Wallace muttered.

"Am I going to prison?"

The silent moment between them proved excruciating for Jake. Visions of him being beaten by fellow inmates in prison flooded his brain. He couldn't handle a place like that. His mother would never speak another word to him as long as he lived. If only there was some way for him to take back all he had done.

"Never speak of this, and never, ever, try something this stupid ever again."

Jake rose on the verge of tears.

"Am I fired?" Jake asked.

Wallace thought long and hard.

"Just get out of my office now."

Jake felt a rush of relief for being able to vocalize what tore at his brain for hours. He could only hope Dr. Wallace would be able to do something to spare him from being locked up forever.

35

In a basement room without windows, one of only two in the entire facility, Dr. Wallace stood over a woman strapped to her bed. The stench of mildew hung in the air. He checked her forehead with his hand, took up a towel to wipe her face down, then stuffed another small cloth firmly into her mouth. She tugged at her restraints but to no avail. Satisfied with his preparations, Wallace retreated to his instruments on a trestle table against one wall, where he set a number of dials. Trembling hands placed each at their maximum setting. Wallace paused as he stared at the dials.

Kit tugged at the straps, staring at him with terror-stricken eyes. She had no inkling of what was about to happen, this being her first time in this room.

Wallace refused to speak. No words of reassurance, no comforting touch. He knew what he must do. There would be no questions, no inquiry, no answering to a superior. All could go back to the way it should be in the asylum.

Hours later as patients moved about, Thompson snared Wallace on the staircase leading to the second floor as he emerged from the basement. So consumed by his thoughts was he, that at first he merely stared blankly at the nurse.

"Is it true Kit's back?" she asked.

Wallace paused before answering.

"Canton police found her unconscious in an abandoned farmhouse, poor thing. I'm attending her."

Wallace continued up the stairs, passing Tesqua coming down. When Tesqua stopped beside Mana, Mana bobbed and weaved as if evading a diving bird, then he straightened back up. He held an empty wastebasket. Tesqua had learned to ignore Mana's idiosyncrasies as nothing more than his lame attempt to maintain his foolish ruse.

"I wish I knew what's in that file Barry keeps on me," Tesqua said.

"You really think it matters?" Mana offered.

"It matters to me why they locked me in here."

On Nathan's approach they moved from the hall toward the day room. As they reached the door to the day room, Mana glanced back at the locked key cabinet behind the nurses'-station desk. The gesture snared Tesqua's attention, but he had no idea why Mana had shown an interest in it.

36

Wallace returned to his office, sat behind his desk for many minutes staring out the window at a fading sun. Miles of vacant land surrounded them. No one could see, nor would even know, this asylum existed if they never ventured down the unpaved rutted road leading to this place. After ten years here, Wallace had hoped for more. A promotion would have given him the opportunity to advance his career. Now he believed this place, and even his research, had failed him. He felt like the Bureau's bastard child, stuck in the middle of nowhere, away from the rest of the family and forced to live off leftover scraps. He should have been grateful for the opportunity, considering how his life had started out, but he wasn't.

He leaned forward over his desk, removing a death certificate from the side drawer. For a moment he stared at it. Then he filled in 'Kit Standing Bear' for the name. He pondered for a time as to cause of death. Finally, he entered pneumonia before signing the parchment. He would create some supporting notation in her medical file, after which he could file it away with the rest of the deceased patient files. No one need ever know what really happened to the poor woman. Another Canton secret would die and be buried away, never to be revealed again.

He picked up the telephone on his desk, the only one in the building, to ring for the grave diggers. Once completed, he removed a clipboard hanging behind the desk on a nail, where he added Kit's name along with a series of numbers to the sheet already containing more than two dozen names of their own.

The matter now dealt with, life could return to the way Wallace wanted it at his asylum.

A quiet month passed. No questions surfaced regarding Kit. The nurses along with Dr. Barry accepted that the police had returned the unconscious woman to the asylum in the later stages of pneumonia. Her subsequent death had been the result of exposure to the elements after having somehow walked out of the facility. Wallace assured Barry in private that someone, possibly Jake, had forgotten to lock the door to reception, allowing Kit to wander away during a moment of inattention by the orderlies. Wallace's monthly report to the Bureau of Indian Affairs indicated only that two patients had expired during the reporting period, both from illness. A untarnished record meant everything to Wallace's future.

****

Tesqua hated checkers. An unchallenging, juvenile game that all too often ended in a draw when opposing players attained any level of competence. But checkers was the only game doctors allowed in the day room. Card games were more interesting, certainly more fun and challenging, but there were so many sore losers that Wallace ordered the cards permanently removed.

Tesqua left the checkers on the table, throwing up his hands in defeat in a mock ceremony to concede victory to Paraquo. Old Paraquo giggled in triumph. He never seemed to catch on that Tesqua designed his moves to ensure Paraquo's victory. Tesqua came to enjoy the smile on Paraquo's face, along with the glint in his eyes when he won. Tesqua could only vaguely remember his own father's smile; it had been so long since he had seen it.

Old Paraquo concentrated so hard on the simple game that it seemed cruel to steal those inconsequential victories from him. Besides, Tesqua learned winning was least important. Having someone to talk to and confide in who wasn't crazy, or someone who might be of help sometime in the future, took precedence over victory. Paraquo, being an elderly cripple, and for the most part dumb as the ox in the field, would be of limited value, but he might still provide some use to Tesqua when the time came.

It became difficult for Tesqua to even think about time. The daily medication they administered kept his faculties somewhere between full mental acuity and stumbling-about dizziness. It took more effort to think about his home, family and what he really wanted, which was to be free of this place.

Mana abandoned his solitary perch at the window facing the giant oak, now growing greener with each passing day. In those brief moments when they might per chance pass by the open reception-room door, they could even catch a puff of fresh outside air blowing against their face.

Mana motioned Tesqua with a head nod. Tesqua followed him across the room.

"Something's going on," Mana commented with eyes roving the day room.

Then he motioned toward the nurses' station. Through the glass, serious faces huddled at the desk. Eyes moved from the orderlies to the patients on the other side of the window.

Something big was about to happen.

Mana slowly perused the day room. Everything remained exactly the same as it had been every other day for as long as Mana could remember, except ...

Across the room, Grano sought to be invisible in the corner. His massive girth prevented him from hiding amongst other patients, but that was exactly what Grano attempted to do. When their eyes met, Grano turned away, lowering his head until his chin rested against his chest.

"There." Mana pointed out Grano for Tesqua.

"What do you think?"

"We will know soon enough," Mana replied. He indicated to Tesqua that Wallace had now joined the worried group at the nurses' station.

"Find a new place to stand," Mana ordered, wandering away when the door opened.

Nathan, Jake and the other orderlies dispersed to round up patients as if they were cattle that needed to be herded back into a corral.

"Hey, it's too early. We don't have to go back to our rooms," a Cherokee with a limp right arm argued while Jake tugged him along. He resisted, but only momentarily. Jake's burning glare drilled fear into him.

"Shut up," Jake scowled.

Tesqua and Mana both knew this was no time to provoke the orderlies. Something had raised an alarm in the staff. Something was about to explode. It became imperative they learn what. Information gleaned is information useful to their own cause.

Tesqua and Mana entered the hall with Nathan close behind. Mana noticed as he left the day room that Grano had lingered behind. An orderly half his size now funneled the seemingly complacent Indian out.

As Tesqua and Mana approached their rooms, a fight among patients broke out in the hall. Nathan rammed an elbow into Tesqua's back, fearing he might enter the fray, then slammed his door shut.

Mana entered his room voluntarily, closing the door himself. From his window, he watched Grano slip around the fight in the hall that now entangled three orderlies with six patients. While the orderlies struggled to separate the patients, Grano withdrew keys, one of which he jabbed into the reception-room-door lock. For a brief moment, no one noticed Grano's actions. He actually thought he might get his shot at freedom.

Then an orderly spied Grano's intent. He lunged for the giant Indian. But Grano threw the poor man half his size into the pile on the floor, pinning Nathan and Jake beneath him.

Grano fumbled with the key in the lock, heard it clank when it released, then he pulled the door wide open. *One more door to freedom.* Grano, however, advanced only as far as the inner reception-room door.

Nathan abandoned the fight in the hall to jump Grano before he could set one foot into freedom. Jake followed suit a second later.

Nathan whacked Grano clean on the jaw with everything he had, causing the giant hulk to topple backward into the asylum hall. Grano's head met the floor with a horrible thud. He landed unconscious. For a long moment all stood still, staring at Grano's massive girth motionless before them. Then Jake closed and locked the reception-room door.

Wallace intervened a few moments later, grabbing the keys still clutched in Grano's limp hand. He tossed them to an orderly.

"Lose them again, you're fired," Wallace snarled.

As Tesqua and Mana watched through the windows in their doors, Grano's arms drooped lifeless while three orderlies lugged him from the floor onto a gurney so he could be rolled away.

Tesqua stared out his door window until the hall went dark. He remained in that same position until the next day's sunlight spread across the floor where Grano had lain. *How could he ever hope to escape this place?*

The whispers sweeping the day room that day debated Grano's fate. Was he dead or alive? Mana watched at the window facing the giant oak for diggers. When none materialized by the time they left for dinner, he concluded somehow Grano had survived the fall. Soon the huge Indian would return to the day room. Mana shouldn't have cared what happened to Grano after the way the hulk beat him in the past, but he did. For all his shortcomings, he was still one of them. They would have lost another to this terrible place.

Tesqua, on the other hand, believed the fall had killed Grano. He insisted by the next afternoon there would be diggers preparing a larger than normal grave.

At day's end Nathan was there to shove Tesqua into his room when the time for lock down came. This time Tesqua resisted.

"You could be the next one dead," Nathan said barely above a whisper.

Tesqua stood just inside his room while Nathan slammed the door and locked it. Tesqua watched as Nathan went by on his way back to the nurses' station. After a few moments, the feet went up on the corner of the desk. Grano had been a fool attempting escape during daylight hours. Certainly, when the huge Indian realized the staff learned of the missing keys, Grano had no choice but to make the best of a feeble opportunity to dash for freedom. For Tesqua, another lesson learned. He stored it away in his bank of knowledge about this place. Like pieces of an intricate puzzle, someday he would assemble all he knew in a way that led him to freedom.

He knew he must be prepared for his opportunity when it finally came. As a result, he conditioned himself to exist on only a few hours sleep each night. Their drugs seemed to keep him awake, and he knew when he finally escaped this place, he would be on the move for days without sleep or food. He must do everything necessary to remain ready.

An hour later, Thompson passed on her way to the desk. She arrived to find Nathan working on the paperwork.

"I'm going to do the drug inventory," she said, taking up a clipboard and leaving Nathan to his work.

But moments after Thompson disappeared down the stairs, Nathan passed Tesqua's room, unaware of Tesqua watching him.

37

The door to Evey's room slid open without so much as a squeak. Nathan held his breath as he slipped inside. His heart raced. It was his turn now. He waited a long moment, allowing his eyes to acclimate to the darkness. Nothing moved. That was good. He unbuttoned his trousers, began preparing himself, though little was needed. Excitement swarmed his brain. In a few seconds, he was out and ready. He needed first to be certain his intrusion had gone undetected. No movement came from the bed. After counting to twenty in his head, Nathan crept to where Evey slept. He clamped a sweated hand tight over her mouth, pressing her head hard into her pillow. He wanted her to know he meant business. He wanted her terrified.

Evey jolted awake, desperate to scream.

"One sound, your injun dies."

Evey's terrified eyes stared up into Nathan's. His clamp over her mouth was so hard it forced her to pull her jaw down in order to clear her nose, which then allowed her to inhale.

With his free hand, Nathan crumpled her gown up to her waist. Staring maniacally into her eyes the entire time, he rubbed between her legs roughly, probing with his fingers to open her up. After a few seconds, he forced her legs apart with his driving thighs. He wanted it to hurt. His surge allowed him to thrust his way deep into her.

The agony of his vicious ramming tore into Evey's soul. She lay alone and helpless. No one would come to her aid. She could do nothing to stop Nathan.

She felt his hot breath spray her cheek as he settled his full weight onto her, endured excruciating pain each time he rammed harder into her. She thought only of Mana at that moment; she would endure anything to keep him safe from this animal. Evey knew in her heart that Nathan would surely do as he warned if she refused. Her silent suffering would spare Mana from Nathan's brutality. But nothing could spare her.

His vile act ended in less than a minute, though it felt like an eternity. Spent, he lay motionless atop her.

To Evey, those moments of torture were unending. The memory of her suffering would remain inside her the rest of her life. She cried silently, pounding Nathan's back as if she were stabbing him with scissors.

Nathan jerked off her, and he was out the door as stealthily as he had breached.

Evey cursed him, weeping out of control into her pillow.

****

In the basement one floor below, another vile act began. This one all for the advancement of science. Or so the doctor believed. Wallace leaned over Grano strapped unconscious to a bed.

"Can't have patients escaping. Looks bad to the Washington bureaucrats. I could lose my job. Though, I don't think you'd care," Wallace muttered to himself.

The doctor lifted an eyelid to check Grano's still unresponsive pupil then left the bed to adjust the dials on his instruments lined up on the long table. After making a series of notations on a sheet of paper where he recorded his thoughts, he returned to Grano to stuff a cloth into his mouth. Regardless of whether a patient was conscious or not, he followed his established protocol. He never could be certain exactly what might happen when he closed the switch.

In the drug room, an exhausted Thompson paused while filling out the drug inventory. Her eyes had gone blurry after such a long day. She was so fatigued she kept making mistakes. After her third erasure, she thought it might be best if she just gave up for the night. She could return fresh in the morning to complete her task. But she had inventoried two-thirds of the drug cabinet. She told herself she could tough it out to finish so it would be on Wallace's desk in the morning. He demanded timely, accurate reports from her, despite the fact that he, for the most part, never gave more than a passing thought to proper patient record keeping.

Without warning, the small room plunged into complete darkness. She screamed out of instinct, though she was in no danger. Fumbling about, she crashed into the prep table while groping for the door. A jolting pain ripped up her spine, bringing a grimace to her face. She caught herself on the verge of cursing. Even by herself, in complete darkness, she knew better than to spew obscenities. After all, even in pitch black, God could still see her.

The light returned the same moment her hand found the door handle. Weak for the first second, it then flooded the room full bright as if nothing had happened. She stood there massaging her throbbing hip. Should she return to the drug cabinet or just return upstairs to her station? This night had become nothing but trouble. She realized, however, that she abandoned the drug cabinet unlocked, a critical infraction of Wallace's rules, so she had to return to lock it anyway. That being the case, she would remain, finish the inventory then return to her station. However, this time she propped the door open just in case the blasted lights went out again.

Within ten minutes, she completed her inventory, locked the drug locker and after locking the door to the drug room, climbed the stairs in pain to the main floor.

She just knew her hip would be bruised for days. Maybe she would have Dr. Barry look at it. The thought of him touching her there sent shivers of excitement along her back. Then good sense set in. She could only hope the injury did not worsen, forcing her to miss work. As it was, she could barely afford even one-day's loss of pay. Her absence would certainly mean there would be hell to pay with Wallace for leaving them short staffed. It seemed like they were habitually understaffed for one reason or another.

Her mind cast her pain aside when she returned to the desk to find Nathan still working on the charts. His sweat-dappled brow, coupled with his accelerated breathing caught her concern.

"They're not done yet?"

"Maury again. I had to take him to the latrine. He wets the bed if we don't let him go."

Their conversation stopped when the lights again dimmed, buzzing in a pattern easily mistaken for Morse code.

"I wish someone would bloody fix the damn electricity here," Thompson called out to the empty hall. As if in response to her complaint, the lights returned to normal brightness.

Nathan nodded his agreement, wiping the sweat on his brow.

"You all right? You look faded," Thompson asked.

"Haven't felt well all day," Nathan replied, his voice matching his pallor.

Thompson set the back of her hand against his forehead. He liked the feel of her warm soft skin against his. He fantasized in that brief moment how she would feel beneath him as he thrust into her. That triggered his encounter with Evey to play across his mind. Would Thompson's privates feel just as fantastic? If only he could find a way to force her to perform. He'd need something very serious to hang over her head before she would succumb to such a demand.

"No fever. Oh, shoot. I almost forgot. Before you go, we need a room cleaned. New arrival on the morrow. I'll finish up the charts."

Thompson braced herself, fully expecting an argument. Nathan regularly unleashed his grumpy side as the end of his shift drew near. She prepared to order him if need be.

"Get right to it," Nathan said, wandering off while whistling to himself.

He *must* not be feeling well, Thompson thought as she slid into the chair to take up the next chart to complete.

38

Thompson lurched out of her chair to a continuous buzzer from the reception room. Her first few strides were stiff and awkward, thanks to her bruised hip. It was just after noon; her day had started badly and progressively worsened. After being belittled by Wallace in front of both Jake and Nathan, a patient accidentally struck her injured hip when his balance faltered while exiting the day room. All that on top of having to endure a pain that felt like someone kept jabbing an ice pick in her with each stride she took. The plum-colored discoloration covered most of her hip, extending half way down her thigh. Even an hour in a hot bath the night before had failed to bring relief. Now she half-dashed/half-hobbled to the reception room to bite off whoever's head was attached to the hand on her buzzer.

"What is your bloody prob ..."

As Thompson blurted out her scolding, a barrel-shaped driver slammed a nine-year-old Indian boy into the wall with such force that Thompson thought for sure he had snapped the young lad's back. He was far too small to fill the straitjacket they had secured him into, using additional restraint straps to keep the jacket in place.

Shock seized Thompson's face.

"Leave him be!" she ordered with as much angry force as she could muster under the circumstances.

"Damn little savage bit me. Needs a muzzle with that jacket," the driver offered in his own defense. He clamped his tongue tight in cheek as he held the lad pinned against the wall.

The lad's doe-like eyes opened wide with terror. He struggled but couldn't for all his effort wiggle free of the arm forcing the air from his chest.

Thompson quickly scanned the paperwork to ensure everything was in order. *How could this one be meant to be here?* The signatures were proper and the paperwork contained all the appropriate information.

"I'll have him from here. You okay, Sam, is it? Let's get you to where you're more comfortable."

Thompson scribbled a signature, returning the top sheet to the driver. With the driver still standing there, she hustled Sam in through the reception door, which she then slammed on the driver. The exchange had made her so angry. She would have slapped the bastard had he dared harm Sam further. In the end, she dismissed him, swallowing her fury.

With Sam inside and the reception door locked, Thompson lowered to her knee, which caused her to wince from the ice pick pain again. She immediately released the restraint straps holding the straitjacket in place. The jacket drooped, which allowed Sam to stretch his arms a little.

"There. That must feel better," she said. She smoothed his jostled shoulder-length black hair in the hopes she might erase the terror consuming his impish face. Sam bit his lip on the verge of tears. She could feel his slender body trembling. But he said nothing.

Thompson returned to her feet. She wanted so much to hug the boy, to somehow let him know he would be all right here. However, before she could do anything, Wallace snared her elbow smartly with an angry glare in his eyes.

"For Christ's sake, he's a nine-year-old boy. He doesn't need restraints."

Wallace refused to release her arm.

"When you get your doctorate, you can make that decision. Until such time, you obey my orders. Is that understood?"

Rattled, Thompson snapped her arm free, then she led Sam past the crowd at the day room window. A terrified Sam clung to Thompson for comfort as much as he could in his straitjacket while she escorted him into the room readied for his arrival. Not only would Sam be kept in his straitjacket, but he would also be isolated from the other patients for his first three days in the asylum. Rules were rules, and policy was policy, and Wallace saw no reason to stray even if the patient were a child.

****

Tesqua sat beside Mana and Evey at dinner. Sam's arrival became the talk amongst them, though the women had not seen the boy. Mana wondered how long the little one would be kept isolated from the population before being integrated. Evey seemed unusually quiet this day. They occupied the space without really talking. Something had changed, and Tesqua sat trying to figure out what. Evey usually initiated conversation, prompting Mana to talk during meals. It seemed unnatural to have such long periods of silence.

Tesqua bounced between watching Evey's eyes and her hands. They, too, were silent all of a sudden. He noticed, however, that Evey's eyes tracked Nathan's every move in the mess hall.

Mana all at once slammed down his spoon, collecting stares from those sitting nearby.

"Someone should teach these white people how to prepare meat."

"Yeah," Tesqua responded absently while unobtrusively watching Evey. Her jaw remained tense.

"Are you listening?" Mana snapped, trying to force eye contact with Tesqua, who seemingly stared off into space.

"Yeah. You hate the food here. So what?"

Then Evey placed her thumb inside her fist on her right hand.

Mana stopped. He nodded, slid his right-hand palm-flat on the table. Evey paused. Tesqua could see anger mounting on Mana's face. Evey extended two fingers while curling the other two into her right palm. Her eyes went to Nathan.

Mana tightened on his spoon. His jaw clinched. Tesqua could see anger seething in his friend's eyes.

Evey kept repeating the same four hand signals until finally Mana covered her hand with his. His gesture brought relief to Evey.

When Nathan approached their table, Evey tightened every muscle in her body; she shut her eyes tight. Tesqua noticed she curled both hands into fists, which she forced into her lap.

"I hate the food here," Mana persisted.

"I hate everything here ..." Tesqua added, hoping his agreement would appease Mana. Tesqua spoke, but the entire time he monitored Evey.

Nathan stopped at their table.

"If you're done eating, get your medication and return to your day rooms," he said.

Nathan never concerned himself in the past with Mana's outbreaks. Yet he chose this time to approach their table. When he slid closer, he forced himself between Mana and Evey, where he deliberately touched her shoulder to demonstrate his power over her.

Evey flinched. She stared straight-ahead, avoiding eye contact with the orderly.

An angry Mana bolted up, forcing himself into Nathan while dumping his tray all over the orderly's chest.

"Sorry," Mana said. There was fire in his eyes. His hands had balled into fists.

His ploy, however, forced Nathan to retreat, thereby releasing his hand from Evey's shoulder. Nathan responded by shoving Mana into Tesqua, who remained seated at the table. The clanking metal trays turned all heads toward them.

Nathan grabbed Mana's shirt collar, using it to force him back into his chair.

Across the room, Jake lifted his head from assisting another patient. He started toward them, but Nathan motioned him away. He wanted this moment all for himself.

Mana for the first time resisted. Their eyes locked.

"You think your crazy whore is worth a few days in the restraint chair?" Nathan whispered into Mana's ear. He kept his voice just loud enough so Evey and Tesqua would also hear.

Mana succumbed, returning to his chair.

Nathan smiled wickedly as he released Mana's shirt collar. Then he strolled away without looking back.

"You okay?" Mana asked.

Evey fought down her tears, working as hard as she could to hide a pang that ripped apart her insides, setting fire to her soul. At the moment, she wanted so much to scream as loud as she could and rip into Nathan's face with her fingernails. If she had a knife at this moment, she would surely gut him until he lay dead at her feet. *Could the punishment for that crime be any worse than the punishment they had already dealt her?*

All she could do instead was nod in the affirmative. She left the table as quickly as she could without Mana detecting how Nathan had destroyed her.

"Dinner's over. Back to your day rooms," Nathan said as he stood in the midst of patients all rising to leave at the same time.

Mana accompanied Evey to the nurse handling the medications tray stationed at the door. Tesqua, all the while, scrutinized every nuance of Evey's behavior. There was no mistaking her sudden, unexplainable change. And her change somehow connected with Nathan. Tesqua was convinced of that. He also had his own suspicions of why Evey had suddenly become terrified of the orderly. He had witnessed similar behavior years earlier as a twelve-year-old.

39

Mana returned alongside Tesqua to the men's day room. He felt cheated that his time with Evey had seemed so lifeless. He wished he had been more attentive now, had tried to make her laugh or attempted to engage her with conversation. He had foolishly allowed such a precious moment in his terrible wretched life to expire unfulfilled. Maybe tomorrow would be better.

Mana drifted off into his own space, pleased that Tesqua had allowed him to exist in solitude for a while. Mana stared vacantly at the digger cutting into the earth at the base of the giant oak.

He scanned to find Tesqua across the room, huddled by himself in a corner, where he stared intensely out the day-room window at the nurses' station.

Mana mouthed 'Grano' while indicating the digger outside, which brought Tesqua over to him.

"Tell me what she signaled you," Tesqua insisted.

At first Mana refused. Their hand signals were a secret only they shared. Anger seethed within him.

"Tell me," Tesqua persisted.

"At first we simply created a signal to let each other know all is well. We exchanged signals each time she passed in the hall. Later, we added gestures to allow us to communicate in the presence of the orderlies. Evey kept repeating 'all is not well' and Nathan. Then she indicated I was in danger. Finally, she signaled Grano. Nathan did something to her. For that, I will kill him," Mana said and wandered away when Nathan and Jake entered.

Another day ended. Another day Tesqua faced separated from his family. Another meaningless day imprisoned in this white man's hellhole. A day he would never get back.

Nathan wandered about the room, glancing frequently at Mana while Jake leaned against the wall in a position near the door. As the clock struck nine, Nathan began herding patients from the day room for the night.

Tesqua wandered about in the clusters of patients, lingering to make himself the last man out. When his eyes met Nathan's, he quickly averted his. Tesqua left the day room with a smug Nathan one step behind him.

In the hall, Tesqua slowed abruptly, just enough to force Nathan into his back. Nathan nudged Tesqua forward. When they reached Tesqua's room, Tesqua glanced side to side, confirmed just Nathan followed, then as Tesqua stopped at his threshold, he drew another nudge from the orderly. But this time he sidestepped to trip Nathan, causing the orderly to spill into his room and out of the sight of the other orderlies.

"Hey, asshole," Nathan said.

Before Nathan could regain his balance, Tesqua grabbed a fistful of Nathan's hair, which he used to slam Nathan's face into the floor with all his might.

"You ever touch our women, I *will* kill you."

Flailing his arms, Nathan battled back to his feet. When he came up, Tesqua whacked him squarely in the jaw, knocking him back into the wall. Nathan's scream for help brought Jake to the doorway. But before Jake could force his way in, Tesqua kicked the door shut into Jake's face. He then held it closed with one hand to keep Jake at bay, while swinging at Nathan with the other.

Unfortunately, Tesqua couldn't both hold the door closed and keep Nathan at arm's length for long. Nathan charged, swinging fists with a fury. But Tesqua still slammed in two solid blows to Nathan's face before Nathan knocked Tesqua away, which allowed Jake to crash in and enter the fray.

Together the orderlies wrestled Tesqua to the bed, where Tesqua finally surrendered; the multiple blows to his face took all the fight from him. His wind stripped away by Nathan's last blow into his gut, Tesqua gasped, desperate to refill vacuous lungs.

Thompson rushed in to find both orderlies bleeding from their noses. The bloody mess appeared much worse than it actually was. All three were covered in dark blood—none of it Tesqua's. That gave Tesqua a small triumph over his torturers.

"Restraints! Get Wallace," Nathan barked like a vicious dog looking to attack anyone who ventured into reach.

Thompson handed over leather restraint straps.

Within a minute, Nathan had Tesqua strapped to his bed.

At that moment, Nathan wanted so bad to batter Tesqua's face. He had him helpless on the mattress, but he knew better than that. There were other ways to even the score.

"I got it now. You can go," Nathan said.

"You sure?" Jake asked, visibly shaken.

Nathan gave Jake a dumb look in response. The restraint straps were so tight around Tesqua's body that he'd never move a muscle. Just the way Nathan wanted the smartass injun.

Thompson offered gauze to Nathan to staunch his nose, then she assisted Jake back to the nurses' station. Jake had tilted his head back to slow his bleeding.

Nathan, however, lingered in the room. He had more to accomplish. His face turned from anger to euphoria as he moved in close to Tesqua's face.

"Know what the difference is between nigras and injuns, Testicles? That is what they call you, isn't it?" he whispered.

He allowed Tesqua a moment to contemplate the question.

"Government don't let us kill nigras."

After he spoke, he drew a line slowly across Tesqua's throat with his index finger. Then he laughed just loud enough for Tesqua's benefit.

"Don't fall asleep, injun."

Nathan retreated a step.

"She was worth it," the orderly then said. "And so were the others."

Then Nathan left.

Tesqua's eyes burned at Nathan on his departure.

For hours Tesqua lay awake in his bed. He listened carefully for sounds in the night. He could discern when Mana left his bed. He detected Thompson's soft footsteps as she departed for the night. Nathan passed in the hall twice. Tesqua had learned to recognize his nemesis' determined footfalls.

When exhaustion overwhelmed him, Tesqua fell fast asleep.

Sometime later his door opened without a sound. Shadows created by the moonlight bleeding in crawled across his face. Then a sheet came down over his head, awakening him. Fists pounded his face and chest in rapid fire. The cloth did a poor job of muffling Tesqua's screams. But that was what his attackers wanted.

Then the pounding stopped.

Tesqua's night screams went silent. The door closed. The pungent smell of stale nicotine remained behind, identifying his attacker.

With the morning, a battered Tesqua sat motionless in the restraint chair, facing the doorway. Nathan had secured the straps extra tight, causing Tesqua's feet to lose all sensation. It felt like a thousand pins were jabbing into each of his feet. He worked his digits as much as possible to keep some blood circulating. The pain from the chest strap constricting his breathing felt like fire. The strap forced him to take short rapid breaths.

But for all his suffering he felt at peace. For what he had done was right. And he knew it. Nathan may feel he had won in their exchange, but from now on, he will know that Tesqua would be on the attack if he continued his sick abuses of Indian women. Tesqua recognized the look in a woman's face when she had been violated. He had seen it in his cousin when they were young. The pain he witnessed in Mesachawa's eyes when he learned of what had happened to her stayed with him. He also knew he would carry Mesachawa's image with him forever.

Barry's entry stole Tesqua from his private thoughts. Tesqua realized now the absolute cleverness of Nathan's ploy. After their exchange, they had slipped into his room to beat him viciously about the face. Barry would only conclude the bruising came from their exchange earlier that same evening. The doctor would never suspect that Nathan had doled out his own midnight justice. The night screams he heard so frequently in this place held new understanding. He could only wonder what other violence the orderlies leveled upon the patients.

But in that moment Tesqua decided it would be his mission here to see Nathan punished for his crimes. Some way, somehow he would punish him.

"I thought we agreed you were going to control your anger. I went out on a limb for you. After all I've done to help you ... Tesqua, I am disappointed," Barry said.

Tesqua offered a vacuous stare through eyes half shut from the bruising, but he said nothing. There were no words an Indian could give a white man capable of changing the way they thought of him. Tesqua knew that for certain now. His only allies in this place were his kind. Even Thompson would turn against him if she were placed in such a situation.

Barry settled onto the bed.

"I want to help you. I sincerely do. But I feel betrayed. How do we fix that?"

Tesqua remained silent. Barry rose. Tesqua followed Barry with the one eye that had not swollen shut. Dare he trust this one? He wanted to. He needed someone here in which to place his faith. Everything about Barry conveyed a bond Tesqua had not known previously with a white man. Yet if he erred at this moment, if he trusted him, would it cost him? He wondered what worse they could do to him than lock him away from his wife and child with no explanation as to why and no indication of when he might be set free. They would never care to understand how he felt, nor why he did the things he did.

Despite wrenching pain along his jaw, Tesqua parted battered lips, ready to speak, but his effort came too late. Barry had left the room. Maybe it was for the best. Maybe Barry should remain an outsider.

Tesqua stared at the wall, allowing his mind's eye to picture Celia smiling back, proudly holding their son. Tesqua knew in his heart that they would both be proud of him for what he had done. They would understand why he did it.

Hours later, Tesqua had no idea how many, since a thick blanket of listless gray clouds obscured the arcing sun, Nathan entered. He eased the door closed, lingering just inside long enough to be certain Tesqua was awake. He wanted the Indian to see him. He wanted Tesqua to know who was in the room.

Nathan's face remained empty, emotionless. Maybe he had come to loosen the straps? Tesqua's feet had lost all feeling. The orderly casually circled, hands in his pockets. He stopped behind Tesqua.

Tesqua squirmed the little he could, trying to glimpse Nathan's actions. None of his straps had been loosened, so he had not come to release him.

Nathan's hand came without warning to clamp Tesqua's mouth shut. Then he pinched off Tesqua's nose. The pain of his grip against his already tender jaw ripped through Tesqua's brain like lightning bolts. The stench of a hand tainted by the latrine piss bucket crawled up his nose.

For the first moment, Tesqua remained calm. Then as his oxygen became spent, he felt the explosive pressure build inside his chest. Panic surged in. He tried to inhale. The clamps sealing his mouth and nose prevented air from getting in. He must breathe. His chest caught fire; his brain swam, screaming for oxygen. He rocked his head violently, desperate to break the hand free just enough to suck in even a slight breath of air.

But the head restraint strap, along with Nathan's hands, kept him from shaking the clamp free. Tesqua's eyelids fluttered. His eyes rolled back into his head as he teetered on the brink of unconsciousness.

Finally, Nathan released him.

With a great sucking hiss, air gushed into Tesqua's lungs. He coughed out the stinking stale air.

Nathan circled into Tesqua's limited field of view. The orderly's face held a maniacal smile beneath wide glaring eyes. He brought his lips to Tesqua's ear.

"It's that easy, Testicles," Nathan whispered.

In that moment, Tesqua understood from Nathan's eyes that he could and would kill. For all he knew, Nathan may have already killed other patients trapped here. And deep in Tesqua's heart, he knew it would ultimately come to that between them.

A shadow crossed as Nathan departed. In time, the room fell into darkness. Tesqua fell asleep in the chair out of sheer exhaustion.

41

Tesqua awoke to a burning throat. Buckled straps laced his torso from his shoulders to his thighs. However, now he was prone. The last he remembered he had been upright in the restraint chair with his head strapped to the backrest.

Tesqua tested the restraints securing both wrists to the sides of the bed. They held fast. When he rotated his head sideways, he could see Wallace hunched over a long table with many instruments on it.

"What are you going to do?" Tesqua asked.

"Help you. Don't be afraid," Wallace replied.

"I do not fear you."

"I sensed that the day you arrived."

Wallace came to him at the bed. Using petroleum jelly as a base, the doctor affixed two quarter-size metal saucers onto Tesqua's temples. The cold from the metal crawled along his skin. They remained in place while Wallace returned to his table.

"Fear is a much under-appreciated emotion, don't you agree? But fear is important. It keeps anger in check. It is our fear that keeps us from making foolish mistakes. You Apaches,

176

however, are known to be fearless. It follows then that fearless men are incapable of restraining their rage."

"Do not do this."

"Tesqua. That's what they call you, isn't it?"

Wallace connected wires to the discs on Tesqua's temples. He checked each one to make certain both were secure.

"You'll require a larger dose."

While ruminating over his dosage, Wallace returned to his table, where he stared for a long moment at the array of instruments. He could increase the voltage but leave the current adjustment where he had initially set it. He understood that the current he released into the body was more dangerous than the voltage. Then he adjusted the current dial a little higher before turning back to face Tesqua. He would have to think further, though, about the duration. The duration was the trickiest of the three variables. Too long and injury resulted. Too short and he risked seeing no measurable results.

"And you call us savages," Tesqua uttered.

He gravely feared what was about to happen. In his heart, he believed Wallace intended to kill him while he lay there on the bed. Tesqua sought something to fix his eyes on as a way to hide his fear.

"I never called you that."

Wallace's gaze turned distant, as if the doctor had drifted off deep within his own thoughts. He absently completed his preparation by stuffing a waded-up cloth into Tesqua's mouth.

"Otherwise you might bite your tongue off. Difficult to explain away something like that."

Wallace reconfirmed his settings before leaning in close to Tesqua.

"I just want to help you, savage."

Tesqua stared in horror as Wallace, back at his table, set his hand on a knife-switch the size of his palm. Tesqua balled his fists, tugging at the leather bindings.

Wallace hesitated, but just for a moment, as if to recalculate every detail in his mind. Satisfied, Wallace closed the knife-switch.

Tesqua arced off the bed as fire raged through his entire body. Every muscle turned rock hard against his will until he thought his heart would explode. He tried to scream from the horrific pain, but he could only rip into the cloth stuffed in his mouth. His teeth tore at the material as if he were ripping flesh from bone. Desperate to escape the agony, his mind shut down for the remainder of the time the electric current coursed through his body.

The lights buzzed like the clamor of a thousand bees, dimmed until almost no illumination remained, then flickered for what seemed an eternity.

Snap!

Tesqua's left radius bone cracked in two. His arm bent up queerly in two places.

The lights returned full bright.

Tesqua at last breathed deeply to refill empty lungs. His head felt like someone had battered it with a hammer. He turned for a look at Wallace, but before he could focus, his eyes rolled back into his head and he collapsed into unconsciousness.

Wallace returned, placing his stethoscope to Tesqua's chest.

****

Mana stood before the window facing the giant oak. His eyes remained closed while he soaked in the warm rays plying over his body. His hand pounded the sill as outside a digger tossed dirt. For a moment, he smiled. They were not digging for him. A moment later, his smile turned to dread. Tesqua was absent from the day room this day.

Patients roamed about, most oblivious to Mana or the others in the room. Paraquo rolled by. He also took notice of Tesqua's absence. When Nathan entered, Mana abandoned the window to approach him.

"Where is Tesqua ... Jimmy today?"

"Find someplace to stand. I don't have time for you right now," Nathan snapped without making eye contact.

Mana began pacing with the voracity of a caged animal. On each pass at the window, he paused to stare out at the digger. With a grim face, Mana continued pacing, muttering incessantly. *Had he lost his only friend in this place?* Had Wallace finally succeeded in breaking Tesqua's spirit?

"No. He can't be ... I'm gonna kill ..."

Mana watched more dirt fly. His eyes bounced from the digger at the giant oak to Nathan across the room. Who was to blame for this?

****

On the second floor, a smiling Barry strolled into Wallace's office. He settled into a chair across from him while Wallace wrote on the clipboard. It had been a rare day for the younger doctor. He had very few pleasant days at the asylum, so he decided he must learn to enjoy them when they came.

"You're recording Harold's death as a head injury?" Barry queried.

"He hit the floor hard. After lying unconscious for hours, his heart stopped. I accept partial responsibility. I'm in charge."

"What do the numbers mean?" Barry asked, staring at the clipboard with ruffled sheets full of numbers accompanying the names.

"Locators. The government believes it unnecessary to provide grave markers for Indians. First number is the row starting from the giant oak. The next is left or right of the tree. The last is the number of paces to the burial site. You should know, just in case."

Wallace returned the clipboard to its hook. It had Grano's name at the bottom of the top sheet.

All Barry could focus on at that moment was the number of patients the list represented. A single line entry on a sheet of faded paper providing a burial location was all that remained of them. Was that all they meant to anyone here?

"That it?" Barry started.

"Well, no. Of course, I also write the Indian agent at their reservation. The agent in turn notifies the family. It's not a perfect system, but it at least allows us to keep track of them."

Barry's smile vanished. His mind churned over the fate of the patients in this place. He lost all the exuberance he had brought with him into Wallace's office. He knew in his heart how to measure success in this profession. He had yet to witness that here. Not a single patient committed to Canton had been returned home to their family.

That clipboard served as a barometer of their efficacy—a constant reminder every day of those who came to this place seeking safe haven and help, but who never left. Part of Barry wanted to leave this place. The more dominant part demanded he stay. His work here had yet to be completed.

42

The hall outside was too quiet, dreary when Wallace entered Tesqua's room. The doctor stood for a long moment just inside the doorway, a smug but unseen smile upon his face.

"How are we feeling?"

On his bed, Tesqua turned away with pain and difficulty from the plaster cast on his forearm to face the wall. He was free of restraints and hoped to keep himself out of them, at least for a while.

"Let's have a look. I had a difficult time setting the arm."

"How did I break my arm?"

"You don't remember?" Wallace said dryly.

Tesqua stared at him for a long moment. He searched his brain as deeply as he could yet dug up no answer to that question.

The smile on Wallace's face set Tesqua's nerves on end.

Wallace instead leaned forward to examine Tesqua's temples carefully. Early in his experiments, the metal discs left telltale burn marks where the electricity entered the body. Wallace had discovered that by employing that thin layer of petroleum jelly on the disc before applying it, he improved conductivity, and eliminated the markings left by his treatment. He couldn't be certain, but he surmised that he sacrificed very little, if any, current when using the jelly.

However, with still so much to learn, and his only teacher in Austria, he had to experiment on his own. Brief telegrams crisscrossing the Atlantic detailed each doctor's progress and formed the only bond they shared. But in reality only one would publish their breakthrough findings and receive the accolades for their work. And Wallace wanted it to be him.

"Do you remember anything of the past two days?"

Tesqua thought hard. He remembered being strapped to the restraint chair. Then he awoke to his arm in a cast and every muscle aching as if he had been working the fields without rest for a week.

"Intriguing."

Wallace speculated in that moment that maybe Tesqua could endure a higher current. He made a mental note to recalculate Tesqua's treatment plan for the next time.

The fact that Tesqua's temples displayed no evidence that anything had occurred just two days before pleased Wallace. So did his results, at least the absence of any abnormal physical manifestations of the treatment. Previous attempts had caused temporary speech impediments on some, debilitating twitches on others. He still needed to determine the full psychological benefits of shock treatment before he could make his findings public. But time was of the essence. From Von Forrester's telegrams, Wallace surmised the Austrian's research was leaps ahead of his.

Wallace receded to the door, stopping to turn back to Tesqua.

"It's troubling that you're unable to recall the circumstances which caused your broken arm. Memory blackouts would indicate we still have a ways to go to cure you."

"Cure me of what?" Tesqua lashed out.

"Your heritage."

Tesqua slammed his casted arm against the bed, grimaced from the pain it sent into his brain. As hard as he tried, he could not bring back the memory of how his arm came to be placed in the cast. That terrified him.

Wallace wandered from Tesqua's room, passing Jake pushing the linen cart, which he had parked outside Mana's room.

Jake entered the room with a sheet from a clean stack on the cart. Despite the menial tasks he performed, Jake never once complained. At least not to where anyone could hear.

As Thompson walked down the hall toward the day room, she passed Tommy, a Navajo who had resided at the asylum longer than Thompson had, suffering from a debilitating left-hemisphere tremor that made walking or holding things in his right hand difficult, if not impossible. Since Arizona doctors could find no physical explanation for Tommy's condition, they passed it off as a mental condition; thereby enabling the Indian agent to commit Tommy to the asylum in the hopes doctors there might find some way of treating his malady.

Wallace, however, never even attempted to treat Tommy's condition, so Tommy would never have an opportunity to be cured, nor ever leave this place, which seemed to suit most everyone involved in Tommy's case.

Tommy's affliction also affected his speech, which made committing him to the asylum so much easier, but made it difficult to work with him. As a result, most everyone avoided

Tommy, who learned to live in the silence that accompanied his disease, whatever it might be.

"Where we going, Tommy?" Thompson inquired.

Most left Tommy to himself. Even Thompson had difficulty at times dealing with him. The orderlies mostly just ridiculed him.

"La ... la ... lay," Tommy started. He had to stop when ejecting the single-syllable word from his mouth became impossible. He sucked in a deep breath, preparing for another attempt.

"Do ... do ..." He stopped again, pounded the side of his face as if attempting to jar something back into its proper place inside his brain so it could begin functioning properly again.

"He ... ad ..."

Thompson endured the torturous moments of silence between Tommy's syllables. She had a thousand other things to attend to, but felt she should wait for him to finish, since she posed the question in the first place. At least she could wait until he finally pieced together a meaningful word or two.

"Hurts," Tommy blurted, offering a flicker of a smile for his accomplishment.

Thompson placed the back of her hand to his forehead, concluded in that second Tommy seemed feverish, then she scanned down the hall.

"Very good then. Jake's finished tidying your bed. I need to do something, then I'll come check your temperature. You may have a fever."

Tommy turned to continue down the hall to his room. But he moved unusually slow, even for Tommy. After Thompson walked away, he snatched a sheet from the linen cart, stuffing it under his shirt.

In the day room, Mana stared out at the giant oak dressed in richly colored fall textures. After a two-day absence, Tesqua finally rejoined him. Mana stared at Tesqua's cast.

They had talked so much over the years, it seemed there was nothing left to talk about.

"How'd you break the arm?" Mana asked. He knew even before asking the answer he would receive. It was another mystery of this place.

"I don't know," Tesqua said. The despair in his voice saturated Mana's brain.

For many minutes neither spoke. Mana stared out at the giant oak while Tesqua's eyes roved the room.

"Itza chu," Tesqua said unexpectedly. "Soar free like the eagle. Escape."

He spoke the words more muttering to himself than engaging Mana in conversation. Yet the words sparked something in Mana's brain.

"Complacency is what will allow us to escape. But how?" Mana said.

"Don't know yet."

Tesqua smiled. His eyes brightened; he looked at the giant oak with different eyes.

"Itza chu," Mana replied.

Mana's slight head nod indicated Nathan, watching them from across the room. When they walked away from each other, Nathan's eyes followed Tesqua as he roamed to a corner opposite from Mana.

Neither noticed Sam's departure from the day room when an orderly entered a few moments later. Sam dashed into the hall to find Thompson busy at her desk.

"Whatca doing?" he asked with his beaming innocent smile.

"Working. Hi, Sam. What do you want?" she said while she continued her work.

"Can I go back to bed? I'm tired," he asked, fidgeting with papers as he leaned on the desk, watching her work. "What are these for?"

"Did you collect up all your bits and pieces?"

"Yes, ma'am. Can I have one of these?"

Sam held up a paper clip.

Thompson smiled in the affirmative.

Sam then unfurled his fist to display a few bits of string and a pair of black buttons, to which he added his new acquisition.

"Oh, I bloody forgot about Tommy. Sure. Come on, a nap might help."

Hand in hand, Thompson led Sam down the hall. Having Sam there added a new dimension to her life. For a brief time each day, she had a child to care for. And Sam was a delight to have around. He made her smile and sometimes even laugh. Something she rarely had the opportunity to enjoy in her life.

They reached Tommy's room only to find him absent. So Thompson continued with Sam to take him to his room.

When they reached the staircase, Thompson screamed. Sam stared.

Tommy dangled from the railing of the first floor landing in a noose fashioned from the sheet, attaching the opposing end to the railing. His dangling body swung side to side with the arms out rigid.

Barry rushed up in response to Thompson's scream. Appraising the scene in a glance, he raced to the landing to release the sheet from the railing. He also held Tommy up, but his effort came much too late. Tommy had expired minutes before anyone came upon him.

Wallace, Nathan and Jake rushed up, converging from different directions. Together they lowered Tommy to the floor, laying the body out. Barry checked the carotid then shook his head.

"Despite all our efforts, Tommy has found a way to accomplish what he's wanted to do since arriving," Wallace commented. He walked away, expecting Barry to handle the necessary details to close Tommy's patient file for good.

Jake covered Tommy with the blanket Thompson provided, then he, along with Nathan, lifted him onto a gurney. Wallace now had yet another death certificate to complete ... another name and number to add to his clipboard, and life would continue on in the asylum.

Tesqua, free of his cast, pushed Paraquo over to Mana at the window so he could watch the diggers near the giant oak, which was now devoid of leaves. Soon winter would set in, making them cold and miserable again. The past three months had seen a food shortage, causing Mana to long for the day when he might be able to eat meat prepared they way he liked it—not cooked until they seared all flavor away.

Months had passed without progress toward his plan for freedom. With winter's imminent approach, he would have to hope for opportunity to come to them in the spring.

Everyone in the day room waited for the women to visit. It had been days since they had been allowed to mingle. Mana interpreted that as yet another bad omen.

Tesqua leaned with his back against the glass, watching Nathan move about the room.

"Sixty-four," Mana said.

"Another riddle? Sixty-four what?" Tesqua replied.

Mana merely pointed. Tesqua turned, though he knew what Mana indicated.

"Graves. Sixty-four graves since I arrived."

"One for each of us," Paraquo said. Then shaking his head, he rolled away.

"We would need a way to incapacitate ..." Tesqua began whispering. But he had failed to make certain no one was within earshot of their conversation.

Mana's face alighted. Nathan closed in, only a few paces away.

"Oh no ..." was all Tesqua could get out before Mana smashed him in the face with his fist.

"Charley, now you're a problem?" Nathan said.

Mana, hiding his smile, surrendered to Nathan's full nelson to be dragged away while Tesqua held his bleeding nose, he himself hiding a smile. Nathan must never suspect them of conspiring. And the only way to ensure that was to divert Nathan any time he might have reason to be suspicious. Even though Nathan maintained a closer eye on Mana and Tesqua than the others in the facility, both remained convinced Nathan would never figure out what they planned. At least their freedom depended on it.

****

Tesqua and Mana spent the ensuing weeks avoiding each other in the day room. To the orderlies it appeared their fast friendship had fallen into disrepair with little possibly of being salvaged. Exactly what they wished Nathan to believe. Tesqua and Mana learned to communicate with simple nods or half-smiles or crude hand gestures.

Tesqua waited across the day room until Mana left his window in favor of a chair at the table. Then he wandered over to the window where Sam stared out at snow-covered fields. Though significantly colder near the glass, nothing could deter

Sam from gazing out at a life he would never have. He wore only his asylum shirt with no blanket to keep him warm.

Tesqua removed his blanket to wrap the lad the way a mother swaddles her baby to stave off a winter wind. Sam looked up at him with innocent brown eyes full of hope, and for a brief second, Tesqua felt like he was looking down at this own son.

"What do you see out there?" Tesqua asked.

"Oklahoma."

"Oklahoma's the other way. That's north. That where you're from?"

"I miss my mother."

"And not your father?"

"Father left us. You a father?"

Tesqua scanned before answering. None of the patients knew anything about his personal life. Only the doctors knew his intimate details, and Tesqua thought it best if it remained that way. Yet Sam's pleading eyes and innocent voice disarmed him.

"Yes."

"You miss your children?"

"Every day."

Tears welled in Sam's eyes. Then they overflowed, rolling down his cheeks. He tried so hard to be brave, wiping them away as quickly as they appeared. But there came too many for him to handle. His sobbing became audible. Then he let go, crying uncontrollably with such force that it choked off his breathing.

"I want to go home," he blurted when he could finally suck in a breath.

Though clumsy, since Tesqua had never dealt with a child before, he attempted to soothe Sam with an arm around the lad's shoulder. He brought him closer, but he couldn't bring himself to hug Sam. There would come a time when Tesqua would leave him behind for his own freedom, so maintaining a distance from the lad would make that time easier to handle.

"Warriors don't cry. It'll be all right. We all want to go home. It's just not possible right now."

Sam wiped away his tears, drawing strength from Tesqua's words. He had never even thought of himself as a warrior, but Tesqua saw him as one. Somehow, Tesqua had inadvertently found the right words. He took Sam's small hand into his and together they stared out.

"I think I see Oklahoma, too."

Sam laughed. The young one's moment of simple pleasure sent chills up Tesqua's spine. He would make his son laugh. They would smile together every day when they were at last together again. He would never, ever, leave Celia alone. Not even for one night. He would hold her every night while they slept, and savor the ecstasy of their making love. He so longed to touch her.

As a digger slinging his shovel over his shoulder trudged up the rise to the giant oak, Tesqua quickly eased Sam from the window. That was one bitter reality he wanted to spare Sam from for as long as possible.

"Think you can beat me at checkers?" Tesqua offered. Their moment of despair having passed, Sam returned to the little boy they had all come to care about.

"You bet," Sam chimed.

At that moment, Thompson entered the day room. She scanned, stopping when her eyes met Sam's. Her heart crumbled at the sight of his tear-stained cheeks and the brave little man trying so desperately to cling to someone, anyone, who might give his life some semblance of natural order.

"Sam, time for Dr. Barry."

Sam left Tesqua's hand to cling just as tightly to Thompson's. For that second, Tesqua could read Thompson's mind through her eyes. They shared an agony over the boy's fate. Thompson really was different from the others in this place. She submerged her compassion deep below the surface, only allowing a glimpse to surface on occasion, perhaps so Wallace might never know she actually felt the pain these people suffered in this place. Yet she was as helpless as them. Or was she? Could she be recruited to help them with their daring plan? Could he find a way to take Sam with him when he escaped this place?

Tesqua scanned the day room. Nathan was nowhere about. They had an opportunity for a meeting. After a minute, Mana joined Tesqua. They roamed to a corner away from the other orderlies.

"Someone must guide him to his vision quest," Mana said.

"Why you looking at me?"

"I was his age when my father took me into the mountains."

Tesqua stopped listening. It was not something he wished to participate in. They should speak of more important matters. But Mana would have none of it.

"An eagle appeared to instruct me on the third night. As I watched, it became a wolf. It said to forego my warrior training to seek the ways of the shaman."

"Obviously you didn't listen," Tesqua snapped.

"I tried."

Both sat in silence for a while.

"I had no vision," Tesqua finally confessed.

"Your father never ..."

"I was twelve. My father took me to the same cave his father had taken him. He was so proud of me. After five days of chanting while fasting, I never received a vision. He was a warrior, as was his father. But his son would not be. I disappointed him. I suspect he never forgave me."

Tesqua walked away. He remained away from Mana until darkness descended upon the day room and the orderlies herded them back to their rooms for the night.

A dozen files scattered Barry's desk with an overflow stacked on the side chair when Tesqua entered. The less Wallace worked with the patients, the more of the burden Barry took on himself. Barry quickly snatched up the paperwork to stuff it into his top desk drawer. So much had been swimming around in his mind; he wasn't sure how to interpret most of it. Much of what he encountered in this place proved confusing, contradictory and confounding to him. It defied the very core of what he had spent his lifetime learning.

"How are you feeling today?" Barry asked. The standard opening each time Tesqua entered his office. Tesqua knew by now that Barry could care less how he felt that day or any other day. His questions were foolish, and for all the time they spent in this office with questions, Barry could offer him no good reason why they imprisoned him here.

"Help me understand why you're here," Barry said.

"You help me understand why I am here. What's in that file you keep on me?" Tesqua replied.

"It's more important that you tell me."

"Tell you what?"

Barry shifted to a file from the stack on his desk.

"What's in your file."

Barry flipped through the sheets, browsing over the material.

"It says the only way we can help you is to keep you here until we resolve your anger."

"Lies."

"What are lies, Tesqua?"

"This place. Your file. The white man."

Barry sat back in his chair, under the mistaken impression he had made some progress, however small. Tesqua needed to communicate. He needed to bring to words what he felt deep inside himself. While both sides talked, neither side listened nor understood.

"Then why do you think you were sent here?"

When Tesqua refused to answer, Barry's optimism died. Both sat in silence staring at each other over the desk. It was vitally important for Barry to find a way to get Tesqua to vocalize what churned inside his head. He had to say the words. He had to recognize that the crime he had committed back in New Mexico was wrong, that his uncontrollable rage had placed him here. That was first step to mental health for Tesqua. Until he took that difficult first step, they could never move forward to the second step.

Tesqua searched his soul. He found nothing. Then he rummaged through the far corners of his mind. In there, he remembered clearly emerging from the lights of a barn after a night of drinking. He stumbled unsteadily toward a dirt road. Midnight approached. The sky was black, moonless. He had consumed way too much alcohol that night. But the liquor allowed him to forget, released him from the burden of what he knew. Celia would be angry at him when he arrived home, but the alcohol also deadened the sting of her wrath.

Suddenly, a burlap sack dropped over his head, rope snared his arms while hammering fists doubled him over. Before he could counter their attack, they pummeled him to the ground and lashed him like a steer, only to drag him away over the rocks. *That* is what he remembered of his last moments of freedom. In a drunken stupor his nightmare began—it had yet to end.

Tesqua stared through Barry, coming back to this horrible place.

"I did nothing. I woke up in jail in a straitjacket. Five days later a white man delivered me here."

"I want to believe you. But your present actions support what's in your file, not what you've told me."

"That sounds like Dr. Wallace, not Dr. Barry," Tesqua shot back.

"Help me believe you. Confide in me. Tell me why you think you were sent here."

"Why? You don't see the truth."

"I'm different. Trust me with the truth."

"The truth! I am Apache. White men believe all Indians are savage. That is the only truth you hear."

Tesqua, frustrated and angry for having to repeat the same words year after year, stomped out.

Barry had no response.

Tesqua returned to the day room to Mana circling, pounding his hand on his leg. Then he stopped at a front window to stare at something. Another patient joined him, then five more crowded the window. Paraquo attempted to roll his way in through the crowd, but they kept him from seeing out. Tesqua retreated to the corner opposite everyone else, where he slumped to the floor. He relished the meager solitude of the moment.

A manure truck stopped with grinding brakes before the asylum, just long enough for an old Indian to lower himself out. His grim face full of pride and tradition took in the building as if he were seeing something this large for the first time in his many years. Its very sight intimidated him. He tried in vain to brush the stench from his clothes. With a wave, he signaled the driver, who sped away without exchange.

The old Indian carried nothing more than a cowhide sack over his shoulder and a blanket bedroll across his back. A wide-brimmed black hat shielded his eyes from the glare of the afternoon sun. He stared for a long moment before ascending the steps.

Once inside, the old man stood in the reception room, facing Wallace on the other side of the glass with Thompson beside him.

"He is fine. He's spoken of you. But I'm afraid you've traveled a long way for nothing," Wallace said.

"Our Indian agent said I would be able to see my son," the old Indian offered. He remained stoic, never shifting position nor releasing any hint of what churned inside his head.

"I determine visitor policy, not Indian agents. A visit now is impossible."

"I must see him, if only for a minute."

The old Indian approached the reception window.

Wallace backed away, throwing an arm out instinctively to protect Thompson.

"Listen to me. With pertussis in the area, I must forbid visitors. My prime concern is for the patients under my care. It would be negligent of me at the least, and dangerous to them at the worst, if I were to grant you a visitation at this time."

The old Indian shook the reception room door violently.

"Let me see him!"

"Vacate these premises, or I'll have you arrested," Wallace ordered. He stood firm, despite the old Indian's persistence that he be granted a visitation.

Finally, the old Indian released the handle. Calm swept over him as he returned to face Wallace before the glass. He stared into the doctor's eyes.

"Allow me to see my son," he said in a defeated whisper. His words became a desperate plea from one man to another.

"Only when it is safe can I allow visitors."

"When will that be?" the old Indian asked.

"I cannot answer that. It could be days, weeks. You must go now."

For a time, the old Indian stood as if contemplating his options. While Thompson returned to her duties at the nurses' station, Dr. Wallace remained at the reception-room window to ensure the old man caused no further disturbance.

After another moment with no words exchanged, the old Indian departed, his spirit broken, his dream crushed once again by the white man.

In the day room, patients peeled away from the front glass. The stir in the hall at the reception door caused quite the excitement for a brief moment. Everyone had crowded the window for a glimpse of the action. It had been months since there had been activity that captured the patients' interest.

Thompson returned to her desk, where Dr. Barry sat collecting his thoughts in the form of notes on a clipboard. He seemed so deeply engaged that Thompson's comments at first passed unnoticed.

"There pertussis in the area?"

She waited for a response. Barry at last noticed her, vacated her chair while taking up his clipboard.

"I'm sorry. Did you say something?"

"Any pertussis in the area?" she repeated.

"No. County Health notifies us immediately of any break-outs. I'd be the first to get the word. They know to contact me directly. Why?"

Barry returned to his notes, wandering away before Thompson could say another word. Only a handful of Indians remained to watch them through the day-room window.

45

Barry sat back in his chair in his office, the room aglow from the weak illumination of a small desk lamp. The hour approached eleven. The day had been exhausting. Barry felt himself slipping into a mild depression. Papers scattered his work surface, but he focused his attention not on what needed his attention, but rather on the flickering yellow flames of a campfire in the midst of a vacant field a few hundred yards from the asylum. The waning days of fall were crowding their way in, bringing cold nights, thanks to a mean wind sweeping out of Canada. Yet for the twenty-seventh consecutive night, the campfire glowed in the darkness.

Barry found himself drawing deeper understanding from the scene that had repeated itself nightly. It became a statement of one man's commitment to his family with his unwillingness to be cast aside by an indifferent system that sought to weed out human compassion from its process. Oddly enough, Barry found himself drawing strength from those slivers of glowing fire.

Wallace entered, appearing equally tired and frustrated. It was not until he settled across the desk from Barry that Barry pulled himself away from the blazing night light.

"Been there over three weeks. There's no pertussis outbreak. He's not going away until he sees him," Barry said plainly.

Wallace stared for a beat. Even in the weak light, Barry could see Wallace's jaw clinch while his hand pulsed in and out of a fist. Whether he liked it or not, Wallace would have to deal with the man.

Barry wanted to say more, so much more, but he refrained. He had so many issues to put on the table between them. Yet Barry either never got the opportunity nor ever forced the opportunity. Before he could say another word, Wallace marched out of the room.

"Goddamn Indians. No one understands..." Wallace muttered with each step until passing beyond Barry's range.

A slight smile crossed Barry's face. The lone man struggling to keep warm in the distant campfire had found a way to force Wallace to yield to the stronger. His persistence, his bond, had won out.

Barry smiled to himself as he shuffled the papers into a neat pile, which he then stacked in the corner. He switched off the lamp before leaving his office in the swell of his accomplishment, though he had done nothing of note for that day. *At least someone had*. He strolled out of his darkened office whistling a tune that had been in his head earlier in the day.

****

The following morning the old Indian stood in the visitors' room despite having two chairs close by. Nervous anticipation crossed his face, yet Barry saw something else in the old man's eyes that triggered an alarm in his head. Most times Barry heeded his intuition, but this time his own excitement had taken the better of him. Patient visits, as infrequent as they were, were mostly positive experiences that aided his treatment programs rather than harmed them. There had been a few isolated occasions where family members triggered difficult memories for patients, and as a result, set treatments back, but Barry could uncover no reason warranting his immediate intervention.

The visitors' room door opened. Tesqua entered. He stood just inside for a long moment, staring at his father. The emptiness in Tesqua's eyes further wrenched his father's already aching heart.

"Son!" his father said with an excitement bursting from his throat. His eyes brightened. In that one moment, he knew enduring the countless nights of cold had been worth every ache in his old, tired body.

"Father," Tesqua said flatly.

Tesqua's father hugged him, but Tesqua made no effort to return the affection. Their awkwardly tense, emotionless moment lingered. Tesqua then sat across the table from his father.

"They take good care of you?"

"There is nothing good here. I no longer understand the word care."

Then a glimmer of excitement crept onto Tesqua's face.

"Have I a son or daughter?" he asked. For the first time, Tesqua had found a way to bring a smile to his face, even if it were only slightly discernible.

"I wanted to come sooner. It was a difficult journey for me. They keep you a long way from our reservation."

Tesqua's face fell. He pressed his hands against the table for support. Those were not the words of a man proud of his grandchildren. His father's drowning eyes struck a pain deep in Tesqua's heart.

"Celia, she died giving birth. Your son did not survive. I wanted to come ..."

The words crushed Tesqua. For a few seconds, his heart stopped. He pictured Celia's smiling face inside his head. He remembered her exquisite beauty on the day they married, the excitement in her voice six months later when she told him they were blessed with child. His eyes misted. *Warriors never cry*, he had said. He scolded himself. He must not reveal weakness to his father or to any of them.

Tesqua buried his head in his arms on the table. He fought with everything he had to force the tears and agony from his brain. He promised to love her always. He had kept his promise.

Only one thing had kept him sane in this horrible place. Only one thing meant enough to him to give him hope that someday he would be back with her again. She was the one constant in his life that gave him cause to take his next breath and nurture his will to leave this hellhole where the white man had imprisoned him.

In that few moments, Tesqua regained his strength. He lifted his head, wiped away all signs of his anguish. They would be the only tears he would shed for her. But in his heart, he would wept for her all the rest of his life.

"He looked so much like you. A proud Mescalero."

Even though his father spoke, Tesqua failed to hear.

"I miss her so much," Tesqua said.

"She missed you every day."

Tesqua's rage reignited into a fury that he kept balled up inside for all the years of his imprisonment. When he clinched his fists, every muscle in his body tensed.

"They stole my life!" he exploded.

Tesqua could no longer restrain the monster consuming his insides. He flew from the chair in a tirade. His father remained seated; he had no reason to fear his son. He had expected this might be Tesqua's reaction. He still had so much to say to him.

Nathan rushed in, followed by Barry. When Nathan lunged for Tesqua, Tesqua grabbed the chair to break it over Nathan's shoulder. Nathan, however, charged undeterred. He snagged Tesqua around the waist while Barry worked to secure Tesqua's flailing arms.

"Let me out of here, you bastards!"

Together Barry and Nathan wrestled Tesqua under control then dragged him from the room.

"Please, do not take him away," his father pleaded, helpless to do anything. He just stood there, a father whose eyes remained locked on his son's.

"Itza chu!" Tesqua shouted from the hall.

Then the door to the visitors' room closed, severing their eye contact. Both feared it would be the last time they might ever see each other again.

"He hurt no one," Tesqua's father yelled, banging on the visitors'-room door and yanking the handle in a vain attempt to get into the asylum proper.

Moments later Tesqua's father abandoned his effort. Defeated, he remained there as Tesqua's screams faded into silence. He tried the door once more before abandoning all hope of ever seeing his son again. A lone tear found its way down his weathered cheek as he left the asylum.

Night came. A restrained Tesqua stared out the window as freezing rain rapped the glass the way insistent children tapped for attention. He could see nothing beyond. He closed his eyes to rain pelting his face. Celia at his side, they ran hand-in-hand naked in the desert. She giggled with the excitement of just being beside the man she loved so dearly. They kissed. Not a passionate kiss, but a kiss between two people so assured of each other's love that neither would ever question their fidelity. Tesqua swallowed her up into his arms to lower her onto an open flat in the sand.

"I love you so, Tesqua," she whispered to him.

The harsh morning's light snapped Tesqua away from his love, drawing her away faster and faster, and regardless of how hard he ran and how far he reached, he could not latch onto her fleeting hand. Nothing he could do would bring her back into his arms. He screamed. But the scream remained inside his dream.

He opened his eyes to Thompson beside his bed. She loosened his restraints, then, instead of leaving, she just stared at him. Tesqua felt her hand touch his. He made no effort to grasp hers. She was part of this place.

"Sorry ... about your wife and child. Dr. Barry spoke with your father after they had locked you down."

Then Thompson left the room.

Tesqua felt no desire to move. No desire to go on. If he could be offered a choice at this moment, it would be to die, so he could journey with Celia and their son. He no longer found reason to live in his place. Nor had he reason to ever leave. Let death come, free him of this prison the white man had locked him in.

For days Tesqua remained in his room around the clock. He refused to speak to Mana, Barry or anyone else. In so doing, Nathan became the prime beneficiary of Tesqua's actions. He enjoyed days of peace, absent the threat of Tesqua's violent outbursts.

But Tesqua soon came to realize that his life would go on in this place. That he must find new meaning and a reason to leave his room. He must never allow the white man to crush him the way they had crushed his father and his father's generation. He must become a voice for the new generation of Indians. He must become part of a nation of people who would find life in a land the white man ripped from their hands. The words breathed life back into his soul. He almost convinced himself to leave his room.

47

Tesqua finally returned to the day room to find Mana sitting at the table, staring out the window across the room. Sam played on the floor with a collection of items he had either absconded from other patients or he had been given. A seemingly content child, he could occupy himself for hours with bits of string and buttons. He rarely caused a disturbance and enjoyed making others laugh. Tesqua could only wonder why the white man had imprisoned Sam in this terrible place. What could a young boy possibly do to anger the white man so much that their only recourse is to lock him away?

The women entered, which brought Mana immediately to his feet. He went to Evey and risked touching her hand as they spoke. He had changed so much since that night in the day room five months ago when they joined in marriage. Seeing them together, Tesqua knew what he did was right. He also realized that Barry must care about them to have been willing to go along with such a bold plan.

Evey sat beside Mana at the table. After many minutes of conversation between them, it seemed they had run out of things to chat about. While Mana turned his attention to the window as he frequently did, Evey removed multi-colored squares of burlap cloth from her pocket. She took to stitching them together using yarn threaded through a blunted needle.

For a time, Mana paid no attention to her activity, instead watching as Lizzie droned on before Ko-nay-ha, who had returned to his state and never again spoke to Lizzie like he had done in the mess hall that day. Ko-nay-ha still existed some-where inside that shell. Mana wondered if he would ever come out again.

When Mana still failed to grasp exactly the meaning of Evey's actions, she held up the pieces of cloth that now resem-bled the first stages of a doll body.

"For the boy?" Mana asked matter-of-factly, concluding it to be a plaything for Sam, though it seemed most unlikely that a boy of Sam's age would show interest in such a doll.

"Not that child, our child," Evey said.

Mana released a wild scream, causing a stir that turned every head in the day room toward the table. His smile brought Tesqua over.

"You're?" Tesqua asked, immediately understanding Evey's activity.

Evey nodded. Her smile stirred something deep within Tes-qua. He had played a part in bringing this new life into their world. Mana's face fully brimmed with pride.

"A father. Me!" Mana whispered. He had never dreamed he would ever be saying those words to anyone.

The moment's excitement turned quickly somber. Tesqua's lips went straight across his face. His brow furrowed as he leaned in close to Evey.

"How did you cut these?" he asked. His eyes narrowed, scanning the room to be certain no orderlies were within range of their conversation.

"They allowed you scissors?" Mana queried.

"No. I instructed the nurse as to what I wished. She cut them for me."

"Where did she keep the scissors?" Tesqua pressed.

He and Mana shared a sidelong glance.

"Her desk. But it is kept locked."

Mana hid the excitement overflowing inside. Tesqua, on the other hand, was less adept at concealing his interest.

"Can you..."

Sam pried his way in to steal their attention, forcing them to let the moment pass for now.

"Tesqua, watch me. I can stand on my head."

Sam kicked his feet up, wavered for that first second, then found his equilibrium. He steadied his legs while balancing on his head.

"See."

He then tumbled, rolled into a ball before jumping back to his feet.

"Ta-dah!"

Evey and Mana applauded. Then Evey hugged Sam exactly the way a proud mother hugs her son. Their embrace sent chills through both of them. Evey's for having a child to hold, and Sam's for having a surrogate mother to hold him.

Tesqua tried without success to show excitement for Sam. His mind still churned over the scissors. They were a long way away, but for the first time since he arrived here, something had surfaced that could be useful. If he could find a way to get his hands on those scissors ... Instinct lifted his eyes toward

Nathan, who looked on through the day-room window from the nurses' station. He must have wondered what they were saying. If he only knew ...

"Now watch. I'll walk on my hands," Sam said, pulling up his drooping trousers to prepare for his next fantastic feat.

Sam suddenly began to quiver out of control. He flopped to the floor, writhing like a snake as foam churned out of his gaping frozen mouth.

Pandemonium!

Patients lurched in every direction, screaming in an attempt to flee the evil spirit that had taken over poor little Sam, pummeling him to the floor in the middle of the room. Indians shoved and punched wildly, all surging at once for the day-room door. One terrified Indian, so desperate to escape this menace, threw himself into the closest windowpane. The glass bowed with a thousand cracks, but the wire embedded in it held the shards intact. Blood quickly spread over the dazed Indian's face as he tried to cover the multiple cuts with his hands.

The clamoring crowd made Thompson's task of reaching Sam all the more difficult. Nathan had to crash through the Indians, knocking some down, tossing others against the wall, wedging a path wide enough for Thompson to squeeze through. Time was critical. She had to reach Sam before it was too late.

Snaking through the current opposing her, Thompson finally reached Sam on the floor. She dropped to her knees to cradle him into her arms, working against his flailing arms to press them against his small body. Sam responded with wild kicks, whacking Thompson's arm.

"Move back. Fetch Doctor Wallace. Someone get hold of his legs."

Sam convulsed, emitting a crude choking sound.

Thompson fumbled with a tongue depressor from her pocket. She could get it to his face, but she was unable get it into his mouth.

"Steady the boy's legs, please!" she yelled loud enough to be heard above the screams reverberating in the room. No one would dare approach Sam except ...

Tesqua lowered himself to the floor beside her. He grabbed both Sam's legs in an effort to steady them. Fear cut into his brain. The evil spirit might leave the boy to enter his body. Tesqua's trembling hands clung to Sam's legs.

Sam's face turned the blue of the sky, which further frightened Tesqua. He so much wanted to release his hold on Sam, fearing if he didn't, the evil spirit would take him instead. But Tesqua held tight. If Thompson showed no fear of this evil, neither would he.

"It's a seizure. We'll get him through it," Thompson said, trying to console Tesqua when she felt him drawing away from the boy.

Sam gagged, desperate to breathe. His bulging tongue had folded back into his throat. Thompson finally worked the tongue depressor into Sam's mouth, maneuvering it to pull Sam's tongue from his throat. Sam's small chest heaved, filling with air.

Observing a fleshy hue return to Sam's face allayed some of Tesqua's fears. Thompson had driven out the spirit; she had saved the boy. So Tesqua edged in closer to Thompson until they pressed against each other.

"He's going to be all right," Thompson said.

Tesqua stared at her. He had never witnessed such bizarre behavior before. With her simple wooden stick, she had somehow banished the evil from Sam's body.

As suddenly as Sam's seizure started, it ceased. Sam fell limp in Thompson's arms. She drew him close to her bosom, electing to slide the tongue depressor from Sam's mouth only after his jaw relaxed, eliminating the possibility of him re-swallowing his tongue. His small lungs moved air in and out while his heart thumped inside his small chest as if he had just run a great distance. His face, though smileless, became peaceful as he slept in Thompson's coddling arms.

"He's okay now. Sam's epileptic. Everyone back to the table for now," Thompson ordered.

Only then did Tesqua release the boy's legs. He returned to his feet to stare down at Sam. His eyes then met Thompson's. She had shown no fear.

The others in the room gradually crept from the corners to return to their chairs. But they kept their distance from the boy. None could understood the true cause of Sam's bizarre actions.

Jake, along with another orderly, crammed in to assist Thompson to her feet. She carried a still-sleeping Sam from the day room. Not a soul dared cross their path as they worked their way into the hall.

48

With the night came dreadful quiet. No moaning, no night screams. Only the faint rhythmic squeaking bed wheels rolling somewhere along the main corridor that descended the ramp to the basement.

Wallace maneuvered the bed down the basement hall himself, turning into the last room on the right. Once inside, he flipped on the light switch, closing the door behind them.

For a moment, Wallace worked over the bed, adjusting the overhead light before setting up his equipment at the long table.

"There will be some pain," he said without turning back toward his patient. When he came around to face the bed, he wore a surgical gown.

A terrified Evey tugged the straps imprisoning her.

"Who is the father?" Wallace asked quietly, as if he were her own father pressing for answers without displaying anger.

Evey gave no response. As he expected she would.

Wallace spread her legs against her will. He positioned himself between them with his tools arranged on a small table easily within arm's reach at the foot of the bed.

"Please. Do not do this. Let me keep my baby."

"This is exactly why none of you will ever be released until you're sterilized," Wallace commented while he prepared himself to solve yet another little problem. This had been a difficult year for him. At times he felt he had lost control of his staff.

Evey's eyes welled with tears. She screamed and cringed in pain when Wallace began his cleansing procedure.

One floor up faint screams rose over the still air. Then the lights flickered, dimming on Mana, who stared out the small window in his door.

****

Tesqua and Mana sat at the table in the day room, each staring off in a different direction. Mana seemed nervous, anxious. Tesqua saw that as a bad sign in a place like this. Mana had for so long maintained a level demeanor despite his years in captivity, as Tesqua put it. It had been days since the women visited. Too many days for Mana. They thought they could remove the Indian blood in them by locking them away in this place. They would never remove the spirit that had made them a strong, proud people.

Paraquo rolled by in another of his ritualistic wanderings about the room. As he passed the table, the day-room door opened. Nathan entered. Mana left the table to approach him.

"The women are coming today?" Mana asked.

"Go sit down," Nathan snapped.

Mana pounded the nurses' station window. Thompson reluctantly opened it, but kept her eyes directed at the paperwork on her desk. Or was she just intentionally avoiding eye contact with Mana?

"I want to see Evey. Why aren't the women coming today?"

"Dr. Wallace's orders. Besides, Evey's ill, has to remain in bed."

Distress consumed Mana's face. Seeing it, Tesqua joined him at the window.

"Sick? How can she be sick? She was fine the last time she was here."

"What's wrong?" Tesqua asked.

Thompson could no longer avoid them at the window. They detected in those evasive eyes that she was concealing something from them. Just the way she looked at them tipped Tesqua off. Something significant had changed in the asylum.

"She's just sick. Give her a few days. I'll let you know of her progress."

Thompson's uncertain eyes, matching a similar tone in her words, told Tesqua something had gone very wrong. She appeared apprehensive about even talking to them. Possibly the result of Wallace's intimidation? Tesqua had seen it before, especially with the nurses after one of Wallace's tirades. Now they needed time to determine if the change in attitude toward them was temporary or permanent. Only time would reveal the true nature of the change … something in great abundance here.

Mana isolated himself from the other patients in the day room. He screamed or whooped at anyone who approached him. That included Tesqua. As he had done since Tesqua first laid eyes on him, Mana pounded the windowsill as he watched out the window at the giant oak. He drew no comfort from the fact that no diggers had climbed the rise to dig at the base of the mighty tree.

At the nine o'clock hour, he left his perch at the window to trail the others out of the day room back to his room for the night. A day without Evey was a terrible thing for him to face.

He would have to wait for tomorrow, hope for good news from the nurse. He wanted to see Evey but knew that was impossible. He must be patient, he told himself repeatedly. Evey will recover from her illness. Dr. Wallace will allow the women to return to the men's day room for a visit. Wallace must. Mana must see her again.

In the darkness of his room, Mana stared blankly at the ceiling. Concern gnawed at his stomach. He told himself a hundred times her illness was nothing serious, that she would recover with their child intact in her womb. Thompson would care for her; she would protect her in this place. Nurse Thompson cared about them, understood what they felt. She would do everything necessary for Evey and their child. But suppose she were unaware of the baby in Evey's womb?

Mana came out of his thoughts when his door jiggled. Nathan was making his nightly check. Then he appeared in the small window with a wicked smile across his face. It frightened Mana to even consider what thoughts might have brought such an evil gesture. Mana took that image to sleep with him that night rather than Evey's beloved smile.

With the morning, Mana threaded around the other patients, slithering snake-like to enter the day room first so as to capture his spot at the window facing the giant oak. He pounded the sill incessantly, mumbling to himself on occasion and frightening away anyone who wandered within arm's reach.

When Paraquo rolled by, Mana lunged at him. Paraquo grabbed Mana's arm, pushing it back into him. They exchanged no words, but Paraquo understood the message. He rolled across the room where he would be safe. The scowl on the old man's face had no impact on Mana.

After a few hours of watching Mana from afar, Tesqua wandered over to him. He leaned against the wall, monitoring the orderlies' movement about the room. Nathan, so far, seemed absent this day. Tesqua used sign language to indicate that fact to Mana, who refused to acknowledge his message.

"At the table. Away from Sam," Tesqua finally said.

"No," Mana replied with a bite so sharp it would have drawn blood if it were teeth instead of words.

"Itza chu," Tesqua said.

"No! Stay here."

"We must talk. Nathan might come in at any minute."

Tesqua tugged Mana's sleeve. Mana ripped his arm free to latch onto the sill. He refused to be dislodged.

"No diggers. Evey's okay," Mana muttered.

Tesqua finally gave up and wandered away.

Evening came. So did Nathan. Tesqua and Mana never spoke that day, which gravely disappointed Tesqua for losing such an opportunity.

As the orderlies locked patients away for the night, Tesqua watched from his doorway as Barry and Thompson tightened their coats while exiting through the reception door. They were stepping out into freedom. They would leave this place to pursue their lives. Tesqua listened to the door lock once they were outside. There would be no freedom for him. He closed the door to his room himself and retired to his bed.

****

Once outside Barry wrapped his collar to protect him from the biting wind whipping across the mostly barren plain.

"I hate winter," he said.

"I hate everything," Thompson replied.

"Bad day?"

"The lad had another seizure. Fighting broke out. It took the orderlies an hour to get everyone calmed down. We have to separate the epileptics. The others don't understand. One of them may try to hurt Sam."

"Well, what do you think?" Barry said.

They stopped before a new black Model A motor car.

"Did you not hear a word I said?"

"I mean this."

Thompson eyed the car with pallid enthusiasm.

"Didn't think Wallace paid you enough."

"Doesn't. Saving since I got here."

"You know how to pilot this thing?"

"Drove it here from Sioux Falls. Learned on the way."

"You've got a single hour's time behind the steering wheel. I must be bloody crazy for going along with this."

Having said that, Thompson still entered the car after Barry opened the door for her.

"You won't regret this," Barry said after sliding in behind the wheel. He switched the ignition switch on, pulled out the choke lever, pumped the accelerator twice before stomping hard on the start peddle twice, which caused the engine to sputter then fire. Then he worked the choke in and out to keep the engine running. After about a minute, it settled into a smooth consistent rhythm. They were ready to venture forth into a new chapter in Barry's life: Complete mobility. He pulled the transmission lever toward him until he found first gear, which took three tries, and with a puttering roar, they were off.

Wallace sat with head in hand facing his instruments on the long table, unconsciously working fingers through his sparse hair as he pondered. He scribbled some numbers on a pad of paper, scratched them out, then scribbled some more. His eyes burned from his long, tedious day. He rubbed them before rechecking his dials to make certain he had not erred in setting the instruments up. He appeared more nervous this night than others. Maybe because he would attempt something he knew no one had attempted before. He would delve into a territory no other man had even considered. While his heart thumped with excitement, his uncertainty chipped away at the edges of his confidence.

He scribbled more notes on the nearby paper. Seeing the numbers on the page caused him to recalculate the equation in his head. After a few moments of reconsideration, he turned his attention to his patient on the bed.

"You okay now?" he asked.

He received no answer in return.

****

Striated cigarette smoke thick as morning fog wafted over the heads in the packed L-shaped room. The old milling warehouse a mile outside of Canton proper, which had sat unused for nearly a decade, had now found a way to bring its owner more cash than he knew how to spend. Jitterbug music pulsed through the crowd of young women in Bob-cut hair, wearing tight, fringed dresses and make-up as thick as the cigarette smoke. They danced before a makeshift stage of plywood elevated by barrels strapped together.

Barry—and a nervous Thompson—settled into a corner booth distant from the music. Thompson crinkled her nose from the smoke as she dug through her purse.

"This is just lovely. We're bloody going to jail, you know."

"Relax, we're medical professionals. This is just a necessary prescription."

"Just because you're allowed alcohol for medicinal purposes doesn't give you license to partake in speak-easys."

Barry winked.

"Quoting the letter of the law, are we? Besides, I have a friend," he confided.

"Bloody wonderful for you."

"No. I mean I have a friend, so we don't have to worry."

"I must say, though, it's exactly what I'd expected."

"You've never been to a speak-easy before?"

Thompson crinkled her nose again, shook her head.

"Not my cup of tea," she whispered.

"Any tea with a shot of whiskey is my cup of tea," Barry replied with a laugh.

He scanned the crowd, drinking in the young women done up in outfits that stoked every man's fantasy. Most were laughing; everyone wore smiles. Barry couldn't remember the last time he surrounded himself with so many lighthearted people.

Thompson also perused the other women crowding the dance floor. But hers were envious eyes. Those women were all vibrantly alive, gorgeous in their make-up, taunting smiles meant to steal a man's heart.

She ran her fingers through her faded chestnut hair in the hopes of making it somehow more attractive. She deplored women who painted their faces with make-up. Yet she appeared to be the only woman in the place without it. She never thought of herself as out-of-date, but this place made her realize how much of the world she missed working in that place. She was too fast approaching forty. She could never compete with the likes of the women in her midst. For a moment, she watched Barry's eyes taking in the dancing, drinking and the animation of the people enjoying their lives. Seemed even the government couldn't prevent people from living their lives the way they really wanted.

How could she ever hope to entice Barry with competition so fierce? She was wrong for this place and wrong for him. She just had to admit it and push foolish thoughts from her mind.

"You need to get out more. There is life outside Canton," Barry said loud enough to be heard over the pulsating music.

"What?" Thompson asked, pointing to her ears.

"There is life outside the Canton asylum," he reiterated, this time in a yell to be sure she heard him.

Thompson laughed a nervous laugh as a gentleman server laid their drinks down. She would do this just this once. With God's help, they would not be raided and hauled off to jail. She could just imagine Wallace's reaction should he ever learn of this.

Barry paid, leaving extra bills on the tray. That's how the speak-easy worked. Patrons paid for the drinks and for the privilege of having someone else assume the risk of prison. But for Barry, every nickel doled out was worth it. He needed to get his head out of the asylum. He needed to be around people who were alive.

The music faded as the band shifted to a romantic ballad.

"You're probably right. I do like it. Not sure why, but I do," Thompson admitted.

"Because it's dangerous."

"Yes, actually. You?"

"Dangerous, uh?"

"Why do you like it?" she persisted. She hoped for a glimpse into Barry's mind. He seemed so out of place in Canton. The opposite of Wallace in every way. Yet he chose to remain there despite the reality of that place. Maybe he stayed to be close to her? Maybe not.

Barry leaned back, took in the room's entire breadth with his gaze. Thompson could not avoid noticing how his eyes grazed over the young, vivacious women spilling into every warehouse corner.

"Makes me feel alive. Gets my head out of that place, back into the real world. At least for a time."

Barry laughed, more to himself, then he downed his drink. He immediately motioned for more from the server who waited attentive nearby.

"I know what you mean," Thompson said. She, on the other hand, nursed her drink.

"I'm not part of that world in there. None of patients trust me. Actually, no one there trusts me," he said.

Barry waited for her response. She hesitated, pondering what kind of retort he expected from her. How much could she reveal to him? If she offered too much of her inner feelings, would he resent her?

"I'm not sure it's even possible to help them," she replied.

"You sound like Wallace now."

Though Thompson hid it, Barry's remark jabbed her in the heart. She loathed the idea that he would ever consider her anything similar to Wallace. She cared about the people in that place. Her heart broke each time Wallace allowed the orderlies to strap a patient into his medieval torture chair. Give her a hammer, she would destroy that monster in a minute.

"Do you think we're doing any good?" she asked after a pause.

A small part of her wanted Barry's eyes looking only at her. But the larger part warned against such adolescent foolishness. At her age, her days of crushes and passionate romance were behind her. She had had that once and lost it. They were mature adults who could no longer foolishly fantasize about the passions of youth.

But a fiery tryst with Barry could be so fulfilling.

"You saying we turn our backs on these people?" Barry said.

His comment kicked her off balance for a second. What was he intimating? How did he really feel about those people locked in that place?

"I'm not the only one turning my back, am I?" she had mustered the courage to fire back at him. Then she thought. Was it a mistake? Would their night end right here, right now? The alcohol crept inside her head, tinkering with her sensibilities.

She rose from her seat when Barry did not immediately respond to her remark. But Barry gently took hold of her hand to return her to her chair.

"We're here to escape work. Have another drink. There must be something else we can talk about."

Barry leaned back, smiled boyishly. He loved this place. The music, the people laughing. Everyone was alive. Everyone had feelings and personality. He motioned for more drinks.

"You dance?" Thompson asked slowly, loud enough to rise above the music cranking up.

"No. You?"

Thompson shook her head.

"Never learned."

"I don't have money. My father does," Barry said. He wasn't sure why or how that comment slipped out, but it had, so now he should deal with it.

"You don't need to explain."

"No, I do. He expects me to fail at any career not of his choosing. I've been dismissed from three other hospitals before Canton. There were no other offers out there. None. Seems no one's willing to take a chance on a radical doctor."

"I won't risk me bloody job."

"Is that what it's about? A job? If we do nothing, then we're just as guilty," Barry said.

He searched Thompson's eyes, exactly where she wanted his eyes to be, but now it tightened her stomach the way he looked at her.

"Where is this *we* coming from? I stuck my neck out. I wrote the commissioner. Wallace told me not to care about these patients. I'm sure he's ..."

Thompson caught herself—too much whiskey.

Barry just stared for a moment.

More drinks arrived. Barry downed his.

"Then this doesn't go beyond Canton," he said.

"What doesn't go beyond Canton?"

"You'd be fired if the BIA in Washington were involved."

"Then you believe me?"

"Of course. But a woman's word gets squashed in Washington. I need something concrete before I can ask for help."

"Try seventy-eight patient deaths in the last three years. Our mortality rate's over thirty percent. Other asylums are between five and nine percent. I checked."

"The death certificates?" Barry queried.

"Pneumonia, pertussis or some other malady."

"All perfectly acceptable."

"Yes. But there's no treatment records. They're all fine one day, dead the next. Couldn't find a single treatment record to support cause of death," Thompson said.

"Could establish purpose to Wallace's negligence," Barry replied.

Thompson searched Barry's eyes while he considered her words. She had never revealed this much to anyone her entire time as an asylum employee. Even her letter to the commissioner only implied that circumstances warranted someone in Washington evaluate the statistics.

****

Wallace stood over the bed with a rolled-up cloth. So many factors had to be taken into account. For each new question he posed in his mind, he realized there were to be at least three answers. If he erred in the current dosage, what could be the most likely consequence? What about duration? Does he lower both the dosage and the duration? Or should he employ a mar-

ginal current but increase the duration? How would he measure the success of his test? Surely, this would be a more
difficult case to form a study behind. How many treatments
might he have to perform before seeing any progress? Did he
expect perfect success? Absolutely not. But there might be
ways in the coming months to validate his theory and show
some measure of success.

"Bite down real hard," he said. He checked the pulse, and
based on his new information regarding heart rate, he returned
to his instruments to adjust the dials further. He scribbled more
numbers on a sheet, pondered for a long moment what he had
written, then re-adjusted the current dial once more.

Sweat beaded his forehead. He wondered how his calculations would be effected. He knew little about how to apply his
experiment to this one. Optimism bubbled under the surface.
Perhaps he would uncover new knowledge that would be
attributed to him in the medical community throughout the
world. He stepped back from his instruments. This warranted
more careful thought.

50

Harsh stage lights mounted on rope loops dangled from the warehouse rafters, illuminating the five-piece band playing their hearts out.

A grim-faced, now tipsy Barry leaned in closer to Thompson.

"We're their dumping ground."

"What?" Thompson pressed.

"A dumping ground. We're a dumping ground. Make trouble on the reservation, Indian agent gets you committed. Problem gone, forever. No one ever leaves here."

Barry leaned back, turned his glass upside down, signaling he wished another.

"But their violent, unpredictable behavior," Thompson countered.

"They're simply angry. We took away their freedom. We stripped them of their dignity without even bothering to try to understand who they really are. We just want to see mental illness. It's our nature."

227

Barry became distracted by the way Thompson's seductive eyes shimmered in the light bouncing off the stage. On impulse he reached across to take her hand.

She snatched it away all too quickly to suit him.

"Sorry, love, if I gave the wrong impression. Better if we just remain work associates."

Why had she said that? She just slammed the most promising man to cross her path in at least five years.

A disappointed Barry turned his attention toward the music.

The moment between them evaporated. She had destroyed it. No, she obliterated it. She allowed her fear to smash her chances for anything good to come between them. But her sixth sense was blasting repeated warnings to avoid involvement with him, and she learned long ago the best voice to listen to was her own.

****

The overhead lights flickered against Wallace's face when he closed the knife switch. Though they dimmed, they resisted going completely out this time, since he had decided at the last minute to reduce the current, instead increasing the duration.

Sam's small body convulsed as if he were in total seizure. His eyes rolled, the cloth stuffed in his mouth muffled his scream, then he went unconscious. It all happened within a few seconds.

Wallace ripped open the knife switch. He had not expected Sam's body to react so violently. Respiratory shock, he had learned through earlier experiments, became a serious concern during such a treatment. He rushed to Sam's side, checked Sam's heartbeat with his stethoscope. A moment later, the stress drained from his face. Then he glanced back at the table to verify the settings on his instruments. For all his thoughtful calculations, he had misjudged the requirements. Wallace removed his stethoscope. He stood staring over an unmoving Sam on the bed.

****

Barry recovered amazingly quickly from his embarrassment, aided by yet another drink. He leaned in to Thompson— and this time—kept his hands folded on the table in front of him.

"We're not helping these people, are we? We all just go through the motions. I don't know if I've ever helped any patient for that matter. Maybe we can't help them. We hang fancy diplomas on a wall to fool ourselves into feeling important," Barry said.

"Now who sounds like Wallace?"

Thompson grew uncomfortable with Barry's inebriation. Her ex-husband drank himself into a stupor, after which he frequently turned violent. Listening to Barry's words coupled with seeing his mannerisms brought back such terrible memories that Thompson had to fight down her erupting urge to get up and leave. But, it was a long walk home if she chose not to ride with Barry in his motor car.

"Maybe my father's right," Barry conceded.

"Wallace ever finds out we even had this talk, we'll both be canned," Thompson said, hoping to steer him away from the topic of work.

51

A glum Mana stared out the day room window at rain pelting the glass. Aside from his pounding the sill, no one would have even known he was there.

Tesqua sat at the table, watching with chin in his palm as two Indians played checkers. Paraquo grunted at one of their moves, shaking his head as he continued across the room. The old man's antics made Tesqua smile. He must now have thought of himself as a checkers master, never realizing that *everyone* he played invariably allowed him to win. Next, crazy old Paraquo would try teaching the others his lame strategy.

Sam dashed in, running to Mana at the window.

"Look! Nurse Thompson gave me an eagle feather," Sam chimed, trying to force the pitch black feather into Mana's face.

"Not now. It's a blackbird feather anyway," Mana said with a caustic edge that Sam failed to detect and heed.

"It's an eagle feather. You're just mad because you wish you had one," Sam protested.

"Get away from me, stupid boy."

Mana ripped the feather from Sam's hand, then he knocked him to the floor with a mean shove to the lad's chest. Sam sat too stunned to say or do anything. Both his butt cheeks stung. It was the first time anyone had treated him mean.

Nathan swarmed in to seize Mana's arm, wrenching it quickly behind his back. Mana offered no resistance. Tesqua moved quickly toward Nathan, holding his hands out in a non-threatening way, hoping to defuse the situation before Mana ended up like he had in the past—in the dreaded restraint chair.

"They're just playing. Right, Sam?" Tesqua offered.

"We're just playing. Mana didn't mean nothing by that," Sam pleaded.

The moment lingered with Nathan still pressing Mana's arm against the shallow of his back. Mana made no effort to either oppose Nathan or even attempt to free his hand. Part of him would welcome the punishment.

Nathan slowly released his pressure, allowing Mana to return his arm to his side. After a moment's pause, Nathan wandered back toward the day-room door, leaving Tesqua with Mana.

"He's just a boy," Tesqua said. "Direct your anger at those who deserve it."

Tesqua's eyes followed Nathan.

"Evey lost our baby," Mana said, all the while locking his eyes on Nathan.

"How do you know?"

"She signaled me when she passed in the corridor two days ago. I confirmed it with Thompson yesterday."

"Lost it, or had it taken from her?"

"Either way, I'll never get another chance to be a father."

"It's no coincidence Wallace has separated us again and now Evey's lost your baby."

Mana turned to stare out the window.

"Itza chu," he said to the giant oak sprawling over their graveyard.

Tesqua nodded reassurance, then roamed over to console Sam, who had plopped himself down in the opposite corner, burying his tear-stained face in his arms. It wasn't the pain that had brought on his crying, it was the rejection that had shaken him deep inside.

"It looks like an eagle feather to me. How do you feel?"

"Leave me alone. You never ask me that. Why do you care now?"

"Because of the other day."

"What happened?"

"You don't remember?" Tesqua seemed surprised.

"I never remember my seizures."

Sam shot his arm out, desperately clutching Tesqua's fore-arm.

"You're not going to leave me? It's not my fault I'm sick. Here, take the eagle feather. It is good fortune."

"It's okay, Sam. I'm not leaving you."

Tesqua realized just how foul his statement was. He would leave Sam behind. Sam would wake up one day and Tesqua and Mana would be gone from his life forever. But Tesqua couldn't think about that now.

He accepted the feather only to stick it in Sam's hair. It stood erect at the back of his head. His lie, like the feather, stuck deep in his throat. He knew a time would come when he would abandon Sam.

"There, now you are a true warrior."

The words made Sam smile. He left Tesqua in the corner, dashing to Thompson at the day-room window.

"When's Evey coming? Can I see her?" he asked through the glass while standing on one of the chairs.

Strolling by at that moment, Mana overheard Sam's conversation. He continued on to the corner with a stone face. However, Sam's words launched an idea in his mind. The lad could be more than just a nuisance after all.

"Evey won't be coming," Thompson started, then her voice dropped to a whisper, "But we'll visit her later, okay?"

Sam smiled, removed the feather from his hair for safekeeping while he retreated to the corner across the room from where Mana had settled. But a few moments later, Mana wandered back over to Sam.

"You must give Evey a message from me. Can you do that?" Mana said as if nothing between the two had occurred.

Sam nodded with excitement.

"Tell her itza chu. Soar free like the eagle. But do it only when you are alone with her. No one else must hear. It's a secret. Understand?"

Sam stared at him puzzled.

"Say it. Itza chu."

"Itza shoe," Sam repeated.

"No. Itza chu. Very important. Can you do that for me?"

"Itza chu. Sure."

Sam wandered away feeling as if Mana had taken him into his confidence and that made Sam feel good.

52

As snow swirled outside his window, with head in hands, Wallace read the telegram unfolded on his desk:

REMARKABLE STRIDES. STOP. HAVEN'T HEARD OF YOUR PROGRESS. STOP. CASE STUDIES ALMOST COMPLETE. STOP. WILL PUBLISH SOON. STOP. ACCOLADES FROM THE PSYCHIATRIC COMMUNITY WILL SOON BE MINE. STOP. VON FORRESTER.

When Wallace noticed Barry passing in the hall, he slipped the telegram away, motioning him into his office with his other hand.

"Dr. Barry, got a minute?"

"Medical profiles. We're behind on record keeping," Barry responded, hoping to avoid having to spend any time with Wallace.

Their relationship had deteriorated the way snow melts in spring, slowly growing smaller until none existed anymore. Barry filled his days with his patients and his somewhat futile attempts to provide some semblance of treatment, while Wallace consumed himself with the asylum's administration. It seemed the government bureaucracy was more than sufficient to keep Wallace out of Barry's hair. And Barry was more than happy to allow those details to be handled without his intervention. The less Barry became involved in asylum administration, the more he liked it.

"It's just paperwork. Let it wait. Something I want to share with you."

An odd excitement crept into Wallace's voice that snared Barry's interest. It was indeed rare for Wallace to display exuberance for anything in this place. Now he was acting more like a kid with a secret itching to share.

Barry paused at the door, desperate to conjure some excuse to sidestep having to sit in Wallace's office while the man droned on about some superfluous detail that no one either here in the asylum or in Washington could care about. Failing to produce a plausible excuse, Barry entered Wallace's office, where he took the chair across from him. He could only wonder how much time he would waste now.

Wallace, however, surprised him when he removed a whiskey bottle from his desk drawer and poured two glasses.

"Sometimes even doctors need a little medicine," he said with a devious smile that showed his yellowed teeth.

Barry accepted the drink with a polite nod. He told himself he would have just one then use the first opportunity to vacate so he could get back to the paperwork at hand.

Before Barry could speak a word, Wallace removed a stuffed file from a locked drawer. That very act sparked Barry's curiosity to a higher level, so now he had to remain—and be cordial—until he learned what was in the file Wallace guarded so carefully with his hands on the desk between them. Here sat a man who had habitually failed to document any patient treatment for years, but who now suddenly produced a file loaded with information. *Maybe there was more to Wallace than could be observed on the surface*, Barry thought, waiting patiently for disclosure.

"Close the door," Wallace said, without taking his hands off his precious folder.

Barry complied. *Time to reveal secrets.*

"I think you'll find this most interesting," Wallace offered, finally releasing the precious worn folder into Barry's waiting hands.

Barry opened the file onto his lap, sipping his whiskey while he read. He became so engrossed in his reading that he failed to notice how carefully Wallace studied his reactions to the words coming off the pages.

After five pages, and Wallace's second drink, Barry lifted his eyes to meet the doctor's. So many conflicting emotions became wrapped up in Barry's eyes that Wallace was at a loss to interpret the doctor's response.

"This is terribly invasive, wouldn't you agree?" was all Barry could offer.

"Yes, but if we can somehow realign the electrical forces controlling the brain, we can virtually eliminate mental illness. That's directly from Von Forrester's hand."

"This is all pure supposition. Nothing I've read could even remotely substantiate such a radical theory."

"But it makes perfect sense. Electrical impulses drive our brains. Suppose those impulses are misfiring. We need some way to force them back into their proper sequence. Violence and anger may simply be manifestations of electrical misfires."

"But how much electricity is too much?"

"I understand your concern. In that regard, it is all trial and error, based on body mass. Everything's there in his notes. He's quite a visionary."

"Trial and error? You're inducing an electrical current into a patient's brain by trial and error!"

Barry's inflections immediately raised the hair on Wallace's neck. Wallace had failed to anticipate such a response. Surely a progressive practitioner as Barry could see the benefits in such a theory.

"It's no different than manipulating dosages of our traditional medicines. We're dealing with an inexact science here. Mistakes will be made. We accept that."

"Not so. Nothing I've read here in its wildest interpretation substantiates such a radical supposition. We have absolutely no idea what kind of damage would be done using something this invasive."

Wallace spoke as if he hadn't heard a word Barry had said.

"So far, memory loss seems to be the only side effect. Combine this with drug therapy, and we can treat epilepsy, depression, psychosis, a whole host of maladies."

"This is not radical. This is simply insane. We can't electrocute these people in the hopes of curing mental illness."

Barry paused. Wallace's words had finally taken root in his brain.

"When you say *we*, do you mean you and Von Forrester? You're not ..."

"No, no, of course not," Wallace quickly injected. "But I hate that a damn Austrian might unveil such a revolutionary cure ahead of us."

Barry closed the file, then he stood, dropping the folder onto Wallace's desk.

"This is unconscionable. We took an oath to do no harm."

Barry set his empty glass on the desk then walked out. It all suddenly became clear to him. What mattered most now was what Barry would do about it.

****

Five days following their exchange in Wallace's office, Barry approached Thompson at the nurses' station while patients wandered into the day room. He knew the risks associated with his action, but he had to do something. With a slight head nod, he signaled her before moving away toward the staircase. *Now or never.*

Thompson hurriedly assigned Jake duties before reaffirming that Nathan remained occupied attending patients in the day room. Then she left her desk to wander up the stairs shortly after Barry. Her heart raced. A knot in her stomach threatened to force her to heave her oatmeal breakfast. All she could think about as she climbed the stairs were the repercussions of her involvement if Wallace caught them.

She felt conspicuously exposed and out of place waiting near the staircase on the second floor. What would she say if Wallace confronted her? She had always been a terrible liar. Wallace would detect her falsehoods immediately. If she ended up spilling her guts to him, it would ruin everything for Barry.

Her hands trembled.

She made fists in an attempt to steady them. She had to pee despite having gone not ten minutes before Barry signaled her. She had anticipated this and secretly hoped Barry would abandon his bold plan. Now she stood tuned to pick up the faintest footsteps on the stairs. Wallace had gone to the basement earlier. Therefore, she would provide Barry advance notice of his return. She could only hope Barry had sufficient time to accomplish what he intended. The urge to return to her station swarmed her brain. She took that first step then pulled it back. Barry needed her.

A minute later, she detected the first echoes of footsteps. Heavy footsteps began their slow rhythmic trek up the stairs from the basement. She advanced without delay to Wallace's office, where Barry sat using the only telephone in the asylum.

"I understand, sir. If you would just be kind enough ..." she heard Barry say loudly as she approached the open door.

He struggled against time and a scratchy connection to get his plea heard. Her silent presence alerted him to the developing danger. He could only hope his message had been understood.

"Thank you. I must hang up now. Thank you again, sir."

Barry cradled the phone, quick to snatch files from a basket on Wallace's desk. Then he hastily joined Thompson in the hall. No sooner had he opened a file when Wallace emerged from the staircase with head hung, his eyes watching the floor before him. Barry and Thompson strolled down the hall quickly as Wallace approached.

Thompson's legs felt like rubber with each step. She just knew Wallace could see the deception in her eyes.

"Perhaps a slightly stronger dose is indicated," Barry said, his eyes locked on the file before him.

Thompson, however, felt particularly vulnerable having no place to focus her eyes as Wallace passed. She locked her eyes on Barry the entire time as if clinging to his every word. Her actions felt forced; she could only hope Wallace might accept them as genuine.

Both sighed as they descended the staircase. Neither looked back to determine if Wallace was staring at them. Barry had never before taken such bold action. If it backfired, it could very well cost him his job.

"Sorry to drag you in. But once I discovered that locked basement door with only Wallace holding the key, I knew I couldn't go on being silent. I fear the worst," Barry said once they had reached the first floor landing.

"And if you're wrong?" she queried.

"Maybe for the first time in my life, I'm not. Trust me."

"That's what me bloody bastard husband said just before he left me for a seventeen-year-old."

As they left the staircase, Thompson headed off toward the nurses' station while Barry pushed through the doors to the women's wing. Now all they could do is wait ... and hope.

53

Sam sat at the table in the day room with his head in one hand, watching the second hand sweep in its arc on the clock. He rapped the surface with his other hand in a nervous way that quickly annoyed the others at the table. He'd lost interest in his things; he spoke to no one at the table. He also couldn't understand what was taking so long. If he didn't hurry, it would be too late. He clutched his feather tightly in his hand, twirling it on occasion.

After a few more minutes, he left his chair to kneel on another at the window to the nurses' station. From his perch, he stared at the top of Thompson's head as she worked over a spread of papers on the desk.

For a moment, Thompson had no idea Sam was staring at her. Then, as if she could feel his eyes upon her, Thompson looked up, saw Sam's patient eyes begging for attention. She shrugged to indicate she had no information for him, then she returned to her work.

Her response appeased Sam for the moment. He drifted away, only to pop back a few minutes later, take up the same position on the chair from which to stare at her through the glass. When she refused to acknowledge him, he rapped lightly with his fingertips.

"I don't know what's keeping him," she said, which this time failed to satisfy the young lad. Sam was just far too cute to ever become annoying.

Thompson had never allowed herself to feel the emptiness of being without a family until Sam came into the institution. Now he reminded her every day of her fallen dream to be married with children. Despite Sam's malady, she would welcome him as her own if she ever got the chance. But Sam *wasn't* an orphan. He had parents, who Thompson was certain missed him every day he was gone. She wondered if they even understood what had happened to their son, what his future was destined to be in this place.

****

Dr. Barry, clad in mask and surgical gown, worked over an elderly Indian man, whose breathing came in such desperate gasps that it appeared each breath he took could be his last. The final stages of Tuberculosis ravaged the old man's lungs.

Every few seconds Barry glanced up at the clock on the wall over the bed. Tipping a cup slightly at the old man's lips, he administered a small amount of medication. The only evidence he had that the old man had taken the medication came from a slight rise of his Adam's apple. Barry remained bedside until a nurse entered with a pan of water and fresh clothes for their patient.

"Fever's stabilizing," he said, moving into the background to allow the nurse to replace him at the bed.

"I've just administered his medication. He should be comfortable the rest of the day. I'll be back to check on him this evening. Please summon me if his respiration or temperature changes," Barry finished as he removed his mask and withdrew to the door.

"Yes, sir," he heard from the nurse on his departure.

As Barry came down the hall toward the men's day room, Thompson tapped the window, which brought Sam flying from his chair to the door.

Sam exited the day room as Dr. Barry hurried up.

"Sorry to be late," Barry apologized as he took Sam's hand.

"There still time?" Sam asked, hopeful.

Barry nodded, displaying just as much excitement as Sam at the moment.

"Can Tesqua come?"

"Sure. But we should hurry."

Sam disappeared back into the day room only to emerge a moment later with a confused Tesqua in tow. The three hurried up the stairs, Sam taking his two-at-a-time, only to wait on the landing for the others to catch up. Sam's smile brought a smile to Barry's face. Tesqua, however, remained unaffected and confused.

Huddled around the radio in Wallace's office, Sam fidgeted in a chair while Barry tuned to the station. Tesqua sat away, eyeing the cavalry hat—with its bullet hole—that sat on the bureau beside the radio.

Static crackled from the box, then it became a squeal as Barry worked the tuning knob with a surgeon's delicate touch.

A choppy voice came in. Barry stopped. The voice smoothed out.

"Ruth already has two home runs. The Yanks have a three-game lead in game four. Unless the Cardinals suddenly come alive, the New York Yankees are gonna sweep this 1928 World Series."

"We got it!" Sam chimed. His face alighted with youthful exuberance. He leaned forward in his chair to be closer to the radio, even though he could hear just fine from where he sat.

"We're going to win, Sam," Barry said. But rather than settle into Wallace's chair, Barry stood beside Sam, watching the lad's reactions as the announcer called the game.

"Come on, Babe, hit another home run. Someday I'm gonna see a game," Sam said, but when he turned around, Barry had disappeared.

Tesqua gazed blankly at the wall. He could care less about listening to the radio. But he offered a facade of interest in order to make Sam happy.

"The Yankee home runs today have been a thing of beauty to see," the announcer said to fill the silence while they waited for the next player to come to the plate.

Barry returned to find Sam staring at the radio on the bureau as if he could somehow see the action on the field. His face broke into an excited grin when Barry handed him a well-worn baseball glove with a pristine ball.

"For me?" Sam asked. He smelled the leather then stroked the glove's pliable pocket after placing it on his left hand. It was too long for his little fingers, but Sam knew he would grow into it in time.

"For you. They were mine when I was your age. I always wanted to ..."

The announcer broke in.

"Here's the pitch .... It's a ball."

"Play second base for the Yankees," Barry continued when the announcer finished. He had forgotten just how exciting a baseball game could be to an eleven-year-old. They had listened to the first two games of the series, but missed the third due to a sick patient. Now they were fortunate enough to listen to the final game, if their Yankees won.

"Tesqua, play catch with me. Maybe someday I'll play second base. Where's second base?"

But even before Sam could pull the ball from the glove, or Barry explain to him the layout of the bases, all eyes settled on the door.

A fuming Wallace filled the doorway.

"What in the goddamn hell?"

"Game four, World Series. Sam and I are Yankee fans," Barry said. But he could see the words meant nothing to Wallace; in fact, they were infuriating him.

Enraged, Wallace swiped at the radio, crashing it to the floor along with the cavalry hat. When Tesqua retrieved the hat, Wallace ripped it from his hands. Only the faded sepia photograph of a cavalry officer remained on the bureau.

"This is my office," Wallace stammered, the veins on his forehead pulsing with rage.

"I thought you were out for the afternoon," Barry tried to explain.

But any effort would be futile.

Tesqua responded quickly to lead Sam out. They scurried down the hall, wanting to get as far away as possible before the yelling started. Tesqua hoped to spare Barry the embarrassment that might come from Sam witnessing what Tesqua knew was about to transpire—a familiar Wallace tirade.

Once they were gone, Wallace clamped onto Barry's arm.

"They're never allowed in here."

"It's the World Series. He's an eleven-year-old boy."

"Damn you! Don't ever cross me again."

Barry stormed out.

Wallace slammed his satchel onto his desk and sat down hard into his chair. When he did, a telegram fluttered off the surface to the floor. He retrieved it, slit it open and read:

SUCCESS. STOP. READY TO PUBLISH. STOP.

Wallace couldn't bring himself to finish. He crumbled the paper, slamming it into the wire wastebasket. He removed his coat, tossed it onto the bureau before pulling a whiskey bottle from his desk drawer. He could only wonder how things at the asylum could become worse.

54

The day began as a repeat of a thousand days past. Tesqua entered the day room to find Mana already at his window staring out at the giant oak. Tesqua wondered how many feet that old tree had grown since his arrival. It certainly appeared much taller, but there was no way to accurately gauge its progress.

Nathan, Jake and two other orderlies roamed the room with little interest in any of the patients. They settled into a corner to chat quietly, looking over at Tesqua on occasion. Because orderlies rotated days off, Tesqua and Mana found it difficult to predict with certainty which days Nathan would be gone. Certainly their best chance for success would be with Nathan out of the building. But Tesqua concluded their success hinged on planning and execution rather than the chance occurrence of Nathan's absence.

Even though Tesqua resisted attaching himself to any women in the asylum, he missed not having the women visit. He knew it must be terribly difficult for Mana to get through each day knowing they imprisoned his wife less than fifty feet away, yet he could have no contact with her. As quickly as that thought came to him, Tesqua banished it. His heart ached whenever he felt his thoughts straying back to Celia. He had to keep her from being in his mind. He had to focus on himself— what he needed to do to get free of this horrible place.

Tesqua had become lost in his thoughts, like he did on so many past days, that when a fight broke out between two Indians across the room, Tesqua at first failed to even react. Maybe it was the length of time here, or the medication they forced into him daily, but the fight stirred nothing inside him.

When Nathan and Jake shoved their way into the fray to gain control, one of the Indians blindsided Nathan with a sucker punch. The flailing fist split Nathan's flesh along his jaw line, stunning him for a few moments and keeping him from assisting Jake, whose hands became entangled trying to secure another of the Indians. In a rage while bleeding profusely, Nathan whacked the Indian who had struck him, knocked him to the floor, where he repeatedly rammed his face into the wooden planks.

"Nathan!" Thompson scolded, when she realized he had lost control.

Her sharp voice made Nathan recognize his actions and stop. He locked the Indian's hands behind him then pulled him back to his feet with the help of another orderly. While they removed the two patients, Thompson cleaned up the blood splattering the floor.

Most of the patients in the day room had merely moved away to avoid the altercation. Some refused to even look at the foray in their midst. No one joined in; no one shouted or yelled. They simply moved away, allowing the orderlies to restore order to the room.

Witnessing that altercation made Tesqua realize they could never fight their way to freedom. Besides, Mana seemed far too passive to even be willing to fight. Maybe that was Mana's plan all along. He would allow Tesqua to do the fighting for him. Maybe he planned to use Tesqua as a decoy while he himself escaped ....

Tesqua wandered over to Mana at the window, who had watched the confusion without emotion, and once it passed, returned to stare at the giant oak.

"Nathan's our biggest threat," Tesqua said.

"Then we incapacitate him," Mana responded so matter-of-factly that it caught Tesqua off guard.

"Great. How?"

Mana smiled as if he had already thought their entire plan through and had handled that detail. While they stood there looking at each other, Sam ran up with his glove.

"Play catch with me."

Tesqua absently caught Sam's toss, but the entire time he watched Mana. Something churned inside that head that Mana refused to share with Tesqua. He had the workings of an escape plan that so far he kept to himself. For a brief moment Tesqua questioned whether their friendship was strong enough to bond them together, or would Mana find a way out for only himself? Tesqua banished the thought. They needed each other not only to survive in this place, but to find their way to freedom.

****

In the infirmary, Nathan sat on an examination table positioned near the window, allowing Barry the full advantage of the sunlight while he stitched Nathan's cut.

"There," Barry said, tying off the final stitch before inspecting his work.

"Can't you give them something stronger. Double it if you have to, if you expect us to keep them under control."

"You the psychiatrist now?" Barry said, washing his hands at the sink before dressing the wound with a gauze bandage.

"Sorry. Just sick of the cowboy and Indian crap all the time."

Barry stared at Nathan while he pressed the final strip of tape into place. Something in that moment sparked in his mind.

"That should do it."

Nathan inspected the bruising in his reflection in the window.

"How long am I gonna look like this?"

"A week, ten days maybe. It's a deep bruise."

"That's just great. I got a date Saturday night."

"That's good. Makes you look tough. Women like that."

"You think? I could tell them I went toe-to-toe with some big ass Joe. He came out the worse."

"See. Absolutely ..."

Barry stopped mid-sentence. He couldn't take his eyes off the bruise blooming on Nathan's face. Maybe it was the way Nathan spoke, or the way the sun played off Nathan's jaw, but it suddenly struck Barry what he had been missing. *How could he have been so incompetent to have missed something so simple?* The answer came to him as plain as the discoloration on Nathan's cheek.

Barry marched out of the infirmary in deep thought.

"Hey, doc, you gonna give me anything?"

"You're good for now," Barry called back from the hall.

55

There were countless days when Dr. Barry arrived at work sickened by the thought of having to face another day in the asylum. So much time had passed and he had yet to feel as if he had made any significant progress with any of this patients. He had tried everything he could think of—that Wallace would approve—to help them; all had failed. Psychiatry was becoming for him so much more than an inexact science; it had developed into a futile attempt to help those who were beyond any reasonable man's definition of help.

Barry's day ended as unremarkable as it had started, despite the lateness of the hour and the fact those twelve full hours of effort reaped nothing in the way of progress.

"Dr. Barry," Wallace called from his office as Barry passed his door. *Oh no, not again*, Barry thought. The last thing he wanted was to deal with Wallace's incessant babble of grandiose dreams.

As Barry entered, Wallace filled two whiskey glasses.

"Not particularly in the spirit," Barry replied to the invitation. He remained standing. He just wanted to get home so he could flop into his bed. He had even lost his desire to eat. He did, however, notice Wallace's advanced state of inebriation. The man must have began knocking back the whisky before dinner time.

"You will be. Stock market crashed. New Yorkers are jumping off buildings. I'm completely wiped out," Wallace informed him.

"Thanks to the government, I can't afford to participate in the market," Barry replied so matter-of-factly that it took Wallace by surprise.

"Thought you came from money?"

Wallace knocked back his shot, promptly poured another, dribbling whiskey on his desk.

"Cut off years ago. Seemed the only way to father's good graces was to become a banker. I guess I get the last laugh after all," Barry said, then he downed his drink.

The whiskey warmed his throat going down. It also quieted the rumblings of his empty stomach. Maybe a few more would ease the frustration swimming inside his head. He took the chair across from Wallace and set his glass down for a refill.

When Thompson appeared at the door, both men stopped drinking.

"Dr. Barry, anything before I go?" she asked.

"No, we're good for now."

"Miss Thompson, stock market crashed," Wallace injected as if intending to shock her also.

"Oh," was all she said. "Will that be all then, sir?"

"Have a good night. See you in the morning," Barry added.

"Very good, sir. Cheers."

Wallace refilled the glasses the moment Thompson departed.

"You expect any impact here?" Barry asked.

"Not an Indian in this country capable of understanding the stock market. I doubt we'll see an increase in admissions. But St. Elizabeth's in DC will be overflowing by year's end. Mark my words."

Wallace tossed back his whiskey and leaned forward to pour another.

****

At the nurses' station desk, Nathan tossed pencils at a cup to stave off boredom. He stopped when moaning rose from down the hall.

"Shut up, you monkey. Go to sleep," he yelled.

He tossed another pencil, this one missing the cup.

Nurse Thompson strolled up while tightening her coat.

"I'll be off then."

"Okey-Dokey," Nathan replied as if he felt compelled by some duty to respond to her statement.

"Oh, stock market crashed today," she added, without knowing why she even said it. She just felt a need to share the news with someone.

"Anyone get hurt?" Nathan asked, then chuckled at his feeble humor.

Thompson ignored his remark, just walked away to the reception door.

****

In Wallace's office, the whiskey bottle sat empty. Wallace sat drunk. Barry sat forced to listen.

"You and I, total opposites," Wallace slurred.

"I've never thought of us that way," Barry responded. But Wallace's comment intrigued him. He would have thought Wallace would have been more guarded with his statements. However, Barry leaned just slightly forward demonstrating interest in Wallace's words, hoping the man might slip, reveal something Barry could use in the future.

"Never had a damn dime. Orphaned at twelve. Father died at ten, mother two years later."

"Sorry to hear. How'd they die?" Barry found himself asking, feigning actual interest in Wallace's life. Maybe he, too, had indulged too much, causing him to lower his guard. Part of him cried out to leave, but another part needed to hear more about the man he worked for.

Wallace grabbed the photograph off the bureau. He stared at it for a long moment.

"Savages at Wounded Knee," he commented as if he were talking to the photograph rather than Barry.

"Really."

"Goddamn Ghost Dancers. Twenty-two years after the fact, I get a look at the Army's official report. A band of rebel Indians. They said they had surrendered their weapons. Then they opened fire on the Army. Twenty-five soldiers died."

"And your mother?" Barry asked. He sought to steer Wallace away from the painful memory making itself evident on his face.

Barry had always thought of his life as difficult living under a tyrannical father who dominated his every waking thought. Maybe there was worse out there that he never took the time to consider.

"All I remember was her having trouble breathing. A neighbor got her to a hospital. Dead two days later. After her funeral, the same neighbor dropped me off at an orphanage."

"Must have been difficult."

"Three orphanages by eighteen. Then the government offered me a chance to go to school. My father being a decorated Army captain when he died opened doors. People felt sorry for me."

"It's late. I should go," Barry said.

"And I'm drunk. I think it's best I leave before I can't find the door."

Barry exited the office while Wallace searched his desk for another bottle.

56

Tesqua sat at the window watching a burnt orange dying sun dip below the horizon. The scene mimicked his life, also slowly fading away. Around him, patients sat or walked without purpose. Sometimes Mana would make him laugh, sometimes spark a fire in his spirit, but most times he existed as lifeless as the rest of the crazy Indians in this place.

The departing sun left the sky black. Darkness overtook him.

"Back to your rooms," Nathan called out from the door. Even Nathan seemed to have changed over the last few months. He seemed to have lost all interest in intimidating them.

One by one, patients filed out like a herd of cattle being funneled through the corrals for the slaughter. If death were to come this night, Tesqua would welcome it. He fell in behind Mana, which made him realize Mana would have no one in this place to talk with, make fun of, or dream about a future that didn't exist for them once he was gone.

While Nathan locked Mana's door down the hall, Tesqua paused in his doorway to inspect the door clasp. He brushed his fingers against it, concentrating on the feel of his skin against the wood.

Nathan moved in behind to nudge him in. Tesqua didn't react. He hoped instead Nathan had failed to notice his clandestine inspection of his prison cell door. *Could he jam the lock so that later he might jimmy it open with something?*

Once inside, Tesqua stood staring back at Nathan through the glass while he locked the door. Tesqua paused for a moment at the side of the door, out of view through the window. He realized what he had felt might be a way out of this place. But this was only one small hurdle with many more to overcome before he could feel freedom's wind against his face.

Tesqua remained beside the door until the sounds in the hall faded. Nathan and Jake would be back at the nurses' station desk, drinking coffee while jabbering about things they wanted to do to the women they met on the outside. They probably never even realized Tesqua could overhear bits of their conversations. For the most part, they spoke of nothing useful to him, but sporadically Tesqua could pick up a scrap of useful information. He knew, for instance, that there were railroad tracks to the east running between this place and Sioux Falls. So once free, the train tracks would lead him to the city.

Tesqua slid closer to the door. He used the weak light falling in from the hall to study the door frame. Nails held the molding solidly in place. It would be difficult to remove enough wood to release the door latch. But there may be another way to get out of his room unnoticed. He retired to his bed to think about a way out rather than fall asleep, despite his exhaustion.

57

While Barry paced, Wallace sat behind his desk with a patient, unaffected face and fingers steepled over his lips.

"You performed a routine physical at admittance as required?" Barry said.

"Correct."

"You noted your findings in his file?"

"The point, please. I've a busy day," Wallace replied, growing impatient with Barry's latest antics.

****

Mana stood off to the side of the latrine while Tesqua washed his hands at the sink. He studied every nuance of Tesqua's face.

"Why did you do it?" Mana asked, searching for any change in Tesqua's eyes.

"Do what?"

"Beat those white men in New Mexico."

"What men? I never beat anyone."

"Your file says you did."

Tesqua's eyes opened wide. He couldn't believe what he was hearing. How could Mana ...

"You read my file? You can read?"

"I told you, my friend, acting crazy serves my purpose. Barry left your file unattended on his desk. I offered to empty his trash, so when he left his office, I checked your folder. It also said inebriation psychosis with violent tendencies."

Tesqua just stared at Mana. If Tesqua were indeed guilty of the crime they accused him of, he disguised it on his face. The genuine surprise in his eyes convinced Mana that Tesqua had spoken the truth and the white man had lied. Even with Mana's bias toward the white man, he still felt certain his friend should be trusted.

"You can read?"

****

Wallace had reached the very end of his patience, surrendering the last of his restraint.

"That's utterly ridiculous. My job is not to scrutinize the Indian agents' integrity. I accept patients duly committed to this facility, providing them the best care possible. Period."

"You don't get it," Barry said, allowing his voice to rise in response to the anger swelling up inside. "They railroaded him."

"Excuse me?"

Wallace's face turned stone hard with his colorless lips tight across his face. Anger seethed just below the surface. What Barry implied tore at the very fabric of Wallace's integrity. How *dare* he accuse him of such despicable acts! Never in his entire professional career had he been subjected to such a vile, caustic interrogation.

"The Indian agent lied and you bought it."

"You dare challenge my integrity, doctor!"

"Did Tesqua present with multiple bruises and contusions consistent with the report provided in his file when he arrived in Canton?"

The words dug in with a lawyer's bite, yet they only fueled Wallace's already boiling anger.

****

Returning to the day room, Mana settled on his haunches into a corner. Tesqua settled likewise beside him. A moody silence swept over them, both staring straight ahead as if in deep thought.

"What means psychosis?" Tesqua asked.

"Means the white man believes you're crazy."

Tesqua hopelessly stared at his scuffed shoes as Paraquo rolled past. Sam, out of boredom, strolled over to Tesqua, but Tesqua ignored him. So, if they believed he was crazy they would never allow him to leave this place. Yet in believing he was crazy Tesqua had failed to get them to trust him enough for them to become complacent. His freedom now seemed a million miles away.

****

Barry's pacing accelerated. He needed to rein in his erupting anger, gain control of himself before he could gain control of the situation. He now believed this could only be the apparent surface of the terrible injustice each of them had unwittingly become a party to.

"Nothing can be done. So I suggest we let it go," Wallace said firmly, his tone indicating finality.

He sought to offer Barry a way to gracefully terminate their discussion. An avenue Wallace felt would allow both men to walk away with their dignity and integrity intact. Somehow, he knew Barry would never accept that.

"Admit it. His hands showed no contusions or signs that he had been in any kind of altercation, did they?"

Barry afforded Wallace only a second to respond, during which time Wallace remained silent.

"He never committed any crime. Paperwork endorsing Tesqua's release will be on your desk by end of day. I suggest you sign it."

Barry's words came out so sharp they carried the undertones of a threat.

"On what grounds?" Wallace asked, maintaining his level calm voice.

"On the grounds he does not now, nor has he ever, suffered from any form of mental illness. There never was anything wrong with him. And you know it. They falsified his paperwork to get him committed for whatever disgusting purpose."

"Waste your time if you wish. But the only way I approve any release is after they're sterilized. Since the government has not seen fit to provide me the appropriate medical facilities, no patient duly authorized under my charge shall be released ever. Am I clear?"

Barry slammed his fist on Wallace's desk.

Wallace lurched back in response.

"These are not the men who killed your father!" Barry shouted, surrendering all control of his sensibilities. The words slipped out before he could stop them. He had allowed his anger to temporarily override his brain.

"Do I make myself clear?" Wallace shouted back, rising from his chair with white knuckles grinding on the desk.

"You've crossed the line with these people."

"And you, Dr. Barry, are dismissed."

Barry stormed from Wallace's office with such anger that he marched down the staircase and exited through the reception door without speaking to anyone. Thompson watched him exit the staircase, saw the frustration consuming his face and turned away from him at her desk. She knew he was best left alone when he wore such emotion.

At nine o'clock that night, Tesqua walked with Mana down the hall while Nathan locked others away.

"I overheard it hours ago," Mana said.

"Doesn't make it true," Tesqua replied.

"They spoke of you. Be careful, my friend. Something is going on."

Nathan came up, shouldered Tesqua toward his room. Tesqua resisted.

"I'm just in the mood to strap you in the restraint chair," Nathan said, smileless.

Tesqua had difficulty reading Nathan's face this night.

The two stood eye-to-eye. Nathan refused to waver. Neither would budge. Then Tesqua entered his room, closing the door himself.

58

Against the first weak rays of an awakening sun, Dr. Barry climbed the asylum stairs, thinking more about what he hoped to accomplish this day than anything else. Hunger growled inside his belly. His confrontation with Wallace proved so upsetting to him that he had skipped dinner and forgotten to eat breakfast. He suspected he had developed stomach problems as a result of the tension between the two over the last few months. But he knew what he must do. He must deliver on his promise. He must make a valiant fight even though he knew Wallace would vehemently oppose his every move from here on out.

Barry removed his keys, slid the reception-room door key into the lock and turned. The tumbler refused to budge. He removed the key, slid it in again and tried to turn. Again the tumbler in the lock refused to yield. He jiggled his key. The door lock remained in place.

Giving up on his key, he rapped on the glass and waited. His stomach convulsed. When no response came, he rapped again, this time a little harder, but not so hard that it might appear insistent.

At last, Nathan strolled up. Barry held up his keys, shook his head. Nathan paused at the door with a peculiar smile on his face. Barry knew without explanation what had transpired. Nathan's smug smile and taunting eyes revealed all the information necessary.

"Wallace's orders," Nathan said plainly.

Barry realized now he had failed to think his idea through to its ultimate conclusion. They had their differences; Barry knew any move would only expand the rift between them. But they were professionals. They had to place patient welfare above all else. He had anticipated Wallace's resistance but had not anticipated Wallace's radical response. He grabbed the door, shook it with great anger.

Nathan just stood there, hands stuffed in his pockets, disgusting grin consuming his face, laughing at the doctor with his eyes. For at that particular moment Nathan had trumped him. He, a lowly orderly, held the power.

After another minute, a straight-faced Wallace appeared at the door. There were no signs of smug pleasure to read on the doctor's face.

"When I said you were dismissed, Dr. Barry, I meant you were fired. As such, you are no longer allowed inside this facility."

"You can't do this!" Barry hammered back.

"I am superintendent of this facility, and I've done it," Wallace replied with an even coolness that let Barry know nothing he could say or do would undo Wallace's decision.

"What about the people you've locked away in here?"

"Your patients revert to my care. Your personal belongings will be placed outside reception by end of day."

Wallace strolled away wallowing in the glow of his accomplishment. He had removed an obstacle to his future success by eliminating Barry. Nathan remained a moment longer, then he followed suit.

"That's not what I mean and you know it. Damn it, Wallace, you can't do this to these people!"

After a moment Thompson appeared. They looked at each other with pain in their faces. Thompson sought to convey her feelings for him and what he stood for with her eyes. She knew if she uttered a single word in his defense, she would find herself on the same side of the door with very few employment options. The nascent depression had clamped a death grip on the nation, making it the worst possible time to be unemployed. Since the crash, thousands upon thousands had lost their jobs on a weekly basis. If she lost her job, it could be years before she could find another. She had no one to turn to for support. Barry had a wealthy family for support. He could find another job, she convinced herself. He could survive something like this. She couldn't.

"I won't abandon them. Tell them," Barry pleaded at the glass. Even in this dark hour, he thought not about himself but rather of his patients. He needed them to know they would not be left behind. Most importantly, he wanted to tell them he understood what had happened to them.

Thompson did all she could do: Stand there in silence.

"Don't you have work to do, nurse?" Wallace sniped from down the hall. He spoke loud enough to ensure even Barry heard his words, as a way of punctuating his statement of power over all who came through those doors.

Thompson wanted to speak, needed to say so many things to Barry, but in the end, she walked away in silence.

59

Five days passed. None of the patients noticed Dr. Barry's absence. Tesqua became the first to raise his concern to Mana, who simply dismissed it. But as successive days wore on, it became evident Dr. Barry was no where in the building.

Agitated, Tesqua and Mana walked the day room perimeter. Their anger festered with each step. Sam followed a step behind, tossing the ball into the air as he walked, catching it in his glove.

"It's three weeks. Wallace canned him I tell you," Tesqua said.

"He's taken a leave, as they say. He'll be back," Mana replied, "Wallace has been gone from this place many times."

"But never this long. I'm telling you, Barry wouldn't be away for this long."

"You speak as if he cares about us. He doesn't really care what happens to us. It is just his job to care," Mana said.

Sam's errant toss knocked Mana in the head, who snatched it out of the air and absently tossed it back to the lad.

"Sorry," Sam apologized, then giggled.

"Now who's a wishful fool?" Mana asked.

"We will settle this," Tesqua said.

Tesqua left Mana near the window facing the giant oak, crossing to the day-room window. He rapped sharply on the glass. Thompson ignored him. She continued her duties at the desk without looking up. She only responded when Tesqua's incessant tapping became a nuisance.

"I need to see Dr. Barry."

"He's not available."

"When can I see him?"

No response. Tesqua revealed anger, shaking the day-room door.

Nathan intervened.

"Let it go, Jimmy," Nathan ordered.

"I want to speak with the doctor," Tesqua countered.

"How about I get Dr. Wallace," Nathan replied, hoping to appease him peacefully. Yet the orderly knew full well this wasn't going to go that way.

"No! Dr. Barry. Now!"

Nathan pried Tesqua's hands from the knob. Then he yanked him from the door. Tesqua spun about, hammering Nathan's jaw.

A bell sounded.

Wallace, Jake and others rushed into the day room to restrain a flailing Tesqua. They gang-tackled him, forcing him flat to the floor with his arms outstretched. From there they wrestled to get him into a straitjacket.

"Leave him alone!" Sam screamed, witnessing the terrible grimace of pain on Tesqua's face.

With all the strength he could muster, Sam fired his ball on instinct into the group holding Tesqua to the floor. The ball whacked Jake in the middle of his back, causing the orderly to recoil and surrender his grip on Tesqua's arm. Tesqua's wild right-cross nailed Nathan in the jaw. Without thinking, Jake backhanded Sam across the face, sending the lad reeling along the floor into the wall.

Mana, who had never once raised an angry hand in his place, could no longer restrain himself. He leaped onto Jake's back, pounding him with both fists.

Thompson intervened to snatch the glove and ball from Sam, who crawled into a corner, where he cried out of control. Another orderly gained a choke hold on Mana to peel him off Jake's back. But not before Mana took a clear shot to Jake's face. The orderly rammed Mana into the wall. Mana's arms fell limply to his sides in supplication. *It felt exhilarating to finally release his anger on his captors.*

****

Strapped in a straitjacket, Tesqua rammed his door until his entire body ached. Then he gave up and slid to the floor with his back against the door.

As day turned into night, Tesqua remained in that same position. No one had entered his room; no one made any attempt to deal with him.

In the hall at the nurses' station, Thompson worked diligently on maintaining the patient charts, not wanting to see some of the good Barry brought to this place fall by the wayside. Wallace walked up, drawing her from her work.

"He reeks of his own waste. He's refused food and water for three days. He's getting weak."

Wallace studied a chart, never making eye contact with Thompson.

"Sir, he's going to die."

"You think I don't know that? You think I wasted twelve years of my life in medical training?" Wallace's words were so caustic that had they been razors, they would have drawn Thompson's blood.

"There were two more fights today. Nathan has eight patients strapped in their beds," Thompson pressed.

Wallace slammed the chart to the desk then marched off.

"I'll be in my office."

Thompson seethed.

In his office, Wallace shuffled through his secret file, rereading old telegrams while organizing sheets of notes he had taken over the past two years. Disappointment painted his face as his eyes moved over the words. The Washington barracudas had failed him. Had Washington provided support, he would have given Von Forrester a run for his money. Now it would all be meaningless once Von Forrester published his findings that would set the psychiatric community on its ear.

Wallace convinced himself he could still continue his work, but there would be no accolades, no fame coming his way. His life would be as meaningless as this place. He would ultimately fade away into old age and obscurity. A new superintendent would take over this facility, and he would end up with nothing more than a meager government pension to live out the last days of his life. Had any of it been worth the effort, he wondered as he sat there no longer seeing the words on the telegrams.

He tucked the papers back into the file with hands that had lost all enthusiasm for his work, this place, even for his life.

"Excuse me, sir?" Thompson interrupted at the door with a voice no louder than the squeaks of a frightened church mouse.

Wallace's backlashes had become so frequent and vicious that Thompson cringed each time she had to approach him with a question or a concern. She wore her apprehension not only on her face, but also in her slumping posture. Her job had defeated her, destroying her very spirit.

"Have you nothing better to do, nurse, than to be my constant annoyance?"

"Sir, Dr. Silk," she persisted, delivering only the words necessary to convey meaning, which had been a mistake on her part, but she blamed Wallace's callousness and mean-spirited attitude toward all the staff in this place afterward.

"What about the damn qua ...?"

Thompson knew she must burst in.

"Sir. He's here," she blurted, hoping her words would drown out Wallace's, since Dr. Silk stood but a few steps behind her in the hall.

"What? Dr. Silk? Dr. Silk!"

Wallace flipped his folder closed just as Dr. Silk entered. Silk carried a tired old frame hunched over with age. All but a few wisps of his white hair had disappeared from a head cluttered with brown age spots. A walnut-shaped nose supported thick glasses, which he adjusted with his right hand before extending it in welcome to his colleague. They had only met briefly a few years earlier at a meeting in Washington, and their encounter, for the most part, had been unremarkable.

"By your candor, I'll surmise you never received my wire," Dr. Silk said with a smile that was neither forgiving nor surprised.

"No. No. I'm sorry. I would have had an orderly meet your train. It is indeed a pleasure, doctor. But to what do we owe this visit?"

Silk paused as if to savor watching Wallace squirm. Perspiration dotted Wallace's forehead. The doctor's palms had suddenly gone sweaty. Indeed Wallace was unprepared for the visit.

"Just routine. Commissioner wants assurance you're using your funding wisely before increasing it."

Silk's words immediately put Wallace at ease, as he had meant to do. *Increasing it*, he had said. After countless reports, letters, even phone calls, it seemed finally the commissioner had heard his plea. Maybe now he would finally offer some long overdue improvements to their aging facility.

"I understand," Wallace replied, constricting his inner excitement. This also could be another of the BIA's 'we really want to help you' routines that never brought needed help to them anyway. It may be nothing more than the Washington bureaucrats' political tap dancing. They so enjoyed tugging the strings of their puppets in the field.

"Then if you don't mind, this old *quack* has a full day planned, so I'll have your nurse get me started."

Wallace swallowed hard.

"Of course."

Thompson led Silk from the office to begin his inspection tour of their facility. The moment he left, Wallace's face turned grim, his stomach knotted—he needed a drink. But he knew better than to pull out the bottle he kept tucked in his desk. He would have to endure these days without it until Silk completed his inspection and departed.

"Fuck!"

Wallace slumped in his chair, muttering something about how miserable his life had become. He buried his face into his hands in exasperation. Then he realized one floor below he had an obstinate, failing Tesqua locked away in his room, reeking of his own waste and severely dehydrated. This day could not have started out worse.

Wallace quickly concluded his best strategy would be to remain out of Silk's way, hope the old man overlooked the multitude of discrepancies in this place, and in the event he didn't, prepare responses for those problems which Silk might likely seek answers. Any involvement Wallace might exhibit would only be viewed negatively upon himself. *Best to just allow the man to perform his duties and hope for the best*. This was probably the only job he performed for the Bureau anyway.

Wallace busied himself tending an old Indian with pertussis. When he next glanced at the clock it was after one, so he rushed out to join Dr. Silk in his office, where over a sandwich, Silk inspected files while Wallace set more on the desk. From the pleasant look on Silk's face, Wallace surmised the inspection might be proceeding well. In retrospect, Barry had done an excellent job of getting the asylum paperwork in order, and it was paying dividends now. He had hoped that Silk, being the typical Washington bureaucrat, would concern himself with administrative matters and overlook the more mundane routine of managing the patients' day-to-day care. He considered Silk more the administrator rather than a psychiatrist, and that could prove very beneficial to him.

After reviewing a few more files, Silk set the stack on the corner of the desk.

"I'm done with these," he offered.

"Shall I have more brought in?" Wallace asked, hoping this phase of the inspection might be over. The more he scrutinized those files, the more likely he would find discrepancies that begged for explanation.

The moment hung between them while Silk adjusted his glasses.

"No. That's fine. I'm ready to move on."

Wallace fought down the urge to follow him out like a lost puppy. The last thing he wished to convey was that he lacked the confidence his facility could withstand the scrutiny of a BIA spot inspection. All he could do for now was hope.

An hour later, Wallace passed Silk sitting in the visitors' room while Thompson escorted one patient out only to lead another in. Another good sign for him. If Thompson hand-picked the patients for Silk to interview, she would be mindful to select only patients presenting the best side of life in the facility. After all, her very job could depend upon Silk's report.

Thompson avoided eye contact with Wallace as he passed. But Wallace felt confident Thompson would do nothing to jeopardize their funding. That same funding kept her employed there.

In the early evening, Silk dined with the staff while Wallace worked in his office. His empty stomach growled, but Silk expected him to remain absent the mess hall while the good doctor conducted his interviews. Wallace relaxed knowing none of his staff would dare speak against him, even under the guise of confidentiality from Dr. Silk. Wallace held absolute power over their employment. Anything they said could be linked back to them if it appeared in a written report. None of them wanted to be walking the streets now.

Wallace stared out at the night for a long time, considering what each of his employees might say. None of them, he felt, would offer anything negative against him or this place. As long as Silk didn't go poking his nose into certain patient rooms, Wallace felt assured his inspection might end well. That would give him leverage to secure an increase in funding. He had wanted so much for this place, but recent events had instilled in him the urgency for a surgical facility. He knew he must sterilize these patients in order to prevent more 'accidents' from occurring.

At the nine o'clock hour, Silk stood by as the orderlies, feigning compassion, assisted patients to their rooms. Jake even helped Paraquo from his wheelchair to his bed, something no one in the facility had ever done for him in all the years of his confinement.

The long, tedious day had taken a toll on the sixty-eight-year-old Dr. Silk. He rubbed red, irritated eyes, his face long and colorless. Despite his fatigue, he used those moments in the hall to scribble notes while orderlies put the last patients to bed for the night.

Dr. Wallace descended the staircase to Silk finishing up his notes.

"Will I see you at breakfast?" Wallace asked.

"Unnecessary. I've enough for my report. I'm off tomorrow for a meeting in Kansas then back to Washington."

"Without much rest," Wallace commented.

"I'll rest on the train."

Silk tucked his notes into his satchel. Then Wallace assisted the good doctor into his coat, all the while hiding the smile stretching ear to ear in his mind. His inspection concluded in only a single day. That could indeed be a good omen.

"Anything to share?" Wallace ventured.

He hoped his casual inquiry might elicit even a small response, revealing some insight into what Silk had thought of the facility, and what he might report to the commissioner.

"Your record keeping lacks discipline. But I concur that housing epileptics separately would ease stress on other patients. Everyone I interviewed, including your staff, had trouble coping with patient seizures. It must be difficult."

"We do our best with what we're given. Perhaps that is just what the commissioner needs to hear."

"Patient fights are a major concern with both patients and staff. More must be done to curb violence," Silk said.

"I have ..."

Silk raised a hand to silence Wallace before he could deliver his canned excuse.

"I understand. Fifty-eight male Indians is more than a handful. I'll recommend funding for an additional orderly as soon I return to Washington. The commissioner will not likely oppose me on that once he knows the facts."

They reached the reception room door. While Wallace unlocked it, Silk gave the hall one more good look.

"A good whitewashing could make the place more pleasant. You should consider that."

"I will," Wallace said, for the first time releasing a smile.

"I'll write my report on the train. That should expedite matters once I get back to Washington."

"Thank you, Dr. Silk. I appreciate your help. I think the bureaucrats don't understand what I do here."

"Don't worry, Dr. Wallace, I'll make sure they know exactly what you're doing here."

The two doctors shared a slight handshake with Silk exiting to a waiting driver in a warm car.

61

A ragged, fetid Tesqua sat in a squat position in the corner of his darkened room. He had no idea anything unusual had transpired beyond in the asylum. All he could focus on was what was around him.

When the door opened, he hugged the corner, curling into a ball as a faint shadow crossed over him, created by light bleeding in from the hall. He expected a beating. They could kill him. He didn't care anymore. He wished they would.

Thompson settled to the floor beside him.

"Don't let them win," she pleaded, her voice conveying all the agony that swelled in her heart. She had been witness to so much evil in this place that she could no longer stand alone uncommitted in the periphery.

Tesqua felt her hand touch his arm. He could feel her warmth, her kindness through the straitjacket. Her words, or more the tone of her voice, cracked the armor he had erected around him. Her touch wormed its way through the canvas, extending its reach throughout his body. He had never felt compassion from any person in this place before. He was feeling It now. Her face remained unseen in the dark, but in his mind's eye, he watched tears stream down her cheeks.

He lifted his head to the faint sparkles of her eyes in the weak light. Were there really tears there? Could she reach him when no one else could?

"Dashtsaah ku," Tesqua muttered.

"What does that mean" she pleaded to him.

"I will die here. Mana is right," Tesqua said. He, after eight terrible years, had succumbed to the wretchedness of this place. They had broken his spirit, crushing everything of meaning inside him, leaving him with nothing more than a destroyed shell waiting to be placed in the ground beneath the giant oak.

"No, Tesqua! *You must live*. You must bear witness to this place. Please, don't give up on us. You have spread hope to so many here. Now you must find hope inside yourself."

Tesqua wanted to speak, but could find no words. He slumped his head back against the wall.

Thompson offered him water. He refused.

The moment hung between them.

Thompson pressed the cup to Tesqua's lips.

"Please."

He drank. Only a small amount, but he drank. Thompson had rekindled a weak flame of hope inside him.

"Thank you," she whispered. Her sobs of joy became audible. She gave him more. He swallowed the entire cup.

"You will not die here," Thompson said, then she left.

Thompson's departure returned the room to darkness, save for a sliver of moonlight that fell into his room.

When Tesqua tried to peer through the darkness, he spied the jutting rock formations of a cave surrounding him. Then a campfire exploded with a shower of glowing embers. Tesqua leaned forward to gather in the fire's warmth. But as he moved

closer, a brown bear rose up on the opposing side of the crack-
ling flames. Tesqua jumped to his feet, withdrawing an imaginary knife. Despite being restrained in his straitjacket, Tesqua
saw himself standing undaunted before the bear, who snarled,
extending ivory claws for attack.

As the firelight danced over the towering bear, the flame
erupted again into a fireball, momentarily blinding Tesqua.
When the flames subsided, an Apache warrior in full regalia
had replaced the bear. The warrior resembled the figure Tesqua
had painted on the day room wall so many years before.

"Sheath your blade, young one," the warrior commanded.

Tesqua knew that voice. It sounded like his father's of
decades ago, when he was vibrant and strong and believed in
the ways of their people.

Yellow firelight danced off the red and black markings on
the warrior's face. His dark eyes glistened.

"What do you want of me?" Tesqua asked, too frightened
to sheath his imaginary blade before such a towering figure.

"They require one with the courage of a warrior. You will
lead them out of their darkness. Guide them to safety against
the bluecoats."

"I am not a warrior," Tesqua responded.

"In your heart you know the truth," the towering figure
retorted with an edge of irritation in its voice.

"Tell me how?"

Tesqua stared at the moonlight pouring in the window,
painting the wall with the giant oak's shadow. The warrior,
campfire and cave vanished. In its wake, Tesqua in his straitjacket faced the wall—no longer cowering in the corner.

He understood now why he had been brought to this terrible place. He knew now exactly what he must do, where his destiny would lead him.

****

Midnight had passed an hour ago. Wallace sat alone in his dimly lit office knocking back whiskey. An empty bottle sat on his desk beside his right hand, a half-full bottle beside his left. The glow of moonlight overhead illuminated his face as he knocked back another shot, whiskey dribbling down his chin.

"You didn't get my wire. Goddamn Barry," he slurred as more whiskey ended up on the desk than in his glass for his next round.

But he had shown them. Silk completed his inspection and departed without the slightest hint of the reality of this place. All his secrets were still safely tucked away from all those money hungry Washington Bureaucrats. Not one understood what it was truly like running a facility that housed the mentally deficient half-breeds of our society. They should spend a week here dealing with these savages if they wanted to understand the true nature of this place. But none of them ever would. They had Wallace to do that for them.

62

Under the table, a small envelope, like the one the doctors used to dispense doses of medication, passed from a withered old hand to a young trembling one.

Paraquo sat at the end of the farthest table in the mess hall. Mana sat beside him. But neither lifted their spoons. Paraquo studied Nathan's pacing a few tables away. Mana avoided eye contact with anyone in the room. Certainly, had anyone noticed his behavior, they might have become suspicious of the two. However, no one would have suspected anything looking at Paraquo.

Mana's heart pounded hard against his chest. He believed that if either Jake or Nathan noticed him, they would know exactly what he was doing. As much as it terrified him, it also exhilarated him. He could think of nothing but being together with his Evey again. He would do anything to find a way to hold her in his arms once more, to kiss her just the way she liked it. Together they would have more babies—many more babies. He would make every one of Evey's dreams come true. He had promised her that, and he meant to keep his promise. Their house would overlook the sprawling plains on which he spent his childhood. His children would grow up in an Indian world, not the white man's world. He understood why he had been brought to this place. He was meant to rescue Evey. He was the chosen spirit. He would achieve what the voices of his ancestors had deemed he must do.

"The wind of the Ghost Dancer, my friend," Paraquo whispered, once they completed the exchange with the envelope tucked safely inside Mana's shoe. It was the first time Mana had taken a breath since they sat down together at the table.

"Will it be enough?" Mana asked.

Paraquo nodded. A sinister smile sprang to his face.

Mana had not seen Paraquo smile since the night he presided over their marriage in the day room.

"The nurses pay little attention to a crippled old man."

When Tesqua entered the mess hall, all heads turned to him. Weeks had passed with no one seeing him. Sam jumped from his chair, crashing it to the floor with a bang. He ran to grab Tesqua's hand to bring him to the table as if he were showing off his father to his friends.

"I missed you. Were you sick? Are you better now?" Sam asked in rapid fire. He sat beside Tesqua, who sat beside Mana while Sam resumed eating his dinner.

Mana smiled.

"Itza chu," Mana said.

Tesqua smiled. He shoveled food voraciously into his mouth like a man pulling himself away from the bitter brink of starvation. He needed every bit of strength he could muster.

Itza chu.

****

In the day room three days later, Tesqua leaned against the wall watching Mana circle. The day appeared so much like any other day in the asylum that no one would have noticed anything out of the ordinary. Yet on this day, Tesqua made eye contact with Mana more frequently. With subtle hand gestures and slight nods they passed signals to each other.

With the thumb of his right hand placed between his middle fingers, Mana signaled Tesqua that all was well with their plan.

Tesqua extended two fingers in his left hand to indicate Nathan. Mana nodded slightly. He placed three fingers of his right hand across his forearm. Tesqua understood that to mean Mana would handle Nathan.

After a time, Tesqua roamed over to the window to stare at the giant oak. A brisk wind gently tossed the branches, and on occasion, leaves fluttered free of their anchors to be carried skyward in the wind. It would be a warm wind, Tesqua thought, a wind favoring them, carrying them back home.

Mana broke his circular pattern to move closer to the window in a way that seemed unplanned. During his meandering in the room, he mumbled to himself with a regularity that was quickly overlooked by those around him. As Mana approached the window, he glanced over his shoulder in the direction of the day-room window for the nurses' station. When he noticed Nathan watching him in particular, he strayed from his path toward Tesqua, signaling with thumb tucked in his fist in his left hand that Nathan was watching. He ended up in the corner away from anyone else in the room.

Tesqua followed Mana from the day room when the call came for dinner. Neither spoke as they collected their food trays to sit apart in the mess hall.

Tesqua finished his dinner first, packing in as much food as he could get. Paraquo even slid his tray over to Tesqua, offering him his dinner. Tesqua signaled Mana 'all is well.'

Mana, however, dallied with his meat, all the time watching Nathan and Jake's movements about the room. *Were they looking at him more frequently this night?* Panic stomped rampant inside Mana's head; he feared he had slipped up, given away their intent. He thought about each move he and Tesqua had engineered over the past months to ensure nothing they did might be interpreted as even slightly out of the mundane.

Tesqua offered a puzzled frown when he noticed Mana had left a plate half filled with food. What was wrong? Mana knew what he must do.

Mana signaled back 'all is well.'

As they did every night after dinner, Tesqua took his medicine from the small cup provided him by Thompson. This time when he crumpled the paper cup into a tight wad he concealed it in his clinched fist unnoticed. Then he wandered from the mess hall to return to the day room.

But on this night when Tesqua reached the first floor, he diverted to the latrine when a passing orderly turned his back toward him. Once inside, Tesqua spit his medicine into the sink. Smiling, he waited. Minutes later Mana entered. He also spit his medicine into the sink and waited with his own smile while Tesqua exited the latrine. This had been the third successive day they had succeeded in avoiding the white man's medication. So far, luck had blessed them.

The next two hours passed without event. Mana and Tesqua watched as patients sat and stared. Tesqua wandered away from Mana to find a wall to lean against opposite the day-room window.

As he stood there, Paraquo rolled toward him. Tesqua tried to hide the panic creeping onto his face. *Had something gone wrong?* This wasn't supposed to happen. Everyone knew the part they must play. Everyone understood exactly how this night was to be executed.

Tesqua breathed easier when Paraquo stopped before him long enough to fold his medicine pouch into Tesqua's hand.

"It is who we are," was all Paraquo said. Then he rolled away to settle beside the day-room door.

Tesqua's eyes immediately went to the window overlooking the nurses' station. No one was looking in. No one had seen Paraquo and him exchange words. Relief slipped out between Tesqua's dry lips.

Tesqua placed his thumb between his middle fingers in his right hand. Mana released a sigh of relief across the room.

All is well.

A few minutes later, Paraquo asked if he could return to his room early. Nathan reluctantly came up to wheel Paraquo into the hall.

Amidst the flow of patients in the room, Tesqua positioned himself just inside the day-room door. Mana eased his way over from his place at the window facing the giant oak to maintain a distance of three paces behind Tesqua.

Their plan had been set into motion—neither looked at the other as they waited. Everything had to be timed perfectly for their scheme to work. Their freedom was at stake.

As Paraquo rolled through the doorway from the day room into the hall, he began moaning in great agony, clutching his shirt with a fist as he slumped from his chair to the floor.

Thompson rushed in from her desk. She and Nathan knelt over Paraquo on the floor.

Tesqua exited the day room, insinuating himself between Thompson and the nurses' station. Other patients gathered just outside the day-room door to watch. Once Tesqua settled into place, Mana slipped from the day room. He crossed without wasting a step to the desk, where he removed a key from the drawer. This phase of their plan had to take place in a few seconds, and it couldn't be rehearsed. They would have one chance at this. If they failed, they would never get another chance. Mana thought only about doing everything correctly.

As Nathan and Thompson worked on Paraquo, Tesqua make certain he shielded Mana's movements from their view. If Paraquo performed well, they would be too busy attending him to notice what was taking place just a few feet away. Paraquo clutched Nathan's leg to hold him on one knee.

Mana unlocked the side cabinet, where he carefully and silently extracted a set of keys. He held them tightly in his left hand as he locked the side cabinet again with his right. Then he returned the key to the desk drawer.

With all the other patients watching Thompson, Nathan and Paraquo on the floor outside the day room, no one noticed what Mana had accomplished. Jake never once looked up to check on the other patients.

As Mana blended back into the crowd, he nudged Tesqua, who in turn passed a hand signal to Paraquo. Tesqua's movement was so slight that only someone looking for it would notice it. For another minute or so, Paraquo continued his writhing in agony. Then he became still.

"I think he's better now," Thompson said. She, along with Nathan, helped Paraquo come to a sitting position on the floor.

"The pain has gone," Paraquo said.

"Was it chest pain?" Thompson asked.

"Like someone squeezing my heart right out of my chest," Paraquo replied.

With Thompson and Nathan's help, Paraquo returned to his wheelchair, so Nathan could push him to his room.

Tesqua returned to the day room to find Mana across the room staring not at him but rather at the day-room door. But his hand signaled 'all is well.'

Minutes passed. Nathan returned to the nurses' station but did not return to the day room. Mana moved to his place at the window facing the giant oak. After a minute, he left, crossing to the other side. On his journey, he passed Tesqua. As they passed, the keys moved soundlessly from Mana's hand to Tesqua's. No one witnessed the exchange. Thompson worked with Nathan at the desk outside the day room. Tesqua and Mana completed the operation successfully, though neither revealed even the slightest sign of victory on their faces.

They still had much to accomplish in the hour remaining. Yet one more vital link to their freedom plan came under their control.

Mana watched the clock from his perch. He moved to the window when he noticed Thompson take up her purse from the desk drawer. He rapped on the glass.

"I need to use the latrine," he begged.

Thompson, true to her nature, never hesitated. She unlocked the day-room door, which allowed Mana to exit. No one ever doubted Mana's trustworthiness. He almost always gained free reign in the asylum—now he would use it to their benefit.

Thompson slipped into her black sweater, buttoning it before making her way to the reception room door.

"You're sure you're going to be all right with him? I can stay," she said, turning back.

"I'll be fine. He said he was feeling better. If anything comes up, I'll ring Wallace."

Nathan's response seemed to appease Thompson, though she still hesitated with indecision before making her way out the reception door. A moment later she was gone, leaving only Nathan outside the day room at the desk with Jake leaning against the wall in the corner of the day room.

Mana released a silent sigh of relief when Thompson finally decided to leave for the night. Her continued presence would have disrupted their plan.

Tesqua watched Nathan set his coffee cup down on the desk. He followed by kicking his feet up on the corner, exactly like he had done a thousand times before after Thompson departed for the night.

"That's it, get nice and comfortable," Tesqua mumbled.

Seeing Mana emerge from the latrine, Tesqua banged the glass boldly to pull Nathan's attention toward him. Jake remained out of position across the day room to witness the actions about to transpire.

"What now, you monkey?" Nathan asked.

"I'm hungry," Tesqua moaned.

"You know there's no eating after dinner."

"I need some meat. I'm sick of potatoes all the time."

While Tesqua kept Nathan distracted, Mana eased up beside the desk, where hidden in his palm he emptied his small envelope into Nathan's coffee cup.

Mana smiled as the powder disappeared, after which Tesqua abandoned his whining. He watched Mana stroll back into the day room. They were careful to take up positions away from each other in the room and away from Jake, who seemed more interested in watching the second hand sweep the clock than observing them.

Yet both kept an eye on Nathan.

Minutes ticked painfully by. The coffee cup sat untouched.

Tesqua checked the clock for the fourth time in less than two minutes. It was 8:55. Now both watched Nathan. Mana risked easing closer to Tesqua. With his right hand, Tesqua extended two fingers, curled the other two and extended his thumb. Mana understood that all was not well. Something had gone wrong. Mana risked approaching Tesqua.

"He's not drinking," Tesqua said, an edge of panic creeping into his voice.

"What do we do?" Mana whispered.

"Have faith and wait."

Mana's patience evaporated a few moments later.

"Your turn to die," Mana said under his breath, moving to the window to rap on the glass.

"What do you want now?" Nathan said, clearly irritated by Mana's intrusion into his private thoughts.

"Nurse Thompson asked me to empty her trash and clean up before I retired."

"Tomorrow," Nathan said. He wanted nothing to do with any of it.

"No. I promised her tonight."

"Great."

Nathan pulled himself from the chair as if it took great effort then unlocked the day-room door. Mana went right to work at the station, collecting up the half-full wastebasket to empty it down the hall. When he returned, he took the metal coffee pot from the hot plate as if he planned to clean it.

Nathan held up his cup.

"Pour me the rest," he instructed.

Mana gladly complied.

Instead of drinking, however, Nathan again set his cup down and this time got to his feet.

"Back to your rooms."

The steaming cup held Tesqua's attention as he passed the desk on his way to his room. Paraquo had advised them that the powder takes more than an hour to work. Nathan would have to drink his coffee once they had settled into their rooms. Tesqua remained certain Nathan would not disappoint them.

Nathan nudged Mana along, clearly dismayed that he had to get up for Mana to do something as frivolous as emptying the trash can.

Tesqua paused in his doorway. Jake came up a few moments later to push him in.

Uncertainty seized Mana's face. They were so close now.

63

Midnight approached. A fulgent glowing moon rose high in a clear night sky. Tesqua had lain silent in his bed for nearly three hours. By now, Jake would have wandered off to fall asleep in some out-of-the-way corner of the asylum, as he always did after tucking everyone safely away.

Tesqua eased to the door. Ever so carefully, he checked in both directions down the hall. Then with a sharp twist, he jammed the door handle hard. The door unlatched. He held it tightly in place for a few seconds. His heart lurched. The first step to his freedom had worked.

The hall outside his room remained silent. So far so good. The door eased open noiselessly—just a crack—and stopped. More silence. He pushed it open enough to extract the waded-up paper cup from the door catch. He felt the refreshing breeze of freedom sweep across his mind. Soon it would be against his face.

Tesqua eased his head out just enough for a view down the hall. All remained still, save for his pounding heart and pitched breathing. His pulse accelerated. At the nurses' station outside the day room, Nathan slept with head back, his feet up on the desk. If he downed all his coffee, he would never wake up. With luck, the cause of Nathan's death would remain a mystery long after they were gone. Wallace would find a way to blame Tesqua, but he wouldn't care. He would be a thousand miles away by then.

Exhilaration swarmed over Tesqua. Shoeless, he slipped from his room, crept slowly down the hall to Mana's door. Without so much as a single sound, Tesqua unlocked Mana's lock. The door opened. Silently, Mana slid out into the hall wearing an asylum shirt with a Ghost Dancer painted on it. He handed another to Tesqua, which for a brief moment crinkled Tesqua's concentration. He dismissed it, stuffing the shirt into his pants as they moved on.

Mana frowned. They would need the aid of the Ghost Dancer spirits if they were to succeed this night.

Mana led the way through the doors to the women's wing.

"Daneezhe," Tesqua muttered.

Mana glared at him.

"Just we only," Tesqua translated for his friend.

He had opposed this next part of their plan right from the beginning. But Mana refused to be dissuaded. Regardless of how much it complicated matters, Mana would only go along with the plan if they brought Evey with them. Tesqua had no choice but to agree if he wanted to be free. Now he hoped this wouldn't be the cause of their demise.

Once safely ensconced within the women's wing, they paused. Mana signaled 'all is well.' A moment later, he stopped at a sound emanating from the nurses' station. They listened for footfalls. If the night nurse approached, they intended to knock her out.

"I still think this is a bad idea," Tesqua risked whispering after the hall returned to silence.

"The Ghost Dancers will protect us. The door at the end on the left," Mana whispered back.

He offered Tesqua no other options. They would take Evey or they would return to their rooms. Mana's eyes told him that much.

"Too dangerous. She'll see us before we get Evey out," Tesqua insisted.

Fear swelled like a raging fire inside him. Their plan had worked thus far, but one mistake could mean failure, bringing about a punishment Tesqua loathed to contemplate. Flashes of the restraint chair sent a ravaging shiver up his spine. How much more torture could he take if they were caught?

"Then give me the keys," Mana ordered. The determination in his eyes at that moment convinced Tesqua they must proceed with Mana's plan.

"If the nurse moves, I knock her out while you get Evey," Tesqua instructed.

"If that happens, get the scissors in the desk afterward. Then we go for the doors," Mana responded.

Mana left Tesqua near the doors, sneaking along the wall to Evey's room. He unlocked the door without a sound then breached the darkness, praying all the while that his intrusion would not bring a scream.

Mana awakened a frightened Evey with a hand clamped to her mouth to prevent an errant shriek. Evey sucked in her breath ready to eject a scream until she realized her husband was holding her. He kissed her first, then he gave her a Ghost Dancer shirt to put on. They never spoke, Evey understood Mana's hand gestures and knew exactly what was happening and what was expected of her.

A long minute later, they emerged from her room to a still silent hall. Tesqua signaled 'all is well,' allowing them to creep along the wall to join him at the doors. They were more than halfway through their plan, which had progressed without a hitch.

That moment of their coming together was charged with excitement, terror and a faith they had shared since the day they were all united in the day room. Mana clutched Evey's hand so tightly that her fingers went numb. She heard her heart pounding in the silence. She dared not let go of Mana for fear she might never hold him again. Sweat accumulated on her palms, which forced Mana to tighten his grip on her even further.

Their silent snail's journey to the reception doors proved torturously tedious. Each step had to be carefully measured. Tesqua never took his eyes off Nathan's boots protruding out from the desk's corner at the nurses' station outside the day room.

Nothing moved except the three as they crept to the reception door. Mana advanced to the lead then silently slipped the key into the lock. He turned ever so slowly to make certain the mechanism generated no noise as it rotated. The bolt slid back. The door became unlocked. Tesqua already thought he could feel free air against his face.

The reception-room door opened without so much as a squeak. Mana eased the door back just wide enough for each to slip through into the reception area.

A single unlocked door stood between them and freedom's wind.

Tesqua came through the reception-room door last. He took the keys from Mana while a cool night air assaulted them. And freedom. Sweet glorious freedom.

But they were not free yet.

No sooner had they entered the reception area when the cool air forced Evey to lurch into a cough. She tried in vain to muffle the terrible sound. But it was too late. Enough had slipped out to betray them.

"Run!" Tesqua yelled.

"Hey, what the hell!" they heard Nathan yell with his feet dropping from the desk.

Evey and Mana exploded out the asylum's front door. They leapt down the stairs to hit the ground and freedom. But Tesqua was not behind them.

Tesqua had one more task to complete. He remained in the reception area for that vital few seconds necessary to jam the key into the lock and re-lock the reception area door, thereby confounding Nathan's pursuit. He also abandoned the key in the lock. That simple act would hang up Nathan, since now he had to work Tesqua's key out before he could push his key in. Those few minutes could mean the difference between capture and freedom.

A moment later, Tesqua emerged from the asylum. He went airborne down the stairs, accelerating with long strides once on the ground to catch up with Mana and Evey. His bare feet dug into the spongy earth for the first time in a decade.

At last, they were free!

A wonderful night breeze caressed their faces. Tesqua had not felt freedom's wind since entering their prison. They must still traverse a one-mile stretch of open field before reaching the densely wooded forest running northeast from the asylum. But once the trees swallowed them up, there would be no way anyone could come after them until morning. By then they could be ten miles from this dreadful place.

In the moonlight they spied the jagged silvery treeline ahead of them.

But Evey suddenly slowed. Winded after only a short distance, she was overcome by a fit of coughing. She had to stop. She coughed so hard she couldn't take in air. Her lips were turning blue.

Then Mana stopped.

Then Tesqua stopped. He spun in dizzying circles, scanning everywhere at once.

"Come on. They'll be coming," he pleaded.

"I can't," Evey cried, her lungs burning red-hot.

Evey's breathing failed her now. She had felt freedom against her face. She could see the trees that meant their safety in the distance. But she couldn't inhale. She could run no further.

"Take her arm. We just need to reach the trees," Tesqua commanded. Terror crept into his voice. He turned back long enough to see headlights come on in their wake near the asylum stairs.

Tesqua clutched one arm, Mana the other, and supporting Evey's weight, they tried to run on. They ran no more than a hundred yards before they had to stop once again.

The forest fringe seemed less distinct now, like it had moved away to prevent them from reaching it. Tesqua located a woody arched portal that would make the perfect entry point and allow the forest to consume them before Nathan could reach them.

Evey coughed harder, ejecting blood that stained her Ghost Dancer shirt.

"Go. We'll never make it if we try to carry her," Mana said. Inside, his heart was breaking. He couldn't be forced to make such a choice. He knew what he must do.

They stopped. Mana took Evey into his arms to support her. He loved her too dearly to ever leave her.

Tesqua started off with a few strong strides.

He stopped.

"We just have to reach the trees," he pleaded.

"Go!" Mana yelled. "You're free, Tesqua. Itza Chu." Mana shouted at him like an angry father wanting his child banished from his sight. "Go, be free, my friend."

Tesqua tried a few more strides. He could go no further. He stared at the medicine pouch still clutched in his hand. *It is who he is. It is who he is meant to be.*

"You'll never get another chance," Mana said, clutching Evey, who struggled desperately to draw sufficient air into her lungs to remain alive.

Tesqua returned to his friends. He helped Evey up as exhaust fumes and truck headlights washed over them, turning their sweated faces as pale as the moon against the night.

Nathan and Jake jumped from the truck the moment it came to a screeching sideways stop. Nathan pulled out the gun, leveling it directly at Tesqua's head.

"Heathen bastard. I've been waiting a long time for this," Nathan yelled as he sighted down the barrel between Tesqua's eyes.

"No!" Jake screamed. He lunged for the gun at the same moment Mana dove to shove Tesqua out of the way.

Crack!

The gunfire shattered the night.

Evey and Mana crumpled to the ground while Jake wrestled Nathan for control of the gun. Nathan had missed Tesqua. But he wanted another shot. When Jake kept him from getting it, he pulled the gun free to whack Tesqua in the face with three rapid blows, causing the Indian to topple to the ground before Jake could finally wrestle the gun from Nathan's hands.

"You crazy? They had their hands up," Jake stammered.

He kept pushing Nathan hard until he forced him against the side of the truck. When Nathan tried to lunge around him, Jake leveled the gun at him.

"Stop, goddamnit! Why did you do that?" Jake screamed.

Nathan just stared.

Tesqua awoke to darkness. Leather straps caused horrible pain to his head and neck. Moments passed before he realized where he was, what had happened. At first, he thought he might be dead. Then he wished he was when he realized he was back in the restraint chair. How much time had passed, he couldn't know.

He relished his brief taste of freedom. So much so, that he relived every moment of it right up until the gun went off, then he watched his two friends drop and felt Nathan beating him with the gun.

The gag they had stuffed into his mouth kept the inside as dry as cotton. Try as he might, he couldn't swallow.

What day was this? He wondered while he sat there looking for anything that might give him some indication.

"Foolish thing you tried," Wallace said from behind him.

Tesqua flinched, thought at first the voice was an apparition, but he knew that wouldn't be the case. He turned as best he could with his head fastened by the restraint strap to see the doctor, but Wallace remained out of view behind him.

When Wallace at last circled into Tesqua's field of vision, enmity flared between the two men. Tesqua could see him only through his left eye. His right eye had swollen completely shut. His lips felt like they were five times their normal size. Fire raged up his jaw right into his brain.

"Nathan rang the Canton police. Now I have to make a report. You made me look bad in the commissioner's eyes," Wallace said slowly, deliberately, using the words to taunt Tesqua.

Wallace inched closer, hoping for a reaction.

Tesqua refused him the satisfaction.

"You're going to die here. Don't you understand that by now?"

Tesqua closed his eye to Wallace. He felt his heart stop inside his chest. He would never again get the opportunity to escape this place. Wallace would make certain of that. No one would ever come for him. Everything he loved in his life was gone. Now he feared his reckless action had killed the only two friends he had left in his world.

Nothing Tesqua could say would improve his life in this dreadful place. So he remained silent, telling Wallace with his face that someday he would find a way to punish him for all he had done.

Wallace moved to the door, paused briefly then left, never looking back at Tesqua struggling desperately to breathe.

Sam occupied himself in the corner of the day room playing with his feather, some string and a few cans Thompson had given him. He counted the days since he had last seen Tesqua. Nine had passed. No one in the place spoke of him, and every time Sam asked about him, he received nothing but dismissal from the orderlies and Thompson.

At first, he thought Tesqua and Mana refused to see him anymore, that they had gone away, so they wouldn't have to be around his sickness. His father had left for that very same reason. As long as he was sick, Sam knew he would never have anyone close to him.

After tiring of his improvised toys, Sam moved to the window facing the giant oak. He wondered what Mana saw out there that kept him at the window every day. Sam thought hard about his mother, and for a second, he thought he could see her smiling face in the glass. It saddened him, but he stroked his feather to help him through the difficult moment. Would he ever see his mother again? He felt so utterly alone now that Tesqua and Mana had left and that no women ever visited. Nurse Thompson never would give him an answer when he asked to visit Evey. Had she left this place also? Even she had become disgusted with his illness.

****

Tesqua stared out his window at the giant oak standing in lush bloom. Only mild bruising remained on his face, yet he still suffered terrible head pains from his beating. While sunlight moved along his wall from day to night, Tesqua remained in the same position staring at the same thing. Wallace kept him isolated from everyone but Jake, who brought meals and took him to the latrine first thing in the morning before anyone was about and the last thing at night after locking everyone else away for the night. His relief during the day came only from the chamberpot left in his room.

Tesqua had contact with no one, including Thompson. He tried to capture her attention when she would pass his window, but she refused even to look at him.

These foolish people thought they were punishing Tesqua for his actions. Instead, he found sanctuary in his solitude. He welcomed the isolation. Their punishment would never break his spirit. They had committed much worse crimes against him and still he endured.

Tesqua slept fitfully, reliving in his dream his last moments with Celia, followed by his escape from this place that culminated in the moment the gun fired. He snapped awake, clutching his chest as if he had been the one shot. It was morning. Then he thought of Mana. Was he dead? How many days had passed before Tesqua regained consciousness? Did the grave diggers dig two graves while he was unconscious?

The door to his room unlocked. Tesqua remained motionless. Instead of Jake entering as he did every time before, the door swung open and stopped. Jake moved on to the next room.

Tesqua watched Paraquo roll by, who smiled at him. Tesqua smiled back. His punishment had ended.

When Tesqua entered the day room, a jubilant Sam dashed up to him. He grabbed Tesqua's hand so tightly it hurt Tesqua's bruised knuckles.

"I missed you. Were you sick? What happened to your face? Where's Mana? How come I can't visit Evey? You want to try to beat me at checkers? Paraquo's been teaching me," Sam fired rapidly as if he needed to get all the questions out that he had stored up for the last weeks.

Tesqua smiled at the thought of Paraquo teaching anyone checkers. He chose not to answer any of the questions; rather he guided Sam over to the window, where together they stared at the giant oak.

There were no new graves.

"No diggers," Tesqua whispered.

He scanned, found Nathan on the opposite side of the room talking with Jake. Their eye contact lasted but a second. Tesqua read the hatred in those dark eyes. He responded with apathy and emptiness.

A puzzled Sam looked on as Tesqua drifted away.

Throughout the day, Tesqua drifted about the day room. Each time he tried to speak with Paraquo, Paraquo rolled quickly away. It was as if he had failed Paraquo also. When Tesqua tired of staring out the window, he took Sam to the table to play checkers, allowing the lad to beat him time after time. And with each Victory, Sam's smile grew brighter and bolder. *Maybe Sam was why he had been destined for this place? Maybe he was meant to save Sam from the horrors of this white man's prison?*

That evening, Tesqua ate dinner in silence. Afterward, Nathan and Thompson administered medications. When Tesqua accepted his from Thompson, he chanced to take hold of her arm. She knew what he wanted.

"Mana's okay. Evey isn't," she whispered, careful to keep Nathan from overhearing their one-sided exchange.

Tesqua downed his medication, left the mess hall and walked with Sam silently back to the day room. While Tesqua passed Mana's room on his way back to the day room, he risked a peek in the window.

Mana's room was empty.

The next day became a replay of the last, except that Sam no longer badgered him with questions. Tesqua sought peace by staring out the window at the giant oak. Thompson's words kept ringing inside his head, 'Evey isn't.'

They needed someone to lead them out of here. He had let them down. He was not the man he believed himself to be, and less of a man than his father. He had failed his vision quest. His shame would live inside him forever.

When the day-room door opened, Mana entered, his arm resting in a sling. He crossed immediately to Tesqua.

"He never drank the coffee," Tesqua said.

"There was enough in there to kill him. Thank God your Ghost Dancer shirt protected you," Mana said.

Tesqua smirked.

"Not the shirt. Nathan's a lousy shot."

Then Tesqua's face went stone serious. He knew the truth about that night.

"*You* saved me ... not some shirt."

Mana smiled.

"Next time ..." Tesqua said. He scanned to make certain no orderly was watching, then he drew his crooked finger across his throat.

Mana left Tesqua at the window, crossing the room to Thompson at the day-room door.

"What of Evey?" he asked.

"You did a bad thing, Mana. Evey's very sick with tuberculosis."

Mana's face dropped, his eyes glazed over. The reaction to Thompson's words brought Tesqua over. But Mana walked away.

He crossed to Paraquo and spoke to him harshly for a minute. Then he returned to Thompson. Mana placed three red beads into her palm.

"For Evey. They will help her," Mana said.

Thompson looked at him. She knew better but decided to accept the beads when she witnessed the depth of concern in Mana's eyes. If only red beads could save her ....

67

The cool cloth Thompson set on Evey's forehead brought Evey's eyelids up. She tried to focus in the dim light, realized who was at her bedside. She needed no words to know the truth. Seeing Thompson wearing a mask told her enough. She was dying.

"Fever's down a little. You want some water?" Thompson offered. A compassionate smile shone in her eyes.

Evey shook her head, drew in a breath as deeply as she could. The pain of her action shot up her neck into her brain.

"I must talk ..." she released with as much of her strength as she could muster.

"Don't say anything. Mana said to tell you he loves you. He watches at the window every day, hoping you'll get better. In his own way, he prays for you."

Evey shook her head.

"I know I am dying. I must speak. Baby. My baby."

"I'm sorry about that. We were foolish," Thompson said.

"Not Mana's."

"What do you mean, not Mana's?"

Thompson clutched Evey's hand.

307

"Not Mana's baby. Nathan ..."

Thompson squeezed Evey's hand, reading the terrible pain in Evey's eyes, pain not from her disease but from the wickedness of this place.

"Nathan raped you?"

Crying, Evey nodded in the affirmative.

"After we married, I was not with child. I know without doubt. Nathan came to my room, forced me ..."

"It's all right. You must conserve your strength," Thompson said. She could see relief sweep over Evey's face. That terrible secret Evey had carried with her for so long. Now she had to unburden herself before ...

"No need now. I am ready. I needed someone to know the truth," Evey said. Then she closed her eyes. Her breathing eased a bit. She looked at peace.

****

Mana slept soundly on his side with his head close to the window. A hand clamped his mouth, startling him awake. He lurched forward to strike back. But he caught himself when he realized Thompson was the one kneeling beside him. With a finger to her lips, she motioned him to follow silently. Mana complied.

Thompson led him through double doors into a small wing isolated from the rest of the patients. His heart stopped when he came to the isolation room's glass window. Evey lay on the other side, breathing with great difficulty, but breathing.

Mana clutched Thompson's arm for support.

"Let me be with her. Don't let her be alone," he pleaded.

"She's very contagious," Thompson countered.

"I don't care. Let me be with her. I want her to know I love her."

"But she cares. She wants you to live. She wants you to carry on in her spirit. I'll be with her. I promise, Mana."

When Mana touched the glass pane between them, Evey opened her eyes. Tears unfurled down her cheeks.

"She wants you to know she loves you. She's glad you joined as husband and wife," Thompson said.

Mana tried to breathe. He could no longer hold back his tears. He wiped them away as quickly as they came, but he couldn't keep up with the torrent.

"We must go. If Wallace finds out about this ..."

Thompson guided Mana gently away from the window. Evey closed her eyes again. Mana took Thompson's arm, not for support but to bring her to look at him.

"I'm not crazy," he said.

"I know. Evey isn't either," Thompson replied.

Mana needed another look. He turned back to her. His heart was breaking. She was sleeping. She was at peace now. He must hold that vision of her loveliness inside him forever.

****

The following day Mana stared through his tortured reflection in the glass at the giant oak while diggers worked beneath the leafy canopy. Mana wiped his tears before setting his hand to the glass to say his good-bye. But as much he as wanted to leave the window so as not to witness what was taking place, he remained to watch the entire day.

As the day's end neared, with the sun mostly out of view in the west, Mana suddenly turned from the window. He caught Thompson's eyes as she entered the room. It was as if he had felt Evey's spirit passing.

Tesqua, seeing the look on Thompson's face as she stood there, went to Mana at the window. Thompson nodded, wiping a tear from her eye. They needed no words to express their anguish. Mana knew Evey was no longer with them. Her spirit was finally free of this terrible place. She would journey alone for now. But someday Mana would join her.

Thompson then left the day room.

"I failed you. I failed Evey," Tesqua said, plagued with guilt.

Mana turned back to his window to stare at the men working under lanterns to finish the grave.

"For a short time, we were free together, Evey and I. You gave us that. You also brought us back together in this place. I know you persuaded Barry to allow us to marry. I will never forget that, my friend," Mana said.

68

Days passed into weeks, weeks into months until the leaves on the giant oak turned a multitude of reds and browns only to flutter from the limbs. And it seemed that Mana had not moved from that place before the window.

"I hate this stupid game," Sam yelled from the table, where he had been playing checkers with Tesqua. The lad viciously swiped the checkers from the board, sending them sprawling across the floor. He stomped from the table, leaving Tesqua sitting there alone in bewilderment.

After a few moments, Mana went to Sam, who had taken up brooding in a corner.

"What's the matter?" Mana asked. It seemed the only bond left in this place existed between Mana, Sam and Tesqua. Even Paraquo had soured in the last few months, avoiding them as if they were to blame for their failure.

"I miss Evey. I miss my mother. I hate this place! I'm never going to be better. Just leave me alone," Sam yelled as loud as he could. He buried his face in his arms, sobbing softly.

Mana stroked the lad's shoulder, hoping to ease his anguish, but he knew deep inside there was nothing anyone could do short of releasing them to go back home that might help anyone in this place. And going home was not an option. Wallace saw to that.

Mana drifted away, passing the day-room window, where he paused to stare into the hall as if waiting for Evey to walk by, like she had done so many times in the past. And each time she passed she would look at him and smile. Her eyes would convey how much she loved him.

In the hall, Nathan removed a sheet from the linen cart and proceeded into a patient room. His movement stole Mana away from his sweet memory. When he couldn't force its return, he abandoned the window to drift over to Paraquo in the corner.

In the patient room, Nathan stripped the soiled sheet from the bed, tossing it in a crumpled heap near the door. He snapped the new sheet onto the mattress and began spreading the corners when Thompson entered, closing the door behind her.

It took her a moment and a few deep breathes to steady her nerves. During that time, Nathan refused to even look at her; he just kept working the sheet on the mattress.

"Evey spoke to me before she died," Thompson said, her words growing stronger.

Nathan tucked a corner, pretending not to hear her.

"One less crazy Injun," he muttered, just loud enough to be sure Thompson heard.

"She wasn't crazy. She understood what was happening to her every moment of every day and night."

For a moment, the words froze Nathan. Then he tucked the last bed corner before turning to Thompson.

"She wanted me to know the truth."

"Truth?"

"The real father of her baby."

"I'd watch my mouth if I were you. Making accusations you can't prove will get you fired."

"I wasn't sure whether to believe her at first."

"You're out of your mind. I've never touched any women here."

"You lying sonofabitch. Two nights ago, the duty nurse reported you sneaking around the women's wing. You didn't know she was watching you, did you? You raped Evey, you bastard. How many others have you raped?"

Thompson forced herself right into his face. Nathan tried to look away, but she forced him to look into her eyes.

"All right, you want to go toe-to-toe, come on. But before you do, consider who Wallace will believe. Because when you fail, I'll make sure he fires you. It's your word against mine, and your star witness is dead. No one will dare speak against me here. You know that."

Their eyes remained locked, Thompson refused to back down. She had taken so much from the men in this place that here she would make her stand.

"I will find a way. You will be punished for what you did."

"I got work to do," Nathan muttered.

Once the tense moment passed, Nathan returned to the bed.

****

Tesqua stacked the checkers into two neat columns back on the table after retrieving them from the floor. Then he joined Mana and Paraquo whispering in the corner. It appeared Paraquo had finally abandoned his shunning of the two, and while he spoke, he leaned in close to Mana.

"Barry uncovered the truth," Mana said, scanning to make certain neither Jake nor any other orderly in the room could overhear their words.

As Mana spoke, Sam drifted to the day-room door, where he waited.

"Barry tried to help us. I never beat any white men on the reservation. But when I learned our Indian agent used the reservation to run his whiskey, I foolishly confided what I'd seen to my friend, Cha-hay-na. He must have betrayed me, informing them what I had learned."

"Why would your friend do that?"

"He always hated me for marrying Celia. They grabbed me that the night. The Indian agent sent me here to keep me from speaking against him. He knew I could bear witness against his activities."

Mana stared straight ahead. He couldn't bear to face Tesqua with his shame.

"There were three of them. They came in the night. I hid like a coward while they whipped my father until he died. They knew he was a Ghost Dancer. They locked me in here to prevent me from identifying them," Mana said. He hung his head after he finished, refusing to look at either Tesqua or Paraquo.

"Sometimes when the night is quiet, I still hear the screaming at Wounded Knee. We were three hundred strong. They slaughtered our women and children. I escaped their massacre. When I tried to speak the truth of what they did, the army hunted me down and shot me. When I refused to die, they threw me in here. I am probably the last alive whose eyes bear witness to that terrible day. They made certain that I would never be able to speak the truth against what the white man did to us."

"Barry was our only hope," Tesqua said.

When an orderly entered the day room, Sam darted out into the hall unnoticed. Once there, he scurried off with a sheet he snatched from the cart.

A minute later Thompson emerged from the patient room, crossing the hall to the day room, unaware that Sam had just turned onto the staircase. When Thompson entered the day room, the talking in the corner stopped.

At that moment, something terrible swept over Mana—he scanned in panic. His subconscious mind had made a connection to something his conscious brain had overlooked.

"Where's Sam?" he asked with an urgency that arrested both Tesqua and Paraquo.

"At the ta ..." Tesqua stopped mid-sentence.

Sam was nowhere in the day room.

"Where's Sam?" Mana pleaded with Thompson.

"He was here a minute ago," Tesqua said.

"You're sure?" Thompson asked.

Seeing the linen cart through the window, Tesqua yanked the locked day room door.

"Open the door!" Tesqua screamed.

Thompson complied when she realized what it all could mean.

Tesqua, Mana and Thompson spilled out of the day room.

"Sam!" Tesqua yelled.

They sprinted past the linen cart.

"Sam!" Mana yelled.

Nathan exited the patient room, tossing the rumbled sheet onto the cart.

"Jesus God," Thompson prayed as they dashed for the staircase.

They reached the cross corridor and the stairs. Clinging to the railing at the first floor landing, Sam held the sheet with one end tied around his neck, the other to the railing.

"No, Sam," Tesqua screamed.

The feather fluttered as Sam released, his small body dropping like a log into the stairwell.

Tesqua dove for Sam, grabbed the rail and rose to clutch Sam's waist just as he started to swing.

"Help me hold him up," Tesqua pleaded.

Mana assaulted the stairs. Upon reaching the landing, he yanked the sheet free. Sam was gagging, but still breathing.

"Dr. Wallace!" Thompson screamed with all her strength.

Despite his precarious position, Tesqua held the boy up with all the strength he could find.

"Breathe, Sam, breathe," he cried.

Sam gagged. Blood chortled from his throat.

Wallace ran up, immediately taking charge.

"A gurney, hurry! Get him flat so we can clear his airway," he commanded.

While Nathan dashed into a patient room to grab a bed, Wallace and Thompson set to work on Sam. They laid him on the floor, where Wallace held Sam's head immobile while Thompson checked his pulse.

"I've got a pulse," she chimed.

"Check the airway while I keep his head still," Wallace ordered.

Using her finger, Thompson carefully probed Sam's throat to make sure his airway remained open. At the same time, Wallace examined Sam's neck. Everything seemed intact. Sam was still breathing, but his skin had turned cold and clammy, his breathing came in short convulsive bursts.

Tesqua and Mana remained close but felt helpless to do anything for the boy.

"Pillows. Now!" Thompson snapped.

Mana dashed into the closest room, returned with a pillow. Tesqua ran into another room to retrieve yet another. They returned with three pillows in all.

"Can't tell if the neck's broken. Larynx feels intact. Thank God he didn't know how to knot the sheet around his neck," Wallace commented as he worked.

Nathan wheeled a bed to within a foot of Wallace and held it steady.

Tesqua set the pillows on the floor, after which he assisted Wallace and Thompson. While Wallace held the boy's neck rock steady, Tesqua and Thompson lifted him gently, transferring him to the bed.

He stopped breathing!

The moment hung between them. Then Sam sucked in a gasp, heralding he was still alive.

"All right, let's get him into a room. We'll work on him there," Wallace ordered.

But before moving him, Thompson stuffed the pillows around Sam's head to force his neck to remain in one position despite having to roll him down the hall and into a nearby room.

"Very gently," Wallace repeated with each step.

Tesqua could see Wallace sweating. His hands trembled as he pushed the bed, working very hard to keep the movement stable.

Sam's legs twitched during the short journey, but most importantly, his gasping remained steady and consistent. As long as air moved in and out of his lungs, they had a chance of saving him. Thompson held Sam's arms as steady as possible during the transfer.

No sooner had they entered the room when Thompson detected a change in Sam's gasping. Though subtle, it indicated Sam's condition was worsening.

"His airway's closing," she stammered.

She took his head in both hands, carefully shifting it back, all the while hoping the extension would open the airway further. Sam's head felt like he was on fire, a sign she interpreted as another serious degradation in Sam's condition.

They were running out of time.

"Tilt the head further back," Wallace ordered.

Thompson worked on Sam's head as best she could. This was no time to be timid. She had to get the angle exactly right to open the airway. She twisted it ever so slightly left, hoping to allow more air in.

Tesqua and Mana stood at the doorway, Mana clutching Sam's precious feather.

Wallace returned to Sam's neck. The skin had become a vile purple, swelling to twice its normal size.

"I don't detect any fractures, but I just can't be sure."

"We're going to ... Nathan, restraints. We can't risk a seizure," Thompson ordered.

"And my bag. Hurry!" Wallace further commanded Nathan, who dashed from the room.

Tesqua and Mana parted to allow him through. Neither had expected to see Nathan moving with such urgency for one of their own.

"We'll sedate him. That might help relax the muscles in his neck," Wallace added to Thompson.

"I've got a pulse of sixty, but it's faint," Thompson reported.

Wallace glanced up at Thompson for a second then returned to his examination of Sam's throat.

Outside the room, Paraquo, Tesqua and Mana sat cross-legged at the door, forcing Nathan to pick his way through to return to the room.

In the room, Thompson held Sam's twitching arms down on the bed. His breathing had deteriorated further, becoming even more erratic—he was suffocating.

"Damnit, where's my bag!" Wallace scowled.

Nathan rushed in with the bag and restraints.

"Goddamnit. Where the hell did you have to go?"

Thompson tightened her hold on Sam's twitching arms.

"The restraints were locked in storage," Nathan offered.

"On whose authority?" Wallace scowled again.

"Sorry, sir. Barry ordered them away. Didn't want them used indiscriminately. I'd forgotten about them."

Sam was gasping now, fighting harder for each breath. His eyelids fluttered as his eyes rolled around in their sockets.

Thompson released hold of Sam's left arm once she had it strapped tightly down. She lifted Sam's eyelids.

"Pupils dilated. He's suffocating," Thompson called.

"Angle the head back further. His throat's swelling shut," Wallace ordered.

Thompson's arms shook as she tried to angle little Sam's head further back. If she moved it too much, she could break his neck.

"I'm trying," she said.

Wallace grabbed a scalpel from his bag. Sam had only one chance left. And only a few seconds.

"I need to open ..."

Wallace wiped the stress from his face. His hand shook as he found the larynx with his finger. Then he set the shaking scalpel tip to it. But he hesitated.

"Get on with it! He's turning blue!" Thompson shouted to snap Wallace out of the trance he seemed to have slipped into over Sam.

In the next second, there came a loud sucking of air followed by chortling blood.

"He's breathing! We'll get you through. Just keep breathing, Sam," Thompson said, relieved.

Sam's chest expanded to its limit as the boy, for the first time, filled his lungs completely with air.

Relief washed over Wallace's face. He removed a gauge bandage from his bag and set the bloody scalpel on the table beside the bed.

"That's real medicine, in case you've forgotten," Thompson muttered while she dressed the opening in Sam's throat to staunch the blood flow but still allow Sam a clear airway for breathing. A pinkish hue returned to Sam's face. His eyes settled under his lids. Thompson thought she could feel his skin temperature dropping as she monitored him.

For the moment, they had pulled Sam out of immediate danger. He inhaled and exhaled in a regular rhythm with his arms at rest. Thompson stood back, looked at Sam on the bed for a moment before leaving the room.

She entered the hall to fifteen patients sitting outside Sam's door. After weaving her way to reach her desk, she returned with a handful of medical supplies and disappeared into the room. The door closed.

Midnight came. A small light illuminated Sam's face. Thompson sat beside him.

"He's breathing easier. Pulse seventy and getting stronger," she reported.

"Pupils?" Wallace asked from a chair across the room.

"Still dilated."

A faint chant seeped in under the door from the hall.

"What the hell?" Wallace said. He went to the door, where he flung it open to thirty sitting Indians, all chanting in unison very low.

"What's this? Nathan, lock them down," Wallace ordered.

Nathan grabbed Paraquo, who fought him, pulling his hands off the wheelchair. Tesqua stepped in to force Nathan's hands away. Nathan uncharacteristically did not resist. Mana stopped Jake from grabbing the Indian next to him.

Thompson emerged in the doorway.

"It's their way. It's how they pray," she said.

"This is ludicrous. I can't leave them out during the night."

Yet not one Indian budged from the floor. The moment lingered between them. Perhaps this was a battle best not fought. Wallace succumbed to their wishes, motioning the orderlies away. Then he retreated into Sam's room and closed the door.

The patients renewed their chant.

Hours passed. Thompson sat at Sam's bed. Wallace slept in a chair in the corner. Thompson had earlier retrieved Sam's baseball and glove, which she now set on Sam's bed, hoping he would wake to see it. She leaned in very close to him to monitor his heartbeat and listen to his breathing.

"I wish you didn't have to be here. I wish everything was different," she whispered so only he would hear.

There was no movement, no response from Sam. For the present, he seemed to be sleeping. The bruising and discoloration on his neck became the only visible signs of Sam's condition.

Thompson removed a cloth from Sam's forehead, soaked it in the pan of water beside the bed and returned it. His fever had waned through her efforts. That sparked in her a glimmer of hope that Sam would come back to them. But a part of her realized Sam might be lost forever. Nothing they could do would bring him back. And they were severely limited in what they could try.

"How's the fever?" Wallace asked from the corner without opening his eyes.

"Better. Our little friend may just make it. I thought you were sleeping."

"Not sleeping. Praying," he said.

Thompson tightened her hand over Sam's while she recited a prayer of her own inside her head. It took her a few moments to recall the words. It had been so many years since she had sought His help. She could only hope He might still be listening.

The first weak rays of a dawning sun found Thompson asleep with her head on Sam's bed. Sam's hand twitched. It went unnoticed. It twitched again. This time the disturbance spurred Thompson. She bolted awake.

Sam reached out, found her hand and clutched it tightly. A moment later, Sam tried to pull his eyelids up. They resisted. But Sam worked harder at it.

"Thank you for staying with us, Sam," Thompson cried. She clutched his hand while stroking his cheek. The warmth from her touch brought Sam's eyes open.

Wallace jumped from his chair, stumbling over to the bed.

All thirty Indians still sat in the hall, though they had been silent for many hours. The door opened; Thompson motioned them in. Sam sat awake now with eyes that begged forgiveness and a bloody gauze dressing at the base of his neck.

"No diggers," Mana said, standing at the doorway with the broadest smile he could muster.

"No diggers," Tesqua said.

They entered to be beside Sam at the bed.

An exhausted Wallace retreated to the sanctuary of his office with the door closed. With a trembling hand, he filled a glass with whiskey. He stopped for a moment, staring at his diplomas on the wall above his father's cavalry hat on the bureau. Then he threw back the shot and clumsily poured another.

The setting sun found Wallace asleep with his head on his desk and an empty whiskey bottle beside him.

Sam arranged the checkers with his ever-present base-ball glove right beside him. It never left his sight since the day Thompson returned it to him. The glove and ball were the only things he had to call his own, and they reminded him of Dr. Barry. While contemplating his first move he unconsciously rubbed the small hook-shaped scar at the base of his neck.

"Don't do that," Tesqua scolded mildly.

"Do what?"

"You're touching your scar. Nurse Thompson told you not to do that because it irritates it."

Sam tried to stop, but a minute later found his finger smoothing over the ridge of skin.

"Why do you always let me win?" Sam asked.

Tesqua at first ignored the question.

Sam persisted with his stare.

"I don't let you win."

Mana and Paraquo were making laps around the day room. As Mana circled, weaving through patients who might wander across this path, Paraquo rolled along a few feet behind him, duplicating his exact meandering. When Mana stopped abruptly with no reasonable purpose at hand, Paraquo rolled into him.

"Stop following me," Mana growled.

"I'm not following you," Paraquo pleaded with a hint of a smile. There was so little pleasure to be experienced in this terrible place, but Paraquo had found some at Mana's expense.

"You're following me," Mana charged.

"You just happen to be walking faster than me going in the exact same direction," Paraquo explained, hoping to derail Mana's argument.

"That means you're following me, you crazy Injun."

"Correct me if I'm wrong, but isn't that why we're all here?" Paraquo chided.

Mana gave up, roaming over to the window facing the front of the asylum. His attention shifted from a pointless gaze at the open meadow toward the stairs. After a moment, he tapped the glass, which brought others to join him.

From his vantage point, Mana could make out a truck parked before the asylum stairs. There was something behind it, but the girth of the truck blocked all but a small corner of the object from his view. Mana shifted to mash his face flat against the window. The glass felt cool against his cheek. It was as if he could almost feel the summer breeze against his face. For a moment, it rekindled those memories of his brief freedom with Evey so long ago.

The object blocked by the truck was a car. A car with letters on the side of it, but from Mana's angle, he couldn't make out the words.

Paraquo joined Mana at the window. Then others crowded around until all in the day room, except for Tesqua and Sam, were craning necks to get a look at the activity going on out-side.

Finally, Tesqua came over with Sam on his shoulder.

"What can you see, Sam?" Tesqua asked.

"A car with words on it," Sam replied.

Tesqua, sensing what would be the natural sequence of events, carried Sam over to the day-room-door window ahead of the others, giving them the best view of the activity unfolding in the hall. They watched Thompson go to the reception room door.

In the reception area, Dr. Barry rapped the reception window. No sooner had he knocked than Thompson showed up, her face a mix of excitement, surprise and concern.

"Unlock the door," Barry said, his voice restrained yet determined.

"You know I'm not allowed," Thompson replied.

Dr. Silk moved out from behind Dr. Barry.

"You are now," Dr. Silk said, holding up a paper, "By order of the Commissioner of the Bureau of Indian Affairs, this facility is closed. I have duly written authority granting us control of the patients."

Thompson followed her first instinct. She withdrew her keys to comply with the doctor's demand.

"What are you doing, nurse?" Wallace said, appearing behind Thompson.

"Sir?" she said.

"Do not unlock that door," Wallace demanded.

The moment of uncertainty hung between them. Thompson's eyes locked on Wallace's. She could see the anger in his tightened jaw.

"Go to hell, doctor!"

The lock to the reception door clanked. The door opened full wide to Barry, Silk and four police officers, who moved into the asylum and flanked Wallace in the hall. But they made no attempt to arrest or even restrain him. Wallace could only stare in disbelief.

"These patients are now under Dr. Barry's direct care. You, Dr. Wallace, will remove only your personal belongings and vacate these premises. You've been ordered to Washington to answer directly to the commissioner," Dr. Silk said with a voice brimming with pride.

In less than twenty-four hours, Barry completed the necessary evaluations of the eighty-five patients remaining in the asylum.

With the next sunrise, Mana, Tesqua, Sam, Paraquo, Thompson and Barry emerged into the brilliant summer sun, where together they felt the wind of freedom against their faces as they stood on the stairs of the Canton Indian insane asylum. Mana no longer pounded with his right hand.

"You're free," Barry said.

He lowered to one knee to look Sam straight in the eye.

"Sam, after I've completed my work here, I'm taking you back to Oklahoma."

When Barry returned to his feet, Tesqua and Barry looked at each other. Neither knew what was the expected exchange at this moment. Then Barry put his hand out. Tesqua accepted it. They had helped each other.

"You see, my friend, you were just like us," Mana said, "we weren't crazy, either."

They descended the asylum steps with Tesqua and Mana carrying Paraquo's wheelchair, and breathed in the sweet fresh air of freedom. Mana had been confined to the Canton asylum for more than fourteen years, Tesqua over a decade.

Before they could leave this terrible place they had one more thing to do. At the base of the giant oak, Mana laid a bundle of smoking sage upon Evey's grave site. They chanted together to honor her memory.

Epilogue

In 1934, Congress ordered the Canton Indian insane asylum permanently closed. Seventeen patients who displayed no signs of mental illness were immediately released. The remaining sixty-eight patients were transferred to Saint Elizabeth's mental hospital in Washington D.C. for further evaluation.

Ironically, the asylum then became a prison for two decades before it was finally abandoned and ultimately torn down.

Today, a plaque sits in the middle of the golf course on the site of the Canton Indian insane asylum, marking the graves of the Native Americans who died while confined there. No one will ever know if all, some, or even any of them ever required institutionalization there.

Seventy years later, at a ceremony held to honor those who died there, an eighty-year-old Indian chanted while clutching a tattered old baseball glove. No one present knew Sam was the last survivor of Canton.

During its 32-year tenure, the asylum admitted 371 Indians into its care. Of those, 121 died within its walls.

A fence erected around the giant oak and the grave sites prevents golfers from playing shots on this hallowed ground, though few, if any, who play there even understand the meaning of the words meant to honor those who perished.

Despite the congressional investigation that revealed terrible abuse and mistreatment of asylum patients, no asylum employee was ever charged with any crime.